# REDEMPTION

## THE PROTECTORS #8

SLOANE KENNEDY

Copyright © 2017 by Sloane Kennedy

Cover Images: ©Wander Aguiar

Cover Design: © Jay Aheer, Simply Defined Art

All rights reserved.

No part of this book may be reproduced in any form or by any electronic or mechanical means, including information storage and retrieval systems, without written permission from the author, except for the use of brief quotations in a book review.

ISBN-13:

978-1546719625

ISBN-10:

1546719628

CONTENTS

*Redemption* .......... v
*Trademark Acknowledgements* .......... vii
*Acknowledgments* .......... ix
*Series Reading Order* .......... xi
*Series Crossover Chart* .......... xv
*Trigger warning* .......... xvii
*redemption* .......... xix

Prologue .......... 1
Chapter 1 .......... 11
Chapter 2 .......... 21
Chapter 3 .......... 28
Chapter 4 .......... 38
Chapter 5 .......... 46
Chapter 6 .......... 57
Chapter 7 .......... 68
Chapter 8 .......... 72
Chapter 9 .......... 88
Chapter 10 .......... 93
Chapter 11 .......... 101
Chapter 12 .......... 108
Chapter 13 .......... 116
Chapter 14 .......... 125
Chapter 15 .......... 137
Chapter 16 .......... 143
Chapter 17 .......... 150
Chapter 18 .......... 165
Chapter 19 .......... 180
Chapter 20 .......... 189
Chapter 21 .......... 196
Chapter 22 .......... 206
Chapter 23 .......... 209

Chapter 24 225
Chapter 25 233
Epilogue 243

*Sneak Peek* 251
Prologue 253

*About the Author* 267
*Also by Sloane Kennedy* 269

# REDEMPTION

Sloane Kennedy

# TRADEMARK ACKNOWLEDGEMENTS

The author acknowledges the trademarked status and trademark owners of the following trademarks mentioned in this work of fiction:

Olive Garden
Forbes Fortune 500
Honda
Lincoln Town Car
Band-Aid
Spiderman
Porsche

ACKNOWLEDGMENTS

A big thank you to David Palencia for helping inspire these guys and give them the perfect names!

Thanks to Samantha Miller for patiently answering my medical questions!

Lucy Lennox, Levi thanks you for that little tidbit of advice you gave me.

Maria and Corinne, thanks for the extra set of eyes to search out all those pesky typos!

To my beta readers, Kylee and Claudia, thanks for continuing to give me your honest opinions!

And of course, my besties and soul sisters for your continued support –
Mari, Claudia and Kylee

# SERIES READING ORDER

All of my series cross over with one another so I've provided a couple of recommended reading orders for you. If you want to start with the Protectors books, use the first list. If you want to follow the books according to timing, use the second list. Note that you can skip any of the books (including M/F) as each was written to be a standalone story.

*\*\*Note that some books may not be readily available on all retail sites\*\**

***Recommended Reading Order (Use this list if you want to start with "The Protectors" series)***

1. Absolution (m/m/m) (The Protectors, #1)
2. Salvation (m/m) (The Protectors, #2)
3. Retribution (m/m) (The Protectors, #3)
4. Gabriel's Rule (m/f) (The Escort Series, #1)
5. Shane's Fall (m/f) (The Escort Series, #2)
6. Logan's Need (m/m) (The Escort Series, #3)
7. Finding Home (m/m/m) (Finding Series, #1)
8. Finding Trust (m/m) (Finding Series, #2)

SERIES READING ORDER

9. Loving Vin (m/f) (Barretti Security Series, #1)
10. Redeeming Rafe (m/m) (Barretti Security Series, #2)
11. Saving Ren (m/m/m) (Barretti Security Series, #3)
12. Freeing Zane (m/m) (Barretti Security Series, #4)
13. Finding Peace (m/m) (Finding Series, #3)
14. Finding Forgiveness (m/m) (Finding Series, #4)
15. Forsaken (m/m) (The Protectors, #4)
16. Vengeance (m/m/m) (The Protectors, #5)
17. A Protectors Family Christmas (The Protectors, #5.5)
18. Atonement (m/m) (The Protectors, #6)
19. Revelation (m/m) (The Protectors, #7)
20. Redemption (m/m) (The Protectors, #8)
21. Finding Hope (m/m/m) (Finding Series, #5)
22. Defiance (m/m) (The Protectors #9)

*Recommended Reading Order (Use this list if you want to follow according to timing)*

1. Gabriel's Rule (m/f) (The Escort Series, #1)
2. Shane's Fall (m/f) (The Escort Series, #2)
3. Logan's Need (m/m) (The Escort Series, #3)
4. Finding Home (m/m/m) (Finding Series, #1)
5. Finding Trust (m/m) (Finding Series, #2)
6. Loving Vin (m/f) (Barretti Security Series, #1)
7. Redeeming Rafe (m/m) (Barretti Security Series, #2)
8. Saving Ren (m/m/m) (Barretti Security Series, #3)
9. Freeing Zane (m/m) (Barretti Security Series, #4)
10. Finding Peace (m/m) (Finding Series, #3)
11. Finding Forgiveness (m/m) (Finding Series, #4)
12. Absolution (m/m/m) (The Protectors, #1)
13. Salvation (m/m) (The Protectors, #2)
14. Retribution (m/m) (The Protectors, #3)
15. Forsaken (m/m) (The Protectors, #4)
16. Vengeance (m/m/m) (The Protectors, #5)
17. A Protectors Family Christmas (The Protectors, #5.5)

18. Atonement (m/m) (The Protectors, #6)
19. Revelation (m/m) (The Protectors, #7)
20. Redemption (m/m) (The Protectors, #8)
21. Finding Hope (m/m/m) (Finding Series, #5)
22. Defiance (m/m) (The Protectors #9)

# SERIES CROSSOVER CHART

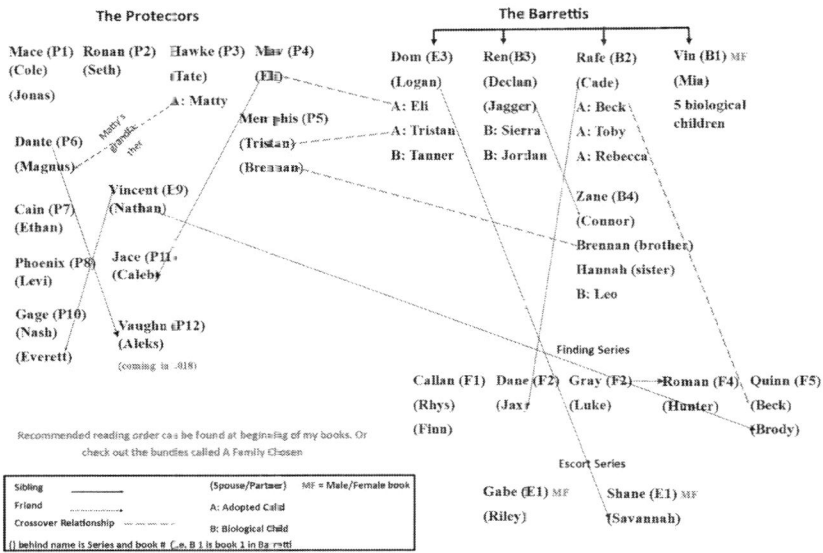

TRIGGER WARNING

Listed below are the trigger warnings for this book. Reading them may cause spoilers:

This book contains references to the sexual abuse of a child and rape

REDEMPTION

re·demp·tion \ri-ˈdem(p)-shən\

Redeeming or atoning for a fault or mistake

# PROLOGUE

## PHOENIX

"Hello, my girl," I said while simultaneously signing the words as soon as the door opened. The little girl beamed up at me as she stood in the open doorway. Her little fingers began moving lightning fast. So fast that I had to interrupt her with a reminder to slow down. Her sheepish grin was almost too much for me.

*"Phoenix, Daddy Seth is taking me to see Ace. Uncle Magnus says I can ride him."*

I smiled at that and bent down to her level since she had to crane her neck to see me otherwise. I'd never met the horse Magnus DuCane owned and had recently brought with him to Seattle after leaving Texas, but I'd heard, or seen rather, Nicole asking her fathers if she could go see the big animal often enough. I suspected the men had a horse-crazy daughter on their hands.

"That's exciting," I said as I slowly signed out the right words.

"Phoenix, hi, come on in," I heard Seth call as he made his way down the hall towards us. I wasn't surprised to see his and Ronan's youngest child, Jamie, in tow, the boy's cherished Spiderman doll clutched between his chubby fingers.

It had been nearly five months since Ronan and Seth had taken in the three orphans as foster children and from everything I'd seen, they'd managed the impossible and made themselves into a family. I knew they were eager to adopt the children and had already started the process of making the situation permanent. While the kids had initially been reserved around both men, they'd warmed up quickly once they'd realized they were finally safe and in a home that would give them the love and security they'd lost after their parents had died in a car accident.

I'd been surprised by Nicole's attachment to me, especially considering both the fact that she was deaf and shy around strangers and that I wasn't what someone would consider a non-threatening guy. With my dark skin tone, heavy build and tattoos, I wasn't the kind of man a kid like Nicole would have gravitated to. But for some reason, she'd been intrigued by me from the get-go and I was more than happy to return her affection.

Even if being around her was both joyous and painful for me at the same time.

"Hey, Seth," I said as I rose and moved into the house. "Heard you have a big afternoon planned."

The young man had his hands full with a couple of jackets, a large tote bag slung over his shoulder and a smaller bag that looked packed full of snacks, sippy cups and several carrots.

And I'd never seen him looking happier.

I'd known Seth for less than a year, and while I hadn't met him before he'd become involved with my boss, Ronan Grisham, it hadn't taken a genius to know how difficult the young man's life had been and how much he'd suffered. At the tender age of fourteen, he'd lost both his parents in a brutal home invasion which had also left him severely injured and traumatized. A few months later, his older brother had been stolen away from him when he'd been murdered by a group of homophobic fellow soldiers. Ronan, who'd been in a relationship with Seth's brother at the time, had been badly injured in the same attack. I didn't know all the details, but I knew enough that both men hadn't really started living again until they'd found each other.

And now they had it all and deservedly so. It was clear as day in

Seth's eyes every time he looked at his children or his husband. The same could be said of Ronan.

I was happy for them, though their joy was a near constant reminder of my own loss.

"Yeah," Seth said with a sigh as he looked at all the stuff in his arms as if trying to make sure he wasn't missing anything. He looked up at me with a big smile. I liked how he signed even as he spoke so that Nicole could follow the conversation. It was a habit I was trying to remember since I never wanted the little girl to feel left out. "Ronan's in the study-"

"I'm here," I heard Ronan interject as he walked towards us. While his eyes were on his husband, I didn't miss the tension in his frame. I couldn't help but wonder if his obvious agitation had anything to do with why I was here. I couldn't tell if Seth had noticed or not, because by the time Ronan reached us, he'd relaxed both his stance and his expression.

"Have fun," Ronan said as he leaned down to talk to Nicole. "Daddy Seth is going to take lots of pictures for me and I'll come next time, okay?"

I had no trouble understanding Nicole's response.

*"Promise?"*

"Promise," Ronan whispered as he signed. Then he was tugging the girl into his arms. Jamie was next, but Ronan stood up with him as the boy clung to him. He leaned in to kiss Seth. "Text me when you get there?"

I was envious of the intimacy between the two men. Every look and every touch they shared spoke volumes. Becoming fathers hadn't changed any of that.

"I will," Seth said softly.

To Jamie, Ronan said, "You have fun with Matty and Leo. Clothes stay on, right?" he said.

Jamie considered him for a moment before saying, "Leo says I can run faster without them."

I stifled a chuckle. I'd seen Magnus's young grandson, Matty, and his best friend Leo take Jamie under their wing at Matty's fathers' wedding at Christmas. Between the superhero shoes Jamie was wearing and his insistence that nudity was a precursor to enhanced abilities, Ronan and Seth were out of luck. They'd already lost their youngest to his hero worship of the two slightly older boys.

Ronan shook his head, but there was no mistaking the grin on his face. "Do what Uncle Dante says, okay?"

Jamie nodded eagerly and then his arms went around Ronan's neck. "Bye, Daddy Ronan," he said softly.

"Bye, Son. See you soon, okay?"

Jamie nodded. Ronan put him down so the little boy could put his free hand on the neck of Bullet, the large German Shepherd that was always wherever the kids were.

"Dante's babysitting?" I asked.

Seth laughed. "He is. He's called me three times in a panic about what snacks to give the kids and to ask if I thought he and Aleks were enough to handle the three boys or if he needed to bring in backup."

I smiled. Leave it to Dante Thorne, Magnus's soon-to-be-husband, to turn babysitting three boys under the age of six into a mission.

"Okay, we should go," Seth said as he gave Ronan one last lingering kiss. "See you later."

Ronan nodded and then he was helping Seth get the kids out the door. I wasn't surprised that the dog was going with them.

The second the door closed, Ronan's mask of contentment slipped away. It was startling to see the level of anger in his eyes. He didn't say anything as he turned on his heel and began striding towards the study. I wisely kept my mouth shut because I knew his fury had nothing to do with me.

Though it was undoubtedly why I was here.

"I need you to look into something for me," Ronan said as he went to his desk and sat down. He punched the keyboard of his computer while I sat down in one of the guest chairs on the opposite side of the desk. The printer began spitting out pages and as soon as it was done, Ronan snatched them up and slapped them down on the desk in front of me.

The first thing I saw was a mug shot of a young man with spiky blond hair and light green eyes. I guessed him to be no more than nineteen or so and a quick glance at the arrest record showed my guess was right.

*Levi Deming, eighteen.*

The arrest report was several years old, putting the guy's current age at 24.

"Drug possession?" I asked as I read the charge. Ronan's group rarely went after people for drugs unless their crimes hurt other people. There was nothing on the report to indicate the kid had committed any other crimes besides being caught with a minimal amount of heroin, not even enough to warrant an additional charge of intent to distribute.

Ronan didn't say anything as he turned his screen so I could see it. The image looking back at me was a still shot of a suburban street. It was grainy and had been taken at night, but there was enough light coming from the street lamps to make out a couple of houses and a car parked in front of one of them. I glanced at the date stamp on the image. It had been taken a week ago.

Before I could ask Ronan why he was showing me the image, it changed to one that was nearly identical. The same car was parked in nearly the exact same spot, but the date was different. It was a day later.

Ronan continued moving forward through the images, four in all. Same car in the same spot four nights in a row.

"These are from a security camera from this house here," Ronan said as he pointed to a spot on the screen across from the house outside which the car was parked.

"Okay," I said, still confused as to why he was showing me the images. A car sitting in front of a house was nothing. More than nothing, actually.

But one look at Ronan and I knew it wasn't nothing. He was practically seething. As a trauma surgeon, the man typically oozed calm and collected, but right now, he was anything but.

"The car," – Ronan pointed at the single car on the screen – "is registered to Curtis Deming, Levi Deming's father."

I didn't respond since the man clearly wasn't done.

"That house," – he jabbed his finger at the house behind the car – "used to belong to Seth's parents."

Tension crept into my bones as I started to suspect where the conversation was headed.

"I've been having Daisy monitor Levi Deming's movements for the past year. When he used his debit card to buy gas at a gas station on Mercer Island where the house is located, she hacked into the security system of the house across the street from Seth's old house and found this." He motioned to the image on the screen.

"You sold that house, right?"

He nodded. "Last fall before we got married."

"That's the house his parents were killed in, wasn't it?" I asked. "And Seth was attacked."

"Stabbed," Ronan said, the fury in his voice barely leashed. "His mother was raped and stabbed to death in an upstairs bedroom while Seth and his father were being held downstairs. Seth was…" Ronan's voice dropped off and I watched him swallow hard. "Seth was tortured to get his father to talk – to reveal the location of a safe that didn't exist. When the men didn't get what they wanted, they slit his father's throat and stabbed Seth and left him for dead." Ronan paused long enough to get ahold of his emotions. I'd seen the man deal with the most brutal of killers and never once had he lost his cool. But now, he barely seemed to be holding it together.

"Three men," he bit out. "One was the stepson of Seth's father's business partner."

"And the other two?" I asked.

"Ricky Deming," Ronan said quietly, though with no less danger in his voice. His finger dropped to the picture on the desk in front of me. "And his younger brother, Levi."

I felt my insides drop out as my eyes fell back to the picture. The guy looked like nothing more than a scared kid who'd gotten in over his head. He was scrawny and pale and slight enough that a stiff wind would likely blow him over, so the idea of him wielding a knife and torturing innocent people before brutally murdering them seemed too far-fetched to believe.

"The stepson is gone – he helped his stepfather kidnap Seth last summer."

I nodded. I'd heard about that. One of Ronan's first recruits into the group, Mace Calhoun and one of Mace's lovers, had helped Ronan find Seth. Both abductors had been killed in the process.

"And the other two?" Clearly Levi was still alive or I wouldn't be sitting in Ronan's office watching the man trying to keep himself from imploding with rage.

"I had Ricky terminated. He murdered his ex-girlfriend, but got off with a sweetheart plea deal. Served less than three years. Before that, he'd been charged in two different rape cases but prosecutors couldn't make the charges stick."

I nodded. "You think he's the one who killed Seth's mother."

Ronan jerked his head in a brief nod.

"And Levi?"

"Served three and a half years for drug possession. Had been keeping his nose clean." Ronan's gaze returned to the computer screen. "Until now," he said ominously.

I had to admit, it didn't look good. It was unlikely the guy knew Seth and Ronan had sold the house. Which meant there was only one reason he was returning to the scene of the crime.

He wanted a second bite at the apple.

Since he'd already know his way around the place, it would make it that much easier for him to make a second attempt to get what he and his brother had missed out on the first time around.

"So, no charges were ever brought against any of them for what happened to Seth and his parents?"

Ronan shook his head. "We decided to give Levi a chance to clean up his act."

I nodded. The fact that the guy had been caught with heroin on him was a clear sign of a possible motive for why he'd go after Seth again. Addicts did stupid things to get their next fix. In the man's muddled mind, Seth would be an easy target, even though he was no longer a child. Not to mention that Seth was an extremely wealthy young man – something that was public knowledge.

I almost felt sorry for the guy. A second chance from someone like Ronan, especially after such a brutal attack on the man who was his entire world, was like winning the fucking lottery. The kid had squandered that...big time.

"I want you to monitor him," Ronan said. "And if he so much as even jaywalks, I want you to terminate him."

Ronan's ruthlessness didn't surprise me, but his level of certainty at how this would all play out unnerved me just a little bit. Not to mention the stakes. If I fucked this up and Levi got another chance at Seth...

I couldn't even consider the possibility.

I wouldn't fuck up, no matter what. I owed Ronan everything. If this kid gave me even one sign that he'd returned to his old ways, I'd take him out with much more mercy than he and his brother had shown Seth and his family.

"You have someone watching Seth and the kids?" I asked.

Ronan nodded. "Seth doesn't know. And I want to keep it that way."

I'd suspected as much. Seth had been struggling with anxiety ever since the attack. It had made him borderline agoraphobic before Ronan had come along. Ronan and Seth had the perfect life now and Ronan wouldn't let anything threaten that, especially not a foolish addict who didn't even have the brains to seek out a new target.

"Consider it done," I said as I stood, snagging the stack of papers off the desk.

Ronan nodded, but didn't stand to walk me out. He looked... defeated. I suspected that came from the fear he was feeling, not to mention the fact that he was having to keep such a secret from his husband.

"I'll send the rest of the information to you," Ronan said. "Last known address, financials, that kind of thing."

I gave him a quick nod and turned to go, but then thought better of it. "Ronan," I said quietly and waited until he looked up at me. "Nothing will happen to him."

A soft sigh escaped Ronan's lips, but he didn't say anything. He merely nodded.

I left the study and headed towards the front door. I couldn't say I was particularly excited about potentially ending the life of young Levi Deming, but Seth and Ronan were family now.

And I always protected my family.

## CHAPTER 1

### LEVI

I'd always hated the rain as a child since it had meant being cooped up inside which, considering the household I'd grown up in, had been akin to torture. But after having spent more than three years of my life not being able to do something as simple as feeling the rain on my skin if I wanted to, I doubted I'd ever have a problem with slogging through the torrential downpours or heavy blankets of mist that Seattle was dually known for. Besides, it made the sensation of the sun warming my skin all the sweeter.

One good thing about the rain was that it meant I'd be less likely to encounter trouble once I set foot outside my apartment.

And by trouble, I was talking about actual Trouble.

With a capital T.

How the guy had figured giving himself the nickname "Trouble" would make him seem tough was beyond me, but apparently, he hadn't relied on the stupid name alone to gain the street cred he'd needed to make a name for himself. And clearly, I wasn't the only one who thought the name was ridiculous because just about everyone called him T.

Even his big brother, Gun.

Yep, that was *his* actual name. Though I'd been told Gun was short for Gunnar which was a Swedish name. Since I didn't even know where to find Sweden on a map, I'd had to take my cellmate Hank's word for it that Gun's stark blond hair, sharp blue eyes and burly body were proof of his Scandinavian heritage. Not that any of that had mattered whenever Gun had cornered me in the shower.

I shivered as the memories washed over me and automatically scanned my surroundings again as I hurried down the sidewalk.

T, whose real name I'd heard through the rumor mill was Hugo, might not be as big as his older brother, but he was proving to be no less dangerous.

A lesson I'd learned within a month of walking out of Washington State Penitentiary after serving three and a half years of a five-year drug possession sentence. T had been waiting for me outside my apartment building. To this day, I still had no clue how he'd found me and when he'd shoved me up against the side of the building and slugged me, I hadn't even known who he was. It had only been when he'd dragged me into the alley next to my building, pushed me to my knees and told me he had a message for me from Gun that I'd realized I'd walked out of one hell and into another.

That had been a year ago.

I'd been at T's mercy ever since.

Except for when he was in jail. I kept hoping he'd be collared for something serious enough to send him to prison, but life wasn't proving to be that kind. At most, he was gone for a couple of weeks at a time, once for an entire month. Every time I'd think maybe it was finally safe to take a deep breath, I'd round a corner and there he'd be.

Of course, it was no less than I deserved.

It was one of the many reasons I never prayed for things to change, though Father O'Shaughnessy had assured me repeatedly that God would be listening when I was ready to talk. I'd believed that line when I'd been a naïve kid begging God to bring my mother home or asking Him to make my dad and my older brother Ricky stop using drugs and alcohol long enough to keep from using me as their personal punching bag…and worse.

I didn't believe in much anymore and especially not in things I couldn't see or feel. And even on the off chance that Father O could convince me that the same higher power existed who'd ignored so many pleas that night seven years ago, my own included, I wouldn't be wasting His time asking for forgiveness for everything I'd done.

I didn't deserve it.

Not from Him.

Not from the young man I'd helped make suffer in the cruelest of ways.

No, T was my well-earned penance. I deserved everything he did to me and then some. If I wasn't such a fucking coward, I'd walk into the nearest police station and finally do what I should have done seven years ago.

Only, it wasn't just about me anymore.

I found some relief from the rain when I reached the bus shelter. On most days, I'd just walk the fifteen blocks that took me from home to St. Anthony's or work, but I was already running late after having had another row with Dina this morning. Our conversation had been proof that I needed to give up the evenings I spent at St. Anthony's before I headed to work, but I was struggling with the idea of no longer volunteering at the soup kitchen Father O ran. Letting T punish my body did nothing to ease the burden on my soul. I knew helping feed a few dozen homeless people night after night wasn't much, but it was one of only two bright spots in my life and I wasn't ready to give it up yet. Though, if Dina had her way, giving up one bright spot was the only way to keep the other one.

Thankfully, the bus was on time and was mostly empty, so I didn't have any trouble finding a seat.

"Hi Carl," I said to the driver with a nod as I slid my metro card through the reader.

"Wasn't sure I'd see you this afternoon," the older man said. "It's barely even drizzling out."

I nearly smiled at that because it was most definitely more than drizzling, but for Seattle, the steady rain, though light, was pretty much a part of the city's landscape, just like the Marketplace and the Space

Needle. Only tourists would feel the need to escape the weather, either by using an umbrella or sticking to indoor activities.

"Running late," I explained. "How's Clarice?"

Carl snorted. "Wants me to take her to the opera for our fortieth anniversary," he groused. "Says I need to wear a monkey suit and everything."

I chuckled. "Better do it," I suggested. "Forty's a big deal."

"Thirty-nine years of dinner at the Olive Garden suddenly ain't fancy enough for her anymore," the older man muttered. "Damn woman."

I patted the man on the shoulder. "Don't forget to get her flowers and act like you're picking her up for your date," I said with a smile before going to the first seat and dropping down into it. Carl grumbled something before swinging the door closed and getting the bus moving.

A chill swept over my body as the warmth of the bus clashed with my wet clothes. Not a good day to have forgotten my jacket, which would have at least offered a bit of protection from the weather. For as late as it was in spring, Mother Nature didn't seem willing to completely let go of winter just yet.

Exhaustion settled into my limbs as the gentle motion of the bus had me seeking out the corner of the seat. I let my head loll against the window as I watched the scenery roll by. Rush hour was starting to pick up so the bus moved at a snail's pace, giving the warmth from the heater a chance to settle over me. Before I knew it and against my wishes, my eyes rolled shut and I was dropped right back into the same nightmare I'd been re-living for the last seven years.

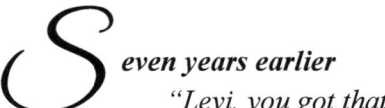

*even years earlier*

"*Levi, you got that?*"

*Before I even had a chance to nod, Ricky's open hand slapped the side of my head.*

"*Stop that fucking daydreaming, you little shit!*" *Ricky snapped.*

*I managed to dodge his next slap, which only served to enrage my brother more and he shifted his whole body so he could lean over the car's front bench seat into the back and grab me by the hair.*

*"You fuck this up for me..." he warned.*

*"I won't!" I cried out as tears stung my eyes. "I promise, Ricky."*

*I held perfectly still as he studied me. It was pitch dark in the car, but it still felt like he could see everything in my eyes. Hell, if he'd been hanging onto my arm, he would have felt how cold I was, as well as the tremors that were violently wracking my body.*

*Ricky shoved me away and I quickly slunk to the corner of the backseat so I was just behind the driver's seat. It wouldn't stop Ricky from getting to me if he really wanted to, but the farther away I was from him, the easier it would be to get ahold of myself.*

*I wanted to laugh at that.*

*Who the fuck was I kidding?*

*I was about to commit so many crimes, I'd easily spend the rest of my life in prison. The idea actually appealed to me for the briefest of moments because it meant getting away from Ricky and my father. But with my luck, they'd stick Ricky in the same cell with me.*

*The car started moving again and I clenched my fingers around the gloves and black ski mask in my hand. Light from the overhead street lamps illuminated the car every dozen feet or so, giving me a partial view of the man driving. Ricky had only introduced him as Jed. I guessed him to be a few years older than Ricky, which put him in his mid-twenties. The guy hadn't spoken to me at all, which was fine by me since he scared the ever-loving shit out of me. Whereas Ricky ran hot and lashed out when he was pissed off, I got the impression Jed was the opposite.*

*Quiet, cold, lethal.*

*I turned my head so I could watch out the window. I hadn't paid much attention to where we were going when Ricky had forced me into the car after telling me I was helping him with a job. Since I knew what kind of "jobs" Ricky did, I'd tried to tell him no, but all that had done was earn me a punch to the side of the head that had left my ears ringing. It wasn't until we'd stopped in a gas station's abandoned parking lot a few minutes ago that Ricky had explained my role in what he'd* said would be a simple burglary if I could just keep my shit together. Apparently, the guy we were going to rob was loaded and we had just one goal when we got to the man's house.

Find the wall safe where he kept loads of cash.

Ricky had gotten excited when he'd explained about that part and he'd looked to Jed for reassurance, which had me guessing this whole thing was likely Jed's doing. Which made sense as we drove past one huge house after another. No way Ricky would have known anyone in this kind of neighborhood.

Hell, Ricky and I weren't even good enough to mow these peoples' lawns or wash their fancy cars.

I didn't have time to dwell on how I'd gotten into this mess because the car suddenly slowed and I watched Jed flick off the headlights as he pulled over to the curb. Houses surrounded us on both sides so I had no idea which one was our target.

"Here," Ricky snapped as he thrust something over the seat at me. I swallowed hard as I realized what it was.

A gun.

"No, Ricky," I said and automatically covered my head when he lunged at me.

"Take the fucking gun, Levi."

I knew that voice. It was his 'I'm done fucking around' voice.

I tried to stifle the whimper that crawled out of my throat as I took the revolver from him. A shiver ran up my spine as the brief image of me turning the gun on him flitted through my mind. But even if I'd had the balls to do it, my ridiculous hope was dashed when I heard Ricky tell Jed the gun wasn't loaded when Jed asked if it was a good idea to be giving me the weapon.

"Mask, gloves," Ricky ordered a moment later.

I watched in mute horror as both men pulled their ski masks on and worked gloves over their hands.

I needed to run. I couldn't do this. I didn't care if we were just taking money from a guy who had plenty of it to go around.

But even as I reached for the handle of the door with one shaky hand, my gaze fell to Ricky's and I saw him watching me. The little bit of light streaming in from a nearby street lamp reflected off the knife in his hand and I knew what it meant. I understood his silent message loud and clear.

Didn't matter that I was his brother, his blood...he'd kill me just the same.

Even knowing the gun wasn't loaded, I carefully put it in my lap before putting on the gloves and then working the mask over my head. It felt itchy and hot against my chilled skin.

The car began moving again, but it only went a few dozen feet before turning into the driveway of one of the slightly smaller houses on the block. Jed had left the headlights off, but I could still make out the house's white siding and dark shutters. It was the kind of house I'd dreamed of living in when I was a kid.

That was back before I'd realized dreams really didn't come true, despite all the shit grown-ups told you.

My stomach crawled as I got out of the car. Ricky had already warned me not to close the door the whole way since it would make too much noise, so I only pushed it against the door frame enough so it would stay closed. I scanned the area around us, expecting the cops to jump out at any second.

I wasn't sure if I wanted them to or not.

But when Ricky grabbed me as soon as I walked around to the other side of the car and wrapped his fingers around my throat, I knew I did want that. I would have welcomed anyone stepping in at that moment...even if it meant spending the rest of my life behind bars. At least then I'd finally know what it was like to have a moment's peace.

Ricky didn't say anything as he held me like that. He didn't have to. I heard him just fine through the painful pinch of his fingers and the stiffness of his frame as he loomed over me.

By the time he released me, I just wanted to get the whole thing over with so I could go home and crawl into my bed and find escape in the only place Ricky couldn't reach me. Of course, after tonight, I had no doubt that if I did manage to sleep, the events that were about to happen would plague my dreams, and Ricky would have a starring role.

Ricky released me with a hard shove that nearly had me falling to the ground. I managed to catch myself against the car and then I docilely followed him and Jed around the side of the house. The gun felt like it weighed a ton as I watched Jed pick the lock on the three-car garage's side door. Once we got inside, I took note of the three cars parked there, but it wasn't until I heard Jed and Ricky's muffled voices that I realized something was wrong and I forced myself to focus.

Horror dawned when I realized the topic of their conversation. They too had noticed the cars and were talking about the likelihood that more than just the man was home and something about that not being part of the plan. They argued furiously for several long seconds and then Jed was moving forward to shove open the door leading from the garage into the house.

"Ricky!" I began in a panic as I realized things had just gone from bad to worse.

Much, much worse.

"Shut the fuck up!" Ricky snarled before hitting the side of my head hard enough to have me seeing stars. I was barely aware of anything as Ricky's fingers closed around my arm and I was dragged into the house into what appeared to be a laundry room. The only light came from a small flashlight Jed was carrying so I focused on it to try to get my bearings. It wasn't until we began climbing a set of stairs that my head cleared. I followed Ricky's silent order to go with Jed.

After that, chaos ensued as Jed went into a big bedroom and turned on the light. The man in the bed startled awake, but Jed was on him before he could do anything more than sit up. Jed hit him hard, then pointed his gun at the woman who was slowly waking up. I was quaking - literally quaking - as I watched Jed force the crying couple out of bed.

"Please, don't hurt my wife!" the man cried out as he tried to go around the bed to get to the woman.

"Shut the fuck up!" Jed snarled and then he hit the man in the head with the butt of the gun. The woman cried out and for the briefest of moments, her eyes connected with mine. I nearly threw up at the sight of her unspoken plea.

*But I did nothing.*

*Not a fucking thing.*

The woman rushed around to the other side of the bed and fell to her knees next to her husband. Blood was trickling down the side of his face.

"Please," the woman sobbed as she cradled the man's head against her body. "Tell us what you want!"

"I want you to shut the fuck up," Jed bit out, his voice emotionless as he put his gun against the woman's head.

She fell silent, her body wracked with sobs as her husband struggled to sit up. He seemed dazed, but he jerked upright suddenly and yelled, "Seth!"

I followed his gaze to just behind me and barely managed to stifle a hoarse shout at the sight of my brother dragging a teenage boy into the room, his gloved hand biting into the kid's arm. The kid was sobbing as he called out to his parents.

"Shut up," Ricky ordered as he put a gun to the kid's head. The room instantly went eerily silent as everyone froze. Then Jed was moving. He dragged the father to his feet and the mother quickly followed. He shoved them forward.

"Downstairs!" was all he said and then Ricky was pulling the crying boy from the room. The parents stumbled past me as they hurried to keep their eyes on their son.

"Levi!" Jed yelled as he followed the parents from the room.

But I couldn't move, couldn't think as I just stood there.

I heard Jed call out to me again and I dimly wondered why he was using my name in the middle of a burglary.

And then it hit me.

Hard.

Because he wasn't planning on leaving any witnesses behind who could repeat my name to the cops.

That was when I leaned over and threw up.

"*L*evi."

Jed's voice sounded wrong. Lighter. Gentler.

"Levi."

I flinched when he started shaking me. I needed to get it together or Ricky would kill me for sure.

"Levi!"

I suddenly jerked awake and nearly fell off the bench. Reality quickly returned as Carl's worried face came into focus. I scanned the bus and saw the few other passengers staring at me in confusion.

"Sorry, Carl," I said as I straightened.

"It's your stop, buddy," Carl said softly as he motioned out the window. I nodded and repeated the apology as I stumbled to my feet.

"You okay?" Carl asked.

"Yeah, yeah," I responded. "Thanks," I added as I pushed past him. Not once in the year I'd been riding the bus had I ever actually fallen asleep, despite the near constant state of exhaustion I lived in. "I'll see you later," I murmured as I hurried off the bus, not sparing Carl another glance.

I was still too rattled by the fact that I'd had my regular nightmare in the daytime.

Of course, I supposed it didn't count as a nightmare since every bit of the events of that night were true.

I felt cold all over as the rain pelted my body. It was only another two-block walk to St. Anthony's, but it felt like a mile. Unlike my walk from the apartment to the bus stop, I wasn't paying the least bit attention to my surroundings as I ducked down the alley that led to the back of the church and the entrance to the kitchen. So, I didn't see him until I was practically on top of him.

"Hello, Princess. Miss me?"

## CHAPTER 2

## PHOENIX

Watching one guy blow another should have been a turn on in most cases, but the sight before me just made me sick. Maybe if the act hadn't been taking place in a dirty, narrow alley surrounded by garbage, I could have found something erotic about the whole thing. Though doubtful, considering the guy doing the blowing was my target. Under normal circumstances, he was exactly my type… lean, slight and almost on the pretty side. But knowing who he was and what he'd done made any attraction I might have felt for him null and void.

I'd been following Levi for only a few days now, and while his routine was mundane to say the least, I hadn't yet seen him do anything that would warrant me putting a bullet in his brain. Ironically, he hadn't even jaywalked when he'd had the opportunity to.

I'd half expected him to return to the property on Mercer Island that had once belonged to Seth's parents, but the guy hadn't strayed beyond his nighttime work at a small Mom and Pop grocery store and the rundown apartment building he lived in. The only other place he visited was the alley between a small church and an abandoned warehouse. The first time I'd seen him disappear down the alley, I'd lost track of him and had assumed he'd used it to get from one street to another. When he'd repeated the move the second day, I'd been ready and had quickly driven around the block to wait for him to come out the other side, but when he hadn't, I'd been left with two options – the church or the warehouse. Since the church had seemed like an unlikely destination for someone like him, I'd gone looking for him in the warehouse, which had turned out to be a squatter's den full of homeless people and addicts, none of whom had run off when they'd spied me among them. I'd spent the better part of an hour looking for Levi, but either he'd managed to get past me or he'd never been there in the first place.

So today, I'd decided I'd need to risk following him more closely. The likelihood that he'd see me was greater, but the benefit was that the alley offered a considerable amount of privacy, so if I was lucky enough to catch him doing something like shooting up, I'd have the proof I needed that he was back to his old ways. But I hadn't expected to find him blowing some random guy. It occurred to me that he could be a prostitute since it wasn't unusual for addicts to sell themselves for the cash they needed for their next fix. But I hadn't seen any money exchange hands before the act and, in fact, Levi had looked less than thrilled to see the big blond guy. The man Levi was servicing was considerably larger than him, though not quite as big as me. His white-blond hair was stuck to his head from the drizzle that continued to blanket the air around us. He was rough with Levi, using his mouth hard and with little to no consideration for the other man. Even when Levi would try to pull back, presumably so he could catch his breath, the blond behemoth would tighten his hold on Levi's hair and just keep ramming his cock between the widely-stretched lips.

As far as I was concerned, the young man deserved everything he got, but I couldn't deny the flash of anger that rippled through me... and it wasn't directed at Levi. I couldn't hear what the blond was saying to Levi, but based on the way his lips sneered as he face-fucked him, I had a pretty good idea. I was close enough to hear the guy's very loud groan of completion as he jammed his dick as deep into Levi's mouth as he could get it, but I couldn't make out any of what he said after pulling his dick free and slapping it against Levi's chin.

His bare dick.

I shook my head at Levi's stupidity. If he was going to sell his ass, he should at least be smart enough to protect it. Not that I was an expert on the habits of prostitutes when it came to oral sex, but common sense dictated that the young man should have at least had the forethought to make his john wear a condom. Between being an addict and this, Levi's days would have been numbered even if I hadn't been tasked with doing the job myself.

I watched as Levi stumbled as he tried to right himself and a flash of fury washed through me when the blond kicked Levi when the smaller man's hands inadvertently landed on the guy's thighs as he tried to stand. Levi's palms hit the ground and I watched as he hung there for a moment on all fours, water dripping off his wet hair which was plastered around his head. An unwelcome thread of pity hit when I watched Levi spit out a small amount of white fluid which I knew wasn't saliva.

I expected the john to leave at that point, probably even without paying considering the vicious kick he'd laid on the young man, but instead, he wrapped his fingers around Levi's upper arm and yanked him to his feet. I heard Levi cry out at the harsh treatment and saw him reach up to grab the shoulder joint of the arm the guy still had ahold of. Levi's eyes instantly dropped and he stood there in silence as the man spoke to him. Frustration went through me at the fact that I couldn't hear any of what was being said. I saw Levi start shaking his head, which was clearly pissing off the other man. Things escalated quickly after Levi let out a hoarse "No" that was loud enough even for me to hear. The blond grabbed him and spun him around causing Levi's back to hit the wall of the building behind him. A vicious punch followed and before Levi could even bring up his arms to block his face, another hit had his head bouncing off the brick behind him.

I forced myself not to intervene, but the thought was short-lived when it became clear that Levi was making no move to escape the man or even defend himself.

"You think you can say no to me?" the man screamed as he

wrapped a hand around Levi's throat. "I own you, you fucking little bitch!"

I'd had enough and I was moving before I could even think better of it. Levi's instincts for self-preservation had finally seemed to kick in because his hands came up to grab the fingers wrapped around his throat. But a hard punch to the gut had Levi gasping for air as he tried to curl in on himself.

"Hey!" I shouted. "Get your hands off him!"

The blond barely reacted to the order, so I wasn't sure if he hadn't heard me or he just didn't give a shit. It didn't matter because I reached him just as he pulled his arm back to deliver another brutal blow. I caught his fist as it flew and put all my weight into throwing him backwards so that he was forced to release his hold on Levi's neck. Levi immediately crumpled to the ground as the blond fell back onto his ass. The man was smart enough not to come up swinging. Instead, he crab-walked backwards a few steps, his eyes full of a mix of surprise and fury. But whatever he saw in my eyes, it was enough to deter him.

"This isn't over!" the man snapped at Levi as he got to his feet and put more distance between us. The man casually straightened his shirt as if he didn't have a care in the world, but I did notice that he kept moving backwards out of my immediate reach. I was half tempted to reach for my gun just to show him that if I wanted his ass in a sling, I'd have it.

I waited until the guy turned tail and hurried out of the alley before turning to confront the young man I'd just saved.

The young man I was supposed to put a bullet through.

"You okay?" I asked, though it was a dumb question to ask since Levi's lip was already swelling and an ugly bruise was forming on his cheek. He was clutching his stomach with one arm.

"Yeah, thanks," he said as he sucked in a few deep breaths. His voice was softer than I'd imagined it would be.

Of course, the only time I'd imagined it always accompanied visions of him telling Seth to shut up as he was being carved up with a knife.

The reminder of who this man was had me stepping back instead of reaching down to give him a hand. Now would be just as good a time as any to pull out my gun and finish this, but I left my hand where it was. As much as I thought this man was scum for the role he'd played in brutalizing an innocent family, Ronan's orders had been clear. And while giving head to a guy in an alley wasn't the most moral of behaviors, it was hardly illegal since money hadn't appeared to change hands.

"You need me to call someone?" I asked. The injuries didn't appear to be life-threatening, but they sure as hell had to hurt.

Levi shook his head. "No, I'm okay," he said as he carefully climbed to his feet. Once he was upright, he leaned against the wall to catch his breath.

"You really should press charges," I said absently. "Your boyfriend shouldn't get away with that." Boyfriend was the politically correct word I'd managed to come up with. Because I was pretty sure the blond was Levi's pimp…especially after the free blow job and the crack about owning Levi.

"No," Levi murmured. "He's not my boyfriend…he…he was just some guy who got me mixed up with someone else."

It was the lamest excuse I'd ever heard, but I didn't call him on it. I certainly didn't want him to know I'd seen him performing oral sex on the guy. As it was, I had no clue how to explain my presence in the alley.

Levi's light green eyes came up to meet mine. His gaze swept my body from head to toe and I felt my dick stir at the perusal. That pissed me off, an emotion I couldn't manage to contain, because Levi quickly shrank back against the wall and watched me with fear-filled eyes.

"Well, if you don't need anything else," I murmured as I moved away from him. I wasn't sure why, but I didn't particularly like knowing I'd instilled fear in the guy. Which was ridiculous since he *should* be scared of me, considering what I was likely going to have to do to him.

"Um, wait," Levi said as I turned my back on him.

I took my time turning back around and saw that he'd stepped away from the wall a little bit. He tensed briefly and then glanced at a door on the other side of the alley. "Listen, the kitchen doesn't open for a couple of hours, but if you want to come inside to get out of this weather, I can get some coffee going. Father O wouldn't mind."

"Kitchen?" I asked dumbly.

Levi nodded, but when I didn't react, his features fell. "Um, you're here for dinner, right?" His eyes shifted to the door opposite us and I finally saw a small sign that I hadn't noticed before.

*St. Anthony's Soup Kitchen*
*Hours: 7am-9am & 6pm-8pm*

"Listen, it's okay," Levi said and I turned my gaze back on him. "Everybody needs help once in a while, right?"

It finally dawned on me what he was talking about. He thought I was there for a free meal. I was so surprised that I didn't respond right away, which seemed to make Levi more nervous.

"I mean, you don't have to be homeless to need a helping hand…"

His voice dropped off as he scanned my body again and I realized he was taking in my clothes. I wasn't wearing anything particularly fancy – just a pair of jeans and a long-sleeved black shirt that I wore untucked so it would hide my gun, which was at the back of my waistband. But my clothes were clean and in good shape – not necessarily the typical clothes of someone living on the streets.

"You work here?" I asked as I glanced at the door again.

Levi nodded and then winced slightly before lifting his hand to steady his jaw. "I'm one of the volunteers. Father O lets me open and get set up so I can leave a bit earlier to get to my job on time."

"Father O?"

"Father O'Shaughnessy. He's the priest here." Levi fell silent for a moment. "Why don't you come inside? I think there's some leftover turkey – I could make you a sandwich while you wait. It's…it's the least I can do for what you did for me."

It was a terrible idea. The last thing I needed to be doing was interacting with the guy. But I was also intrigued. Maybe the volunteering was just a ploy to look like he'd gone legit, or maybe it was a condition of his early release from prison. If I could get him talking, I might get him to put the nails in his own coffin.

"Okay," I said.

"Good," Levi responded. A small smile graced his lips, but didn't last long since the move also caused him to flinch in pain. "I'm Levi. What's your name?"

"Phoenix," I answered, not having an issue with giving him my real name. It wasn't like he'd be around long enough to tell the cops about me anyway.

"Phoenix," Levi said softly and I felt my traitorous cock twitch. Fuck, I absolutely could not be attracted to this guy.

"It's nice to meet you, Phoenix," Levi said as he stuck out his hand.

"You too…Levi," I responded as I shook his hand.

And inwardly cursed myself as sparks of electricity fired through my palm and directly to my dick.

A whole hell of a lot of sparks.

Yeah, this was bad.

Really, really bad.

## CHAPTER 3

### LEVI

"Would you excuse me a second?" I asked as soon as I showed Phoenix where he could sit and went to the coffee machine to get it going. My face hurt like crazy and I could taste blood in my mouth along with the lingering flavor of T's cum. I'd hoped to spit all of it out after T had finished, but he'd kept his cock shoved down my throat for so long that I'd had no choice but to swallow some of it.

Either way, it meant yet another round of STD testing. At this rate, the people at the free clinic wouldn't even need to ask my name or what I was there for.

I'd tried a few times to get T to wear a condom, but he hadn't given a shit. But he hadn't hesitated to tell me if *I* gave *him* anything, he'd kick my ass. I hadn't bothered to tell him that anything he picked up would come from one of his numerous "girlfriends" since I hadn't had sex in a few years…not since Gun had decided to make me his bitch in the shower the day after I'd stepped off the prison bus that had transported me from my hellish past to a whole new world of torture and torment.

Being Gun's toy had only lasted a few weeks because Hank had taken pity on me after finding me on the floor of the shower, broken and bleeding from several of my body's openings after Gun had let his disciples take turns using me as punishment for going to the guards and begging for help. As much as I'd deserved everything I'd gotten the moment I'd stepped off the prison bus, I hadn't been able to withstand Gun's brutality. At one point, I'd even begged him to kill me, but he'd merely laughed at me and asked me why he'd get rid of a perfectly good new fuck toy.

Luckily, with T, his brutality was limited to rough blowjobs. I'd learned enough about blowing a guy from Gun that I could usually make T come quickly, and fortunately, he hadn't shown any interest in me beyond using my mouth on occasion. But I suspected my reprieve wasn't going to last because he'd spent much of the blowjob today wondering aloud if he fucked me from behind, would my ass be any different than any other bitch's. His words had scared the hell out of me and I'd worked harder to make him come quickly so he wouldn't push me down on all fours and shove into me like Gun always used to do. T had always made a big show of calling me a faggot and asking me if maybe I was hiding a pussy beneath my clothes because I was so pretty. I guessed it was his way of reminding me he wasn't gay and that fucking my mouth didn't count as being with another guy.

I'd expected T to just leave me there like he usually did after he came, but I'd been surprised when he'd had a new demand this time around.

And as soon as he'd voiced it, I'd wished he'd told me he was going to fuck me instead, because there was no way I could give him what he was asking.

Not couldn't…wouldn't.

Most of the choices in my life had been taken from me, either by Ricky, prison, or Gun and T, but there were still a few things I would say no to until my dying breath.

T could beat me, fuck me, even kill me, but I would never hurt another living soul ever again. Even if what he was asking might not physically endanger someone, it would be breaking the trust of someone who'd believed in me…who'd taken a chance on me when no one else had.

T hadn't liked hearing no, and I'd prepared myself for his displeasure, but he hadn't gotten very far with his beating before he'd been interrupted.

*Phoenix.*

Even thinking about the man's unique name had me searching him out. I found him watching me intently and I suddenly realized I'd asked him to excuse me for a moment, but hadn't heard his answer. Shit, how long had I been standing in front of the coffee maker, my finger on the start button?

"Sorry," I mumbled as I pressed the button. "Be right back," I added as I hurried from the kitchen. There was a private bathroom near the storage room where the non-perishable food items were kept. I avoided the mirror as I searched out the small bottle of mouthwash I kept beneath the sink. I'd gotten smart after the first time T had confronted me on my way to the soup kitchen and bought a couple of bottles of the strong antiseptic-style liquid in the hopes it would offer some protection against any diseases T sent my way, in addition to helping get rid of the disgusting flavor that no amount of juice, water or coffee could mask.

Once I'd gargled for several minutes and spit the mix of mouthwash and blood into the sink, I looked up to study myself in the mirror. All in all, the damage wasn't as bad as it usually was. I guess I had Phoenix to thank for that. My thoughts drifted to the man waiting in the other room for me as I began dabbing at my cut lip with some wet paper towels.

For starters, the guy was huge. Not that that was a surprise since at 5'9, I couldn't even be considered average. Phoenix had to be at least six inches taller than me and probably outweighed me by 75 pounds or more. Even Gun hadn't been that big. I hadn't missed the tattoos on the man's dark skin where the collar of his shirt had shifted as he'd knocked T to the ground, nor had I been able to look away from his piercing eyes which were so dark, they looked almost black.

Phoenix's hair was cropped short and he had a neatly trimmed beard that framed beautifully wide, full lips. I was inexplicably intrigued by those lips, which wasn't the norm for me since I tended to shy away from guys like him...hell, any guys these days, since my only experiences with sex were something I'd rather forget, but was condemned to remember and apparently repeat if T got his way.

Which he would.

I sighed as I studied my reflection. Why was I even thinking about all this? Not only was the man in the other room likely not even gay, but the last thing I wanted was to get involved with someone.

Involved?

I laughed out loud.

Guys didn't get involved with me. They fucked me. They used me. My body was my form of payment and nothing more. Hell, my body wouldn't even react to my own hand anymore. In what universe would I have a normal reaction to a good-looking guy like Phoenix?

Yeah, I'd felt a little flutter of excitement when I'd first gotten a good look at him, similar to what I'd felt when I was a kid and I'd gotten assigned Kyle Verona, the most popular kid in the eighth grade, as my lab partner. Back then, I'd often found myself battling to keep from popping a boner whenever Kyle would brush up against me as he leaned in to study the contents of our beaker, but nowadays, unwanted erections weren't something I had to worry about anymore. I'd thought that the mysterious flutter was gone too, but apparently not, because my stomach was currently doing little somersaults and I was eager to get back out to the kitchen at the same time that I wanted to hide out in the bathroom for the rest of the evening.

I shook my head and dismissed my errant thoughts that were clearly just a result of Phoenix riding in on his white steed to rescue me. I should have told him he was far too late.

Seven years too late to be exact.

I forced myself to finish cleaning up and made my way back to the kitchen. A shimmer of disappointment went through me when I saw the chair Phoenix had been sitting in was empty. But the unexpected sadness only lasted long enough for me to round the corner and nearly run right into him where he was standing in front of the coffee machine. He put his hands out to catch me by the arms just before my body made impact. Electricity danced beneath my skin at the contact, despite the fabric of my shirt separating us from being skin on skin. I couldn't stifle the gasp that escaped my lips as the sensation shot throughout my entire body.

Phoenix instantly dropped his hands and stepped back from me and I saw the same look he'd given me outside…the one that had set off warning bells in my head.

He hadn't looked at me like he wanted to fuck me…I would have preferred that look compared to the one I'd seen then and was again seeing now.

It was the same look he'd given T after he'd thrown him to the ground.

Cold, deadly anger.

I automatically stepped back. "Sorry," I murmured as I took in his tense frame. He shuttered the menacing look quickly and nodded at the coffee machine.

"You forgot to put water in it."

"What?" I asked stupidly, not really hearing his words since I was still caught up in trying to figure out why he'd looked at me twice now like he was regretting not letting T finish what he'd started. Had I done something to piss him off? Maybe I'd embarrassed him with my comment about everyone needing a helping hand? I mean, yeah, the guy didn't look homeless, but I knew looks were deceiving. And I certainly hadn't meant to offend him, but wasn't the hot meal the soup kitchen offered the reason he'd been in that alley?

Phoenix picked up the carafe full of water and poured it into the machine's water reservoir. "You didn't put any water in it." He flipped the switch and I listened as the coffee machine began pulling the water into the tank to heat it.

"Um, sorry," I murmured. I felt foolish for looking so scatter-brained to him. I had a lot of limitations when it came to my intelligence, but I was usually pretty good at following through on tasks, especially if they were part of a routine. But between T's demand in the alley and Phoenix's interruption, I was still struggling to process everything. Especially since I knew T would be back. Hell, I would likely find him waiting for me tonight when I left for work.

"Um, can I make you that sandwich?" I asked as I moved to the refrigerator to grab the supplies I'd need. The soup shelter wasn't blessed with a lot of donations, so the appliances were older and didn't have the capacity to feed as many people as Father O would have liked, but I'd never seen him turn someone away. I'd add some extra money to the locked donation box that sat at the end of the serving line to cover the cost of the extra food for Phoenix.

I felt rather than saw Phoenix behind me, but he didn't linger and by the time I had the meat, mayo and lettuce in my hands, he was back in the chair. I didn't miss the fact that he hadn't answered me, nor had he taken his eyes off me. The sensation of being watched made me uncomfortable, especially since my goal in life was to be invisible, but I forced myself to focus on fixing the food. "I'm sorry, all we have is leftover turkey," I murmured as I worked.

"That's fine."

I worked quickly, but when I reached for the plate with the sandwich on it to carry it over to where Phoenix was sitting, I heard him say, "Would you mind cutting it?"

I stilled at that and shot him a glance. It was a somewhat odd request, but who was I to judge?

I returned the plate to the counter and then took a deep breath as I reached for one of the butcher knives in the small block near the sink, since it would have looked strange to bypass them and search out one of the blunt dinner knives that were kept along with all the other silverware in a basket at the beginning of the serving line.

It should have been the easiest thing in the world to grab the knife and cut through the sandwich. It would literally take the average person a few seconds.

Except I wasn't average.

*Oh God, stop! Please, I swear, I'm telling you the truth!*

I flinched at the sound of the man's voice in my head…as loud now as it had been that night. And the young man's tortured sobs as he'd tried to be brave…

"You okay?"

I jerked at the sensation of Phoenix's hand on my forearm. When had he gotten up and moved to my side? I glanced down to see the fingers of my right hand biting into the edge of the plate so hard that my knuckles had gone bloodless. The knife was sitting next to the plate. The sandwich hadn't been cut.

I let out a choked laugh as I said, "Yeah, sorry, not sure what's wrong with me today."

I *did* know what was wrong, but I certainly wasn't going to tell him. I mean, what was I supposed to say?

*Um yeah, I watched a sick fuck carve up an innocent kid like he was nothing more than a Christmas ham and I stood by and did nothing. And now every time I pick up anything sharper than a butter knife, I'm right back in that house listening to a father beg for his son's life and wishing I had even half his kid's courage so I could do something, anything to stop it all.*

"You took a couple of pretty good hits," Phoenix said softly...so softly that I automatically looked up at him. This time he didn't look angry, just...confused.

That couldn't be right, could it?

"Yeah, I guess," I lied. "Sorry." I looked at the knife again, but when I felt the familiar bile crawling up my throat, I stepped away from the plate. "I should get you some coffee," I practically yelled. I quickly turned my back on him, hoping like hell he'd cut his own damn sandwich.

I took my time getting a mug from the cabinet above the coffee machine and by the time I'd located the container of powdered creamer and the basket holding the sugar packets, Phoenix was back at the small table, his sandwich cut, but untouched in front of him. I filled the mug and took it and the other items to the table. I was barely aware of Phoenix thanking me. "Um, I need to get started on dinner."

Phoenix nodded and waved me away. "Of course. Thank you for this," he said as he motioned to the coffee and sandwich.

I nodded and turned away from him. I was very aware of Phoenix's eyes on me as I started prepping everything, but I was still too embarrassed by my behavior to even consider looking his way or try drawing him into conversation. In fact, I was regretting even inviting him inside to wait for dinner service to start.

The routine of cooking started to relax me and after a while I nearly forgot about Phoenix all together until his rumbly voice had me jumping back from the pot of potatoes I was boiling so I could ultimately mash them.

"Is it okay if I wash this by hand?"

With my heart still racing, I looked over my shoulder at him and saw the empty plate in his hand. A small part of me was pleased to see he'd eaten all the food I'd made for him. I shook off the silly thought and said, "You can just leave it in the sink. I'll wash it in a bit."

The soup kitchen had a dishwasher, but it had broken a long time ago and it didn't make sense to put money that could be spent on other things towards fixing it when it was just as easy, if not a little more time consuming, to wash the dishes by hand. On the days when I didn't have to go to work after dinner service ended, I actually looked forward to the monotony of washing dishes.

"I don't mind," Phoenix said as he moved towards the sink. "I'm one of those people," he added.

"Those people?" I asked.

"You know, the ones who wash the dishes before they put them in the dishwasher. Or have to have everything put in the dishwasher just so."

I chuckled. "My mom was one of those…used to drive my dad crazy, especially after all the shit she gave him for not helping with the dishes."

"My mom too. She and I were constantly reorganizing the dishwasher after the other was done."

"What about your dad?" I asked.

"He and my sister wisely stayed out of the kitchen before and after dinner." Phoenix glanced over his shoulder at me. "The kitchen was my mom's domain…mine too, I guess."

I smiled at that. It wasn't exactly the manliest thing to admit to. "I used to cook with my mom all the time. Dishes were supposed to be my dad and brother's responsibility, but my dad usually got out of it by sweet-talking my mom."

"What about your brother?"

The warmth of the memory dissipated. "Ricky never did much of anything he didn't want to do."

My brother had been one of those kids who'd been born bad to the bone. Although I'd still been a baby when he'd been a small child, I'd heard stories of his behavior, mostly from fights I'd overheard between my parents as they'd blamed each other for how Ricky had turned out. My mother had been accused of coddling and spoiling Ricky too much while my father had apparently used a heavy hand to discipline Ricky, even when he'd been a toddler. The result had been an angry, narcissistic kid with a violent temper and a sadistic streak a mile long. At the tender age of ten, Ricky had stabbed my mother in the hand with his fork after she'd ordered him to finish his carrots. Not surprisingly, my mother had been afraid of him after that and had done nothing to address his increasingly volatile and violent behavior. My father had seemed to fear Ricky as well, because he'd stopped taking his temper out on Ricky and had laid it all on me. I hadn't fared any better with my brother.

But of course, I would have welcomed the beatings if that was all Ricky had been interested in.

My body instantly went cold and I felt the tell-tale numbness start to settle over me. I put my hands on the edge of the stove and enjoyed the warmth that seeped into my fingers from the metal. The heat from the burner flame helped too, but it wasn't enough.

I couldn't do this...not here.

Not now.

Ricky was gone.

I tried to pull up the day the cops had shown up at our door to tell my father that Ricky's body had been found in a culvert by an underpass on the city's south side, but I couldn't hang on to the memory. As sick as it sounded, it had ended up being one of the best days of my life. I'd been standing behind my father when he'd been told his oldest kid was dead. I'd let out this hysterical laugh which had earned me a harsh look from my father that I'd known would be accompanied by a punch or slap at some point after the cops left, but I hadn't cared because all I'd been able to think that was I was finally free. I'd gone to my room and cried.

Big, wet, happy tears.

It had taken me hours to stop and even after my father had kicked my ass for disrespecting Ricky's memory, I'd continued to celebrate his death. A twisted part of me had wanted to go find the cops and ask them if I could see Ricky's body, since I knew my father wouldn't let me go with him to identify my brother at the coroner's office. I'd slept like a rock that night, regardless of all the guilt I still carried around with me.

But despite Ricky's death, his memory lived on in my mind. And it didn't take much to send me back to the days where I'd lie in my bed in the room I'd shared with Ricky when we were just kids and stifle a whimper every time I heard the springs in his mattress creaking. Most times he'd just been turning over in his sleep, but not always.

My vision began to dim as the chill in my body started to spiral out to my limbs. I needed to excuse myself so I could at least escape to the bathroom, but I knew it was already too late. I'd waited too long.

As my knees buckled and hit the floor, my last coherent thought was, even from the grave, Ricky was still winning.

# CHAPTER 4

## PHOENIX

*I* heard rather than saw Levi hit the floor because as he went down, his hand hit the handle of a pot on the stove, knocking it to the ground. Fortunately, the pot was empty so he wasn't burned. I dropped the plate I was still washing and rushed to his side. He hadn't passed out, but he was kneeling on the cold tile, his head lowered and his hands in his lap.

"Levi?" I said in a rush as I put my arm around his back to keep him from collapsing in a heap. When he didn't respond to me, I forced his chin to the side so I could see his face. His eyes were open, but the lids lowered halfway. His expression was completely empty.

"Levi, talk to me," I murmured as I gave him a little shake. His skin felt cold and clammy.

I was in the process of pulling out my phone when I heard a man's voice say, "What's going on here?"

A short, gray-haired man in black pants and a short-sleeved black shirt was standing at the entrance to the kitchen. The white collar gave away his identity.

"Levi?" the priest said quickly as he rushed to us and dropped down next to Levi. "What happened?" he asked, his accusatory eyes snapping up to meet mine.

"I don't know. We were just talking and then he collapsed. I was about to call 911."

"No," the man said, shaking his head. "Can you lift him?"

I nodded and gathered Levi into my arms. He weighed next to nothing so it was easy to stand even without the priest putting his hand at my elbow, apparently to try to steady me. If the situation hadn't been so disturbing, I would have laughed at the slight man's attempt to assist someone of my size and build.

"Bring him this way…we need to get him warm."

Warm? Had this happened before?

I followed the priest to the back of the small space. He led me to a little room that wasn't any bigger than a walk-in closet. There was a tiny cot in the room with a single blanket and pillow on it. A small lamp was on the little table next to the bed, along with a Bible. The only decoration in the room was a plain wooden cross hanging just above the head of the bed.

The priest pulled back the blanket. "Put him here and stay with him."

For his age, the man was energetic, because before I'd even put Levi down, he was rushing from the room. I settled Levi under the blanket. His eyes were still partially open, but he didn't seem to be looking at me. It was an unwelcome reminder for me, but I pushed the thought aside as I put my hand against Levi's bruised cheek.

"Levi, can you hear me?"

The panic crawling through my body was unexpected, especially considering how confused the last thirty minutes had left me.

Ever since I'd followed Levi into the soup kitchen, I'd been studying his movements and reactions and trying to match the man I was watching to the ruthless criminal he was supposed to be. It had started outside when he'd offered to make me a sandwich and let me wait out the weather inside, despite his obvious fear of me. He'd also made every effort to reassure me that there was no judgment for my perceived homelessness or need for a helping hand. In fact, he'd gone out of his way to treat me with respect.

Criminals didn't do that, nor did guys forced into volunteer work as part of their punishment for their crimes. They didn't care about the people they were helping, at least not enough to offer a kind word and gentle smile.

I was sure I'd been overthinking the whole thing as I'd watched Levi move around the kitchen. Despite the mishap with the coffee machine, he'd seemed comfortable with the routine of preparing what would likely be a large meal. I'd still been off-balance by his demeanor, so I'd done something I knew would help me focus on why I was really there.

I'd asked him to cut my sandwich.

Not because I'd actually wanted it cut, but because I'd needed to see that knife in his hand. I'd needed to put him in Seth's family's home, standing over a terrified fourteen-year-old kid and his helpless father. I knew that Levi hadn't been the one to cut or stab Seth because if he had, there was no way Ronan would have let him live, but I'd hoped just putting that knife in his hands for a few seconds would remind me that his inaction had resulted in two deaths and the brutal torture of an innocent teenage boy.

Only, Levi hadn't just snatched up one of the butcher knives and sliced through the sandwich. Instead, he'd stared at the handful of knives for a good minute before he'd finally reached for one with a shaking hand. He'd gotten lost as soon as his fingers had closed around the black handle of one of the knives.

He'd stared at the huge blade as if he'd never seen a knife before and his whole body had locked up like a steel trap. Another minute had passed before he'd finally put the knife down as carefully as if he'd been handling a lit stick of dynamite and then his hand had closed around the edge of the plate as if he'd needed something to hang onto. When he hadn't moved and he hadn't responded to me calling his name, I'd gone to his side to snap him out of his daze.

A daze much like the one he was currently in.

"Sit him up," the priest murmured as he returned to the room, a glass of orange juice in hand.

I put my arm around Levi's back and gently pulled him upright. To my surprise, he didn't fall forward against my chest. It was like he was still with us in some ways, enough to control his body, but his mind had checked out.

"Levi, take a drink for me, please," the priest said as he placed the glass against Levi's lips. Levi obediently took a drink and then another when the priest repeated the request.

"Okay, lay him back down."

The priest took off again, but was back within a minute with another blanket. I helped him tuck it around Levi until his entire body was covered from toe to chin.

"Who are you?" the priest finally asked when Levi's body seemed to relax after a few minutes and his eyes drifted shut. I watched as the man's fingers tentatively reached towards Levi's face as if to touch his injuries. His eyes were heavy with sadness.

"My name is Phoenix Jones," I offered. The man's shrewd eyes narrowed and I knew my name wasn't going to be enough for him, so I scrambled to come up with a legitimate-sounding reason to explain my presence. "I ran into Levi outside and he offered to let me come inside to get out of the weather. I didn't do that to him," I added as I motioned to Levi's battered face.

Before he could question me further, which I could tell he was about to do, I said, "Levi and I were just talking and then he collapsed. You knew what to do…has this happened before?"

The man hesitated before nodding. "It appears to be similar to a panic attack…but more like he gets lost in his head for a bit. He won't tell me what brings them on, but he's had a few since he started volunteering here…that I know of anyway. Since he prefers to work by himself, he could also be having them when no one is around."

"You seem to know him well," I suggested.

"I also know enough not to share personal information about my friends with strangers, Mr. Jones."

Friends?

It was an odd term for the man to use, especially considering Levi was basically an employee.

"I'm just concerned about him, Father," I said softly, and to my own surprise, the statement was a true one. I hadn't expected to have so much trouble reconciling the young man I'd held in my arms a moment ago with the guy who'd help destroy a family for nothing more than a quick payout.

The man's face softened a little as he finally stroked his fingers over the discolored skin on Levi's left cheek. "Levi's a lost soul, Mr. Jones. But unlike many of the men and women who seek my counsel, he appears to have no interest in finding it again."

The image of Levi on his hands and knees as he spat out a mouthful of cum went through my mind. The priest's words had me wondering if the bruises weren't a new thing because he didn't seem overly surprised by them.

"Father O?" Levi whispered as he struggled to fully open his eyes. He immediately tried to sit up, but I put my hand on his shoulder.

"No, my son, you lie down for a bit," Father O admonished, his voice gentle.

Levi's head dropped back on the pillow. A minute passed before he seemed to completely come back to himself. I saw the disappointment and embarrassment in his gaze and when his eyes flicked to me, they didn't linger. He was clearly humiliated.

"Levi-" I began, but stopped when he sat up.

"I'm okay now," he murmured. "Sorry, Father," he added as his eyes fell on the older man.

"Never apologize for something beyond your control."

The man's words didn't seem to comfort Levi at all. If anything, color flooded his cheeks. "I should get back to work," Levi said.

"No, you need to go home and get some rest," the priest responded.

But Levi started shaking his head before the man even finished the statement. "No, I need to be here." When Father O began shaking his head, Levi reached out to grab his arm. "Please."

The one word seemed to spark some silent conversation between the two men. Father O finally nodded his head. "But I'm going to help you."

"No," Levi cut in. His voice softened as he said, "You're already late for hearing confessions, right?"

The priest seemed torn.

"I can help Levi," I said before I could think too much about what I was doing.

Both men looked at me like I'd grown two heads.

"No," Levi said, his voice dropping just a bit. "You don't have to help cook the meal you're going to eat…you already have enough on your mind. We .." He hesitated as his eyes shifted to Father O who nodded. "We want you to be able to relax and-"

"Levi," I interrupted. "I'm not homeless and I didn't come here for a free meal. I was cutting through the alley as a shortcut to get to my car when I ran into you." I didn't mention the circumstances of how I'd met him. "You were so kind to offer me a place to get out of the rain and something to eat, that it got me to thinking about how I'd like to give back." I shifted my eyes to the priest.

"I'd love to help out, if you could use the help, that is," I said to the older man.

There was a hint of suspicion in Levi's gaze, which had me wondering if he'd bought my story, but he remained silent. Father O smiled widely and nodded. "Why yes, that would be wonderful. We could use all the help we can get, isn't that right, Levi?" the priest said.

Levi nodded. "Yeah, that's great."

Father O sobered and then turned his attention on Levi. I watched his fingers curl around Levi's chin. "Put some ice on these," he said as he carefully fingered the bruised skin. "You know where to find me."

Another nod from Levi. I expected it was yet another one of their silent conversations. The priest got up and left the room. Levi shifted and pushed the blankets off his body before swinging his legs over the side of the bed.

"You shouldn't lie to a priest," he murmured.

His observation was a surprise, but I didn't bother to deny it. It *had* been a pretty lame argument.

"Why were you really in that alley?" he asked.

"That's not really what you want to ask me, is it?" I countered.

An uncomfortable sensation floated through my chest as I watched Levi bend his upper body over his legs and let his clasped hands dangle just above his knees. His demeanor was much like what it had been in the alley after the rough blowjob.

"If you tell me who he is, I can help you," I said, shocking even myself. But every time I tried to remind myself that this guy deserved everything he got, I saw him spitting out that cum, his eyes empty, his body broken. It was like he'd accepted that all he'd ever be was some guy who belonged on all fours in a dirty alley surrounded by garbage, waiting for the next man to come along and use his body.

As much as I detested him for what he'd done to Seth and his family, I'd seen enough in the last hour to know he hadn't walked away unscathed. But I also still had more questions than answers. And the bottom line was that I didn't believe in making people suffer for their crimes. I'd joined Ronan's team to make sure justice got served, not to inflict the same torment on my marks that they'd inflicted upon others. Maybe it was a fine line that separated me from the monsters I hunted, but it was there just the same and I knew what side of it I wanted…no, needed to be on.

Levi hung there dejectedly for a moment before saying, "You should go, Phoenix. I really appreciate what you did for me in the alley, but I don't think it's a good idea for you to be here."

When he got up to leave, I grabbed his wrist to keep him next to me. He shuddered and I heard him let out a wisp of air, but he didn't try to pull free of me. On the one hand, I was glad he wasn't fighting me, but on the other, I kind of wished he would.

"Why not?" I asked. "Why shouldn't I be here?"

Levi finally lifted his head and turned to meet my gaze. My heart hurt for him as I saw the tears pooling there. "Because I'd be too tempted to take you up on your offer. What you saw out in that alley… I deserved it…I *earned* it," he whispered. His tears fell and he pulled free of my hold so he could dash them away. He let out a wet-sounding laugh. "Father O keeps telling me God's watching over me…that he loves me no matter what and he'll forgive me for all of my sins." Levi shook his head. "I don't have the heart to tell him God gave up on me a long time ago."

I let him go when he stood and left the room.

Because no matter what, I wasn't going to tell the man I'd been sent to kill that his life was worth fighting for.

Even if the tiniest part of me was beginning to wonder if maybe it was.

## CHAPTER 5

### LEVI

*H*e was waiting for me when I walked through the door leading into the alley. I thought he was T at first when I saw him in my periphery, but my relief as I took in his hulking frame as he leaned against the wall where T had fucked my mouth just a few hours earlier was short-lived as I realized what his presence meant.

Either he hadn't believed my earlier words or he hadn't cared.

The flare of hope that sparked deep inside my belly as Phoenix straightened and began walking towards me felt ugly and wrong. And I knew why.

Because I'd *wanted* him to be there waiting for me.

It was all I'd thought about as I'd worked to get dinner ready.

Darkness was just starting to fall so it was hard to make out Phoenix's expression until he stepped into the light that was coming from just above the door. I wasn't sure what I'd expected to see, but it certainly wasn't the tense anger that lined his face.

Okay, so maybe he hadn't stayed behind to talk more. Maybe whatever I'd done to piss him off was about to come back and bite me in the ass. I dropped my gaze to his hands which were fisted. God, the damage he could do with them. The little flutter in my belly that hadn't left in the three hours since I'd first interacted with him turned into a sharp pang of terror and I automatically stepped away from him until my back hit the door behind me.

I was surprised when he paused briefly and then relaxed his hands. The expression in his gaze eased too, but then he was moving again until he was practically in my space.

"I'll walk you to your car."

"No," I automatically said. "That's not necessary."

"We're not arguing about this, Levi," he said gruffly and then his hand was closing around my arm. His gentle hold only served to anger me.

I yanked my arm free and bit out, "Weren't you listening in there?" as I motioned over my shoulder. "I don't want your help."

"I don't care what you want!" Phoenix shot back and then his body was crowding mine against the door. "You might be okay with putting yourself in danger, but I'm not." His voice softened a little. "Just let me do this, Levi. Tomorrow you can go back to believing whatever the hell you want."

It was a simple request, but he had no clue what he was asking me. But I also saw the determination in his eyes.

"I don't have a car I usually walk to work…it's only about six blocks away. When I'm done, I take the bus home."

"Fine, we'll take my car."

I wanted to tell him that I preferred to walk, but I knew he wouldn't understand, so I merely nodded.

"It's this way," Phoenix said as he turned away from me. I followed him and wasn't particularly surprised when he slowed so that I was walking next to him instead of behind him. The rain had stopped, but the air was cool around us.

"Where do you work?" Phoenix asked as we walked. I noticed the way he kept looking around us and I wondered if he was watching out for T or it was just his normal behavior.

"At a small grocery store. I clean and restock the shelves. Sometimes I help out with bagging groceries if they're busy, but the store closes at nine so it's usually just me after that."

"Do you like it?"

"What? My job?" I asked. "Yeah, I guess so. I like the routine. I'm good at routines."

"I meant the alone part."

I glanced at him in confusion. His dark eyes met mine and I felt a shimmer of electricity flare in my belly. That damn flutter was back.

"You said it's usually just you after the store closes. Do you prefer it that way?"

I dropped my eyes. "Yeah, I guess. It's quiet and I don't have to make conversation." I let out a dry laugh and said, "You've already seen that I'm not so good at the talking."

Phoenix smiled. "I don't think that's true. Besides, I'm not exactly the easiest guy to talk to sometimes."

"I think you're underestimating yourself," I murmured. Sure, appearance-wise, he was as intimidating as hell. But for all his brawn and brute strength, he'd shown moments of gentleness too. Even when he'd grabbed me a few moments earlier and insisted on escorting me to work, his touch hadn't hurt and his words had been firm and demanding, but not forceful.

He didn't respond to my comment, but I could sense him glancing at me now and again.

"What happened back there in front of the stove, Levi?"

I swallowed hard. Between him having seen me blowing T and my mini-breakdown, I hadn't been sure which topic he'd press me for more information on, but I'd figured he wouldn't just let things lie. Didn't make it any easier to deal with, though. So I did what I did best and kept my mouth shut.

"Your brother must have been a real piece of work."

At his words, I stopped walking. "What?"

He turned to face me.

"What would make you say that?" I asked, my heart thudding in my chest.

"You were talking about him right before you..." His voice dropped off briefly. "His name is Ricky, right?"

I nodded absentmindedly. "Was. He's dead."

"I'm sor-"

"Don't," I cut in before he could finish talking. "He doesn't deserve your pity."

I moved past him and started walking more quickly. The sooner I got away from this man, the better. He was far too perceptive.

"Levi, wait."

"No!" I yelled as he once again grabbed my arm. I yanked free of his hold and he quickly put his hands up.

"This is my car," he said carefully as he motioned to a large silver SUV.

Embarrassed by my over-the-top reaction, I nodded and tried to catch my breath. "We should go. I don't want to be late for work."

I wouldn't be, of course, since I'd given myself enough of a cushion to make the walk to work, but I didn't tell him that. I just wanted to get away from him because the roller coaster of emotions he was putting me through was just fucked up.

"No problem," Phoenix said softly. I suspected he knew I was in no danger of being late. I started to approach the car, but stopped in shock when he went to the passenger side door and opened it for me.

I hurried past him and climbed into the car before I completely lost it.

As soon as he closed the door, I let the few tears that had been collecting in my eyes fall so I could quickly use my sleeve to wipe them away as Phoenix walked around the front of the SUV. I turned my head to look out the window as he climbed in. I just needed to keep it together for a few more minutes. Since I'd be getting to work early, I'd at least have a few minutes to myself to try and get it together.

I was glad when Phoenix didn't try to engage me in conversation as I directed him on which way to go. But as soon as he pulled the car over to the curb and I went for the door, his big hand closed over my wrist. "Levi."

I flinched at the way he said my name. I knew I wasn't going to like whatever came next.

"Please, don't," I murmured before he could speak again. I kept my eyes downcast as I tried to ignore the warmth radiating out beneath my skin where he was holding on to me. I chanced a glance at where we were connected and marveled at how much bigger his hand was then mine. His fingers easily encircled my wrist. It would take next to nothing for him to snap it if he wanted to.

"Don't what?"

"Just don't," I whispered, hoping it was enough.

To my shock and disappointment, it was. Phoenix released me. "Take care of yourself, Levi."

I couldn't even find the strength to respond, so I merely gave him a jerky nod and then nearly fell out of the car in my effort to escape the charged air inside of it. My insides hurt with every step I took away from the SUV and I felt another round of tears threaten to fall.

Goddamn fucking hope.

~

I was half expecting to find Phoenix waiting for me the next morning as I left work. I tried to tell myself I was glad when I didn't see him outside the employee entrance, but the fact that I actually went out of my way to walk around to the front of the store just to make sure the big man wasn't waiting there either contradicted my relief.

It was still dark outside considering it was just a few minutes past five. The fog was heavy, but it wasn't raining. Most days, I would have just walked home, but with my latest run-in with T on my mind, I decided to play it safe and catch the bus. The man was likely passed out somewhere with one of his women, but I wasn't going to risk it, especially not after the request he'd made the night before.

I'd been working at Carlisle's Food Market for almost a year now, but for some reason, T had waited until last night to use my position there to benefit him. He hadn't ever confronted me at the grocery store before, so I supposed it was possible he hadn't realized until recently that I worked there, but I couldn't be sure. It didn't really matter because now that my employment with the small chain of stores was on his mind, he wasn't going to let it go.

I'd met Betty Carlisle about two months after I'd gotten out of prison. I'd been job hunting for nearly as long when I'd walked into the store to fill out an application after being turned down by the two dozen other places I'd tried. I'd been half-tempted not to check the yes box for the question that had prevented me from even getting a call from all the previous jobs...the one asking if I'd ever been convicted of a crime. But as desperate as I'd been, I'd been more frightened about getting caught in a lie, though I wasn't sure why, since it wasn't like a lie could send me back to prison.

So, I'd stood at the end of the checkout counter on a quiet Sunday afternoon and painstakingly filled out the application, even if there'd been little to fill out since I'd had practically no work experience except for a few months of working as a janitor when I'd been seventeen years old. Ironically, I'd lied on that application because they'd wanted a high school graduate. Luckily, they hadn't checked to confirm that I'd finished school. And once I'd been arrested for drug possession, the lie hadn't seemed particularly important in the grand scheme of things.

Once I'd completed the application, I'd handed it to the cashier - an older, graying woman in a pink smock - with absolutely no expectation of receiving a call. But as I'd started to leave, the woman had held a pair of thick glasses up to her eyes so she could read the application and had begun asking me questions.

Blunt ones.

*You still doing drugs?*
*You ever bagged groceries before?*
*You good at following directions?*
*You willing to pee in a cup right now?*

I'd answered no to the first two questions and yes to the last two. Two minutes later, I'd been following the woman to the employee bathroom where she'd handed me the cup from a small, at-home drug testing kit she'd snagged from the shelf near the pharmacy section of the store. As we'd waited the required ten minutes for the test to process, she'd launched into a speech about how she believed in giving people second chances since she'd been given her own when she was a teenager. There'd been no hesitation as she'd told me all about her struggles with alcohol when she'd been around my age and that it had nearly destroyed her life. Until a certain someone had forced her to sober up.

That someone had turned out to be Bill Carlisle and he'd been her boss at the time...in the very same store. I'd been shocked to discover I'd been talking to Betty Carlisle, the owner of the store, the entire time. After a stint in rehab that Bill had paid for, she'd spent the next forty years as his wife before he'd died of a heart attack. Together, they'd built a chain of Carlisle's Markets throughout the Pacific Northwest. The stores serviced smaller communities that didn't always have access to the bigger, well-known chain grocery stores. And while Betty wouldn't make the Fortune 500 list anytime soon, the estate her husband had left behind was worth more than I would ever make in ten lifetimes.

After my drug test had come back negative, Betty had put me to work that very same day. In the beginning, I'd worked part-time under the watchful eye of the main nightshift worker, but he'd quit the previous month to go to graduate school in another state, so Betty had offered me full-time work plus overtime for any extra hours she needed me for rather than replacing the guy. The extra money was a godsend and starting next month, I'd be eligible for the health plan.

But if T had his way, I'd lose it all.

And worse, I'd betray Betty, the only other person besides Father O who'd given me a second chance.

T's request the night before had been for me to help him steal prescription drugs from the pharmacy section of the store, which he would then turn around and sell on the street at a huge profit. He'd gone on to explain that he had someone who could give me bottles with fake pills to replace the ones I stole, making it an operation we could milk for a while before being discovered. I hadn't even let him finish the thought before I'd told him no for the second time.

I had no clue how I was going to get out of this whole thing since I knew T wasn't going to just let me say no. I could try going to the cops, but they weren't exactly my biggest fans. Not to mention I was worried they'd somehow link me back to my crimes seven years ago.

And I didn't want to tell Betty because I didn't want her to look at me with suspicion...like she was wondering if I was maybe going to do it at some point. The only option was to let T kick my ass until he realized I wasn't changing my mind...and hope that he wouldn't kill me in retaliation.

Thankfully, the short walk to the bus was uneventful and I'd timed it perfectly so I didn't have to wait very long. The ride home was quick since it was still early and there wasn't any rush hour traffic to battle. I kept my eyes peeled for T as I walked from the bus stop to my apartment building, but my luck held out and I made it into the relative safety of the six-story building. But I couldn't breathe a sigh of relief just yet since I had one more obstacle to get through before I could crash in my bed for a few hours of much-needed sleep.

As expected, my father was sitting at the kitchen table when I entered our small, two-bedroom apartment. It was the same apartment I'd lived in most of my life and while I'd often wondered why my father hadn't moved throughout the years, considering how run-down the place had become, I did have my suspicions about what was keeping him there, though I never voiced them.

There were just some things that people were never prepared to accept.

That my mother was never going to return was one of them.

From all the pictures my mother had shown me when I was a little kid, my parents had seemed blissfully happy early on in their marriage. Even at my young age, I'd recognized their devotion to one another in photographs. But there were fewer and fewer pictures to document my parents' life together after Ricky's arrival. Sure, there were dozens upon dozens of him as a baby, but there'd been very few of my parents. And there were even fewer of me when I'd been born.

Maybe the excitement had just been gone at that point or maybe Ricky's strain on my parents' marriage had started to slowly drive them apart. It didn't really matter because it had taken just one discovery to cause the whole marriage to implode. I'd been there that day when the building's maintenance man had shown up at our door and asked our father to go down to the boiler room with him. My mother had been at work and a then fourteen-year-old Ricky had been off with friends. My father hadn't seen me follow him and the guy downstairs after my curiosity had gotten the best of me and I'd disobeyed the order to stay in the apartment.

I hadn't realized what I'd been seeing at first. My nine-year-old brain hadn't been able to process that depth of depravity. There'd been bodies hanging everywhere...no, not the two-legged kind, but the 4-legged and winged variety. At least a dozen small animals and birds had been strung up from nails pounded into a rafter in one corner of the room. Not one of the victims had had a head. I'd stood there in a state of mute shock until I'd recognized our neighbor Mrs. Hurley's cat among the bodies, the animal's once snow white fur stained red with blood.

At that point, I'd thrown up then and there, not caring that my father would discover I'd disobeyed his order. I'd then promptly passed out.

I'd learned later when I'd heard my father telling my mother about the horrific scene that the maintenance man had found a notebook with my brother's name in it in the boiler room. There'd been entry after entry in the journal describing each animal's death. My father had smoothed things over with the maintenance man and poor Mrs. Hurley, and I hadn't doubted a significant amount of money had exchanged hands, because my mother had railed at my father for keeping Ricky out of legal trouble by paying off the people involved. When Ricky had come home, he hadn't been overly concerned about the discovery. He'd simply told my parents he'd wanted to see what kinds of sounds the animals made as they were dying and then asked what was for dinner.

My mother had begged my father to get Ricky some help, but my father had been adamant that it was something he could handle. That night, he'd threatened Ricky with everything he'd had, including putting him into a psychiatric hospital, but he never laid a hand on Ricky. Likely because he was too afraid of what Ricky would do to him if he did.

Not laying hands on Ricky might have kept my parents safe that night, but it hadn't done me any favors. Because Ricky had not been happy about his torture chamber being taken away from him.

I'd begged my parents to let me sleep with them that night since I'd been terrified of Ricky after realizing what he was really capable of, but they'd assured me that everything was settled.

It hadn't been.

I shook off the memory that was threatening to overtake me as I watched my bleary-eyed father drink his coffee. A small bottle of scotch was sitting next to his mug. I kept my mouth shut as I dug into my pocket for the money I'd withdrawn from my account. Betty electronically deposited my paycheck into my account every two weeks so it was easy enough just to use the ATM at work to grab some cash when I was leaving.

I didn't speak to my father as I placed the money on the table.

"You're late," he muttered.

I knew he was talking about the money because he didn't give a shit about whether I walked through the door on time. I could have gone missing for days, but he wouldn't take notice until the rent came due.

"Sorry, there was some kind of problem with work depositing my check on time," I lied. The truth was, Dina had insisted that I give her the last of the money I had in my account a couple days earlier, so there hadn't been enough until this morning to cover rent.

"Next time you'll start paying in advance."

I bit back the urge to remind him that the only thing keeping his ass from being evicted was my larger share of the rent *plus* the work I did to help the owner maintain the property that helped cover the rent my father and I couldn't come up with in cash. If my father hadn't been so invested in staying in the apartment, I had no doubt he would have spent the money I gave him on booze. As it was, most of his own paycheck went to fund his incessant need for alcohol.

I desperately wished I could just get my own place, but like my father, I too was tied to this place.

"No problem," I murmured. I knew he wouldn't remember the conversation anyway, so I pretty much would have told him whatever he wanted to hear. I ignored my rumbling stomach and went to my room. I had less than three hours before I needed to be up again and I didn't want to spend any of that time in the kitchen making breakfast while my father was still lingering around. I'd eat later when it was time for me to get up.

Because by then, my father would be gone and I'd get to face the best part of my day.

## CHAPTER 6

PHOENIX

Levi definitely wasn't happy to see me when he opened the door to let me into the kitchen. But the fact that he also wasn't surprised by my presence meant Father O had likely talked to him.

After dropping Levi off at work the night before, I'd parked my car on the street alongside the grocery store since I'd figured the guy who was hassling Levi would likely try to go after him again using the employee entrance rather than the busier front entrance. The asshole hadn't shown up and as soon as I'd made sure Levi had made it safely home, I'd gone to my own apartment to get some sleep. Since Ronan had someone watching Seth 24/7, there wasn't the need to stay on Levi the whole time and since I'd identified through learning his routine that he rarely left his building between the time he got home and the time he left to volunteer at the soup kitchen, I'd felt it safe enough for me to go home to get some sleep rather than try to sleep in the confines of my car.

I'd gotten up around lunch time and then headed to St. Anthony's to talk to Father O. I figured getting the old man on my side would make things easier when I showed up for my first shift as the newest volunteer for the St. Anthony's Soup Kitchen. I'd convinced Father O to put me on the same schedule as Levi so that I could give him a ride to work each night. The deciding factor for Father O had been my insistence that I could make sure whoever had put the bruises on Levi's face wouldn't get a second chance. I hadn't told the priest I already knew how Levi had gotten the injuries, but he hadn't seemed surprised that Levi had even ended up with the bruises in the first place...like he'd already known it wasn't a random attack. After I'd gotten Father O's buy-in, I'd gone back to Levi's apartment to wait so I could follow him. Like the day before, he'd taken the bus again, despite the improvement in the weather. Since he'd walked to the church all the previous times, I had to assume he was being careful because of his run-in with the blond asshole the day before.

There'd been no sign of said asshole this time around so I'd waited a few minutes before knocking on the soup kitchen entrance door.

Levi didn't say anything as he opened the door wider, so I followed him inside and remained silent as he gave me my instructions - cutting up vegetables for the stew he was preparing.

As I worked, I let my thoughts drift to where they'd been since the previous night after Levi had asked me to leave the soup kitchen after I'd volunteered to help him finish preparing the meal. My intention had been to go back to my car and wait for Levi to appear from the alley and follow him to work like I normally did, but I'd been too on edge that I'd miss his attacker sneaking into the alley through the end I couldn't cover, so I'd ended up getting out of my car and waiting for Levi by the door. My anger at myself had grown and grown as I'd tried to make sense of what I was doing there...after all, my job wasn't to keep Levi safe. It didn't matter if his entire body was covered in bruises when it came time for me to take him out, I had a damn job to do. And even if it wasn't my job, Seth was my priority because he was family. Levi was nothing to me.

So, what the hell was I doing here? Why was I going through such extraordinary measures to ensure the young man didn't get hurt again? Why, even now, did I want to go up to him and shake him and ask him why he'd participated in such a horrific crime seven years ago? Why did someone heartless enough to stand by and watch a man and his child be cruelly tortured and listen to a woman being brutally raped then go and volunteer at a soup kitchen when he wasn't under any obligation to do so?

That was a piece of information I'd managed to wrangle out of Father O when I'd talked to him earlier. There was no court or probation officer ordering Levi to give back to the community...he was doing it because he wanted to. And from the way the priest had talked about him, the young man thoroughly enjoyed the work and was popular among the men, women and children who relied on the soup kitchen's services. Apparently, the way he'd talked to me when he'd still thought I needed a helping hand was the way he talked to all the people who walked through the soup kitchen's door. He treated them like people. He showed them respect and kindness. He inquired about their lives. Father O had even told me a story about how he'd given up his gloves, hat and coat this past winter to a man who'd had nothing.

I wanted to believe it was an act, but I couldn't deny his breakdown the night before

When he'd been talking about his brother.

To have such an extreme reaction to even the mere mention of his older brother had been a telling sign, and I was starting to have my own suspicions about just how much influence Ricky Deming had had the night Seth and his family had been attacked. Before the drug possession charges that had landed Levi in prison just before he'd turned nineteen, he hadn't been in any kind of trouble. His brother, on the other hand, had had numerous run-ins with the law. Mostly minor things like assault and vandalism.

Everything had changed when Ricky had been in his twenties and he'd been accused of rape on two separate occasions. One of the girls hadn't even been eighteen years old. Initially, both girls had pointed the finger at Ricky, but when the prosecutor had been ready to press charges, they'd both recanted. And then Ricky's girlfriend had been discovered strangled to death in her apartment.

It should have been a slam-dunk case, but Ricky's father had offered an alibi, which had made the prosecutor nervous. So, he'd knocked the charges down so Ricky barely served any time at all. Both

Levi and Ricky had been in prison for an overlapping time period, but not in the same prison and Levi had gotten out before Ricky. Luckily, there hadn't been much time for Ricky to hurt anyone else because Ronan had ordered the man's termination within a month of him being released.

I glanced over my shoulder at Levi who was in the process of pulling some frozen dinner rolls out of the freezer and putting them on several cookie sheets so they'd be ready to go when dinner was just about ready to be served. "Where do you want these?" I asked as I motioned to the vegetables I'd already chopped. Levi glanced at me and I didn't miss the way his eyes lingered briefly on the butcher knife in my hand.

"Um, put them in here," he murmured as he reached into a cabinet above the stove and pulled out a large bowl. His shirt rode up just a little bit and I barely managed to conceal my reaction at the sight of a jagged scar just above his hip bone that ran upwards until it disappeared beneath his shirt. Levi didn't notice me studying him and I averted my eyes when he handed me the bowl.

"Smells good," I said absently as I began putting the vegetables in the bowl. The base for the stew had been simmering for a while now. I moved to his side. "You mind if I try it?"

Levi seemed surprised by the request, but he nodded and handed me a clean wooden spoon. I tried the soup and nodded. "It's good."

He studied me for a moment. "But?"

"No buts," I said, handing him the spoon.

"What?" he asked. "Is it missing something?"

"No," I began.

"Please, tell me."

"It's really good, Levi," I reassured him. At his look of worry, I patted his shoulder and then reached into the cabinet and found the spices I was looking for. "Do you trust me?" I asked as I opened the top of the container of allspice.

The look in Levi's eyes was hard to acknowledge. I'd meant the question in terms of him trusting me not to ruin dinner, but he was clearly thinking about the question very differently.

He managed a nod.

"A dash of this," I said as I added the allspice. I reached for the paprika. "And about half a teaspoon of this. It'll give it just a little more kick." I stirred the spices in and then got another clean wooden spoon and dipped it into the broth. I took a taste and then held the spoon to his lips so he could try the rest of it.

Levi didn't move as his eyes held mine and just like that, the air around us changed and I realized why. My dick went from interested to hard as I stared at where Levi's lips were hovering near the edge of the spoon. The same edge where my lips had been just a moment ago.

I held my breath as Levi finally leaned forward and closed his mouth over the spoon. His eyes lifted to meet mine as he swallowed. The sight of just a little moisture clinging to his lips was my undoing and I was dropping my mouth to his before I could even consider my actions.

The sound of the outer door slamming had Levi jumping back just before my mouth came into contact with his.

"I'm here!" I heard a woman's voice call out.

Levi stared at me, wide-eyed with flushed cheeks. My own body was screaming at me to grab him, uncaring that we were no longer alone. I gripped the spoon in my hand as if the action could somehow keep me from reaching for him.

"Hi sweetie, sorry I'm late," the voice said and I barely noticed the young woman round the corner. She seemed oblivious as she shrugged off her jacket and dumped it and her purse on the small table against the wall.

"Oh," the woman said when she finally realized Levi wasn't alone. I forced my attention to her and that seemed to knock Levi from his daze.

"Sherry, this is Phoenix. He's a new volunteer. Phoenix, this is Sherry."

"Hi, Sherry," I said as I reached out my hand to her.

I barely heard her as she welcomed me and began making small talk, because my eyes strayed back to Levi who'd dropped his gaze.

"Um, I'm going to go start getting things ready up front, okay?"

The confusion in her voice finally seemed to get through to Levi because he looked at her and nodded. "Um, yeah, okay. Do you need help?"

Sherry looked back and forth between me and Levi and shook her head. Where she'd been friendly before, her eyes were clouded with suspicion as she pinned me with her gaze and took a step closer to Levi. "If you need anything, just call out, okay?" she murmured to him as she patted his arm.

He nodded.

I received what I was sure was some kind of silent warning from the girl before she left. If I hadn't still been reeling from the near miss with Levi, I would have smiled at the thought of the petite girl threatening me with bodily harm if I hurt the young man across from me.

Levi was the first to move. He moved past me to stir the soup again. "It's really good. Thanks. I'll remember that for next time."

It took me a moment to realize he was talking about the spices I'd added.

"No problem. They're my mom's secret ingredients," I said as I tried to get back on track. I took the spoon I was still holding and went to the sink to clean it off.

"Tell her I'll take the secret to my grave," Levi joked in an attempt to get us back on even footing.

But his words struck a chord and pain seared through my chest.

"Phoenix, are you okay?"

I glanced at him and saw him watching me with worry. I nodded and tried to smile, but wasn't sure I managed to pull it off. "I keep thinking it will get easier." I shifted my eyes back to the sink. "You'd think after six years, it *would* be easier."

"What?" Levi asked, his voice soft…and close. I sensed rather than felt him at my side.

I shook my head. Luckily, Levi seemed to realize what I couldn't say.

"I'm sorry," he offered. I felt his hand come to rest in the middle of my back and begin moving in large circles in an attempt to soothe me.

"It hits me when I least expect it," I admitted.

"How did it happen?"

"Car accident."

"I don't know what to say," he murmured as he dropped his eyes.

I shifted so I was facing him and then used my fingers under his chin to lift his face, but I didn't say anything. I loved how warm his skin was. My curiosity got the best of me and I lifted my thumb so I could trace it over his lower lip. When I reached the cut near the side of his mouth, I paused.

It was a brutal reminder of who this man was and why I was here.

I dropped my hand. "We should probably get back to work. Dinner starts soon, right?"

Levi nodded. I wasn't sure, but he seemed almost disappointed. We continued our work in silence, but my body refused to stop reacting to the close contact we were forced to work in within the narrow confines of the kitchen.

When the dinner service started, I joined Levi, Sherry and a young man named Patrick on the serving line as people began filing in through the main door leading from the church into the seating area. It was startling to see the wide variety of people the soup kitchen served. Sure, there were the typical-looking older men with scraggly beards, unkempt hair and tattered clothes who eagerly collected a bowl of stew along with rolls and a side of salad, but there were also people I never would have pegged as needing a helping hand. A young woman with three small children in tow was the most heartbreaking because she looked barely old enough to take care of herself, let alone three kids. And the look on her gaunt face...like she could lie down at any moment and go to sleep and gladly never wake up.

I knew some of these people were there by choice, since not everyone who lived on the streets was necessarily looking for a better life. But I suspected the majority had fallen on hard times due to anything from financial problems, dealing with mental illness or not being able to escape the lure of drugs and alcohol. And while everyone took the allotted amount of food they were allowed to, I could tell most were ashamed to have to hold out their hand.

As I watched the men, women and children come and go, I watched Levi too.

Whereas I'd been wondering what each person's story was, Levi either already knew or he didn't care because he interacted with all the people like he'd known them a lifetime. He asked the adults questions about how they were doing and pulled smiles from the kids with teasing jokes. They weren't vagrants who couldn't get their lives together…they were people needing a hand…his hand.

Frustration coursed through me once again as I tried to make sense of things. So far, nothing about Levi fit. Maybe if he'd gone the path of the straight and narrow after the attack on Seth's family, I could have accepted that he was a changed man or that he was trying to seek redemption through this small act of kindness. But for whatever reason, he'd chosen to use drugs which had landed him in prison. And prison didn't rehabilitate people, despite that being their supposed intent. No, after three years locked behind bars with the worst of the worst, Levi couldn't have come out a better person than when he'd gone in. I'd seen the proof myself with the blond behemoth who was anything but a model citizen. Not to mention the fact that Levi had returned to the scene of his and his brother's crime not once, but several times. None of that bode well for him.

So why was he here? Why after Father O had told him to go home after his mini-meltdown had he been so adamant about finishing his shift?

I was so distracted that I almost missed Levi saying his goodbyes to Sherry and Patrick as he removed the hairnet and latex gloves we'd all put on before serving the meal. His eyes connected with mine briefly, but he didn't say anything and he turned away before I could tell him to wait for me. I caught up to him in the small room at the back of the building that had the bed in it. He was in the midst of pulling on his jacket when he glanced over his shoulder at me to where I was standing in the doorway. He looked apprehensive and I couldn't blame him. I was still on edge about the almost-kiss. Even now, I wanted to walk into the room, close the door behind me and urge Levi down on the bed so I could feel his entire body pressed up against mine.

"Did you need something?" he asked, his voice uneven. My presence was definitely rattling him.

"I'll give you a ride to work."

I expected him to argue, but he dropped his eyes so he could fiddle with his zipper. He shook his head and then tried to move past me where I was still standing in the doorframe. I didn't like the look of dejection in his eyes, so I shot my hand out to stop him and then brought my other arm up to block him from ducking back into the room.

"What?" I asked.

He shook his head slowly. "If you're going to do it, just do it already," he finally whispered brokenly.

"Do what?" I asked softly.

But instead of answering me, Levi ducked under my arm, but not to leave the room. Instead, he went back inside of it and then tugged at the zipper of his jacket before taking it back off again. "Would you close the door at least?" he asked as he lifted his eyes.

Curious, I did as he said and stepped into the room, closing the door behind me. Levi averted his eyes and then his fingers were reaching for the button on his jeans. Understanding dawned as a single, stifled sob left his throat right before he reached for his zipper.

Rage went through me, so profound that I wanted to hit something. But I doused my anger and reached Levi in two strides, grabbing his wrists before he could push his pants down.

"No," I said simply, because I needed a moment to calm down before doing anything else. To think he was putting me in the same category as the bastard who'd degraded him in the alley the day before had bile crawling up the back of my throat.

Levi hung there for a moment before pulling his hands free. He zipped his pants up, but didn't move away from me like I expected. To my horror, he reached for the button on my pants instead. "Can you wear a condom, please?" he asked as his fingers popped my button free. "I can still make it feel good."

"Levi, stop," I snapped before I grabbed his hands to keep him from sliding my zipper down.

"What is it that you want, Phoenix?" Levi yelled, his voice thick with tears.

"For starters, I want you to look at me," I said, softening my voice.

Since I still had ahold of Levi's hands, he couldn't do anything about the tears that slipped from his eyes. He forced his head up, but it took several long seconds for his eyes to connect with mine.

"All I want is to give you a ride to work," I murmured.

"I don't believe you."

The admission surprised me, mostly because it took balls to call someone a liar to their face, especially someone so much bigger and stronger. Or maybe he just didn't care about the potential consequences.

Levi pulled free of me and stepped back, though with the bed behind him, there wasn't really any place for him to go.

"I don't know why you were in that alley yesterday, but I know it wasn't to become a volunteer here. You stuck around even after I asked you to leave and then this afternoon, Father O told me you're working here now and that you just happen to be on the same schedule as me. What am I supposed to think?" he asked. "I saw the way you looked at me in the kitchen. You know what I let T do to me."

I didn't miss his slip, though I didn't have time to dwell on the fact that I now had a name to go with the asshole who'd roughed Levi up yesterday.

*T.*

"So, you think I'm no better than that fucker?" I asked as I moved closer to him. "You think my only reason for being here, the only reason I looked at you like I did in the kitchen was so I could get my dick down your throat or up your ass?"

Levi didn't answer as I closed the distance between us until my body was brushing his. He was forced to crane his neck to look up at me.

"The offer for the ride is just that, Levi," I said softly as I reached up to cup his jaw with both my hands. "As for what happened in the kitchen," – I dropped my mouth so that it was hovering just above his for a moment before I skimmed my lips up his jaw in a featherlight caress – "I guess we'll just never know because contrary to what you think, I don't believe in taking what should always be freely given."

I forced myself to release him and stepped back. Levi was breathing hard and I could see his body shaking. "I'll wait outside for you for five minutes. If you still want that ride, be out there before then. If not…"

I didn't bother finishing my sentence because it wasn't necessary. I turned and left the room, having absolutely no clue if I'd see Levi outside in less than five minutes or not. It wouldn't change anything if he wasn't there, since I'd still be following him, but I couldn't deny what I wanted the outcome to be.

It was that thought that had me glancing down at my watch.

Four minutes and fifty-five seconds to go.

## CHAPTER 7

### LEVI

"*Ricky, don't!*"

"*Shut up, you fucking little coward!*" Ricky hissed. "*Let's see if you'll go running to Mommy and Daddy after this!*"

"Levi?"

I jerked back to the present at the sound of Father O's voice. With ice still flooding my veins, I looked up to see Father O watching me with concern from the doorway.

"What time is it?" I asked as I searched out my jacket on the bed.

How long had I been sitting here like this?

"Is he still here?" I didn't give Father O a chance to answer before grabbing my jacket and saying, "Sorry, Father, I have to go."

What I was doing was beyond stupid, but that didn't slow me down. If anything, it got me moving faster.

*I don't believe in taking what should always be freely given.*

God, I wanted so badly to believe him. Because if what he was saying was true, that moment in the kitchen…that moment where I hadn't been able to look away from him, where I'd been staring at his beautiful lips and wondering what they would feel like against mine… had been real.

As I pushed open the door leading to the alley, that hated voice crept into my head.

My brother's voice.

*So what, you think you deserve a guy like that, you pathetic little shit? You're a murderer*

I came to a stop as I sucked in a breath. No, I hadn't actually wielded the knife that had ended two lives and destroyed a third, but wasn't I just as culpable? More so, even, since I'd stood by and let it happen? Like the man who stood on the beach and watched another drown? No throwing him a lifeline or calling for help.

I was struggling to catch my breath as I stood there. What *was* I expecting? Friendship? Romance? To know what it felt like to be kissed, since I didn't think the surprise smooch Lisa Larkin had laid on me in the first grade counted?

I couldn't have any of those things. I mean, what was the point? Even if I could somehow get past the fact that I didn't deserve a guy like Phoenix in my life, what would happen when he found out who I really was? Hell, he didn't even need to know about what had happened seven years ago to hate me.

I automatically tugged my sleeve down on my wrist and then shook my head.

No, I couldn't risk spending any more time with him. I couldn't *want* like that. It would make my already bleak world so much worse.

The thought was well and good, but as soon as I lifted my gaze and saw Phoenix standing on the other side of the alley, his back to the wall and his dark eyes on me, that flutter in my belly exploded into a feeling unlike anything I'd ever known before. And the relief that I hadn't missed him…

I shook my head even as I stepped into the alley and let the door swing closed behind me. He didn't move towards me, but he never took his eyes off me either as I approached him.

I'd let myself have this one thing. These few minutes where I could pretend I was someone else. I'd be a regular guy who was allowed to feel excitement and anticipation. I'd let myself imagine what it would be like if Phoenix leaned down and kissed me and I'd walk by his side and dream of him reaching out to take my hand in his. And when my few minutes were up, I'd go back to being who I really was…Levi Deming, coward, weakling, murderer.

I was okay with adding selfish and foolish to the list of my crimes if it gave me the chance to pretend even for a little while that the last seven years hadn't happened.

Phoenix straightened once I reached him. His lips pulled into a slight smile, but he didn't say anything and neither did I. I just fell into step next to him and followed him from the alley to his car. He opened the door for me again and waited until I was seated to close it behind me. Maybe I'd add the sin of pretending we were on a date to the ever-growing list.

"I'm glad you came, Levi," Phoenix said as he climbed into the SUV.

"I'm sorry," I blurted out.

"For what?"

I slid my eyes so they were looking through the windshield instead of at him.

"For thinking you were like *him*." I knew I'd slipped up earlier and mentioned T by name, but that didn't mean I wanted to say his name again…hell, I didn't want any part of him in this moment.

"Tell me his real name, Levi. I can help you."

I shook my head before turning to look at him. "We should probably go. I don't want to be late."

Phoenix studied me for a while before starting the car. My body was trembling, but I didn't know why. I wasn't scared exactly. It was something else.

I didn't realize what the feeling was until Phoenix stopped the car a few minutes later and grabbed my wrist before I could get out. His thumb began stroking over my skin. I both wanted to tear my hand free so I could escape the car, and crawl across the console into his lap.

What the hell was happening to me?

"Levi?"

His voice brought me back to reality and I realized I'd missed something based on the expectant way he was looking at me.

"Sorry, what?" I asked.

"What time do you get off work?"

"Um, late…or early I guess, depending on how you look at it. Five o'clock tomorrow morning."

He nodded and released me.

What would I do if he leaned across the console and kissed me? What *could* I do to make him do just that?

But he remained where he was and the embarrassment of my train of thought had me scrambling to get out of the SUV. "See you tomorrow at St. Anthony's?" I asked before I remembered that none of this was real. I was supposed to be telling him not to come back.

"Yeah, see you tomorrow," he murmured softly.

I forced myself not to look back at him as I closed the door and hurried towards the grocery store's employee entrance. But just before I opened the door, I did look back.

Only, he wasn't there.

Disappointment curled through me, but the lingering warmth on the inside of my wrist where he'd been stroking me reminded me it hadn't been a dream, not entirely anyway. I hung onto that sensation for the rest of the night as I cleaned floors and stocked shelves. And it was still there when I stepped out into the early morning darkness and rounded the corner the next morning, intent on heading for the bus stop.

And it lingered even as my eyes fell on the familiar silver SUV sitting alongside the curb and the man leaning against the side of it.

# CHAPTER 8

## PHOENIX

"Come on in," Ronan said as he opened the door wider for me. I hadn't seen Seth's car in the driveway, so I suspected we were alone. Which made sense since Ronan likely didn't want his husband around when I gave him my first report on Levi Deming.

It had been a week since I'd begun trailing Levi and while I'd given Ronan a couple of brief phone reports over that time period, I hadn't shared a lot of details with him since I was still in the information-gathering stages of my reconnaissance.

Normally, I had no issue with these kinds of briefings, but nothing about this case was normal. And I wasn't relishing what I was about to do.

Lie.

No, not about everything.

But there was quite a bit of information about what I'd been up to the last week that I would need to leave out of my report because I just had no explanation for what I'd been thinking.

Starting with the rides I was continuing to give my target.

To work.

From work.

Hell, I was supposed to pick him up this afternoon to take him to St. Anthony's for our shift tonight.

And I had absolutely no explanation whatsoever for the insanity that had taken over me three mornings ago when I'd been waiting for Levi outside the grocery store. To say he'd been stunned to see me was an understatement. But right after I'd taken in his look of shock, I'd watched his lips pull into a soft smile that had punched right through to my heart. I'd seen Levi smile when he interacted with the soup kitchen guests, but it was nothing compared to the beautiful expression that had stolen across his features that morning.

Or after I'd asked him if he wanted to go to breakfast.

He hadn't even hesitated to say yes, which had surprised me. He'd been nervous at first as we'd sat down in this little diner just a few blocks from his work, but as we'd started to dig into our food, he'd begun pelting me with question after question about myself.

Questions I'd had to skirt around or answer with half-truths.

Like what kind of work I did that would allow me to be sitting on the curb waiting for him at five o'clock in the morning and spending my evenings volunteering at a soup kitchen.

My response about being a consultant in the security industry seemed to have satisfied him well enough that we'd moved on to other topics. Safe ones like what kind of movies we liked and what we did for fun.

Typical date conversation.

Except it hadn't been a date.

Not really.

Because I couldn't be dating a man I was supposed to kill.

"Have a seat," Ronan said as he motioned to the same chair I'd been sitting in a week earlier when I'd gotten the assignment. I'd been so certain then of what the outcome would be.

But now...

"Daisy ran the name you gave me. One guy fits the bill," Ronan said as he handed me several pieces of paper. I'd told him about T after Levi had let the name slip a few days ago. I hadn't been sure the information would be enough to learn anything useful about the man who'd assaulted Levi, but as I reached for the pages, I knew the alias had been enough.

"His name is Hugo Larson. He's done time for assault, breaking and entering and drug possession. He's got an older brother named Gunnar who's doing life at WSP, the same prison Levi did his time at. The brother is in for murder," Ronan explained.

I nodded as I studied the rap sheet in my hands. I didn't see anything about T being a pimp, which meant what I'd seen in the alley with Levi hadn't been about prostitution. The fact that T and Levi shared a connection through T's brother wasn't a good sign for Levi.

"So, you didn't hear anything else when you heard Levi call the guy by his name?" Ronan asked.

My insides tightened at the question. I hadn't told Ronan about Levi performing oral sex on T or that I'd intervened. I didn't have a good explanation as to why I'd left that detail out.

"No," I said as I lifted my eyes and looked directly at Ronan. If I kept my eyes down, he might figure out I was lying.

*You just need more time to figure things out,* the voice in my head reminded me. It did nothing to ease my guilt, though. This man had given me purpose after I'd lost everything. He'd let me be a part of his family.

Did I really want to risk losing that for Levi? For a man I knew without a shadow of doubt had participated in a brutal crime that he'd never had to pay for?

Ronan drummed his fingers on the desk. "So, all he's done is go to work, home and this soup kitchen thing?" he asked.

I nodded. "He sticks to the same routine. There hasn't been any sign of T since the encounter in the alley."

Ronan's jaw was tight as he nodded. I could tell he was frustrated. I found myself holding my breath as I waited for him to speak.

What the fuck would I do if he said to pull the trigger anyway? The fact that Levi was consorting with a known criminal was potentially enough for Ronan to decide the young man's fate.

"Keep on him," Ronan finally said, clearly unhappy with his own decision.

I nodded and quickly stood. "I've got a stop to make before I head back there…he'll be heading to St. Anthony's in a few hours."

Ronan nodded and his gaze softened. "How's she doing?"

I merely shook my head because he knew the answer to his own question. The answer wouldn't change anytime soon…or possibly ever.

"Seth and Tristan were talking about stopping by for another visit soon."

Another round of guilt went through me even as warmth flooded my system. "She'd like that," I murmured. "I'll call you if there's anything new," I said in a rush as I hurried to get out of there.

As I made my way towards the front door, I shook my head.

I couldn't lose this. I just couldn't. They were my family. Levi was no one to me…he was a job and nothing more.

I ignored the inner voice calling me a liar and left the house. I hated myself for the brief hope that went through me that maybe today would be the day Levi finally proved to be the man he'd been that night seven years ago. But on the heels of that thought came that damn inner voice again.

*Liar.*

~

"It's my turn to pay," Levi said as he dug out his wallet. "And don't think I don't know what you did yesterday," he said with a shake of his head.

"What?" I asked innocently as I took a sip of the little bit of coffee remaining in my cup.

"You waited until I went to the bathroom to ask the waitress for the check," he scolded.

I smiled at that. We'd been having breakfast together every morning at the same diner since that first morning I'd picked him up after work and I'd somehow managed to pay the bill each time, but Levi had insisted the day before that he'd pay. Since I could tell from the young man's worn and limited wardrobe and less than ideal living conditions if his shitty, run-down apartment building was anything to go by, I knew money wasn't something he had a lot of. I watched as he carefully counted out the money. His eyes lifted to mine briefly and I saw his cheeks color in embarrassment.

I wanted to tell him he had nothing to be embarrassed about, but I suspected it would have the opposite effect and humiliate him even more.

It wasn't something I'd started to notice until this past week as I'd spent more time in Levi's presence. I'd first picked up on it in the kitchen as we'd been preparing dinner. Whenever Levi had to deal with a measurement or counting something out, like how many spoonfuls of an ingredient to add, he took an inordinate amount of time to do so. I'd made the mistake of interrupting him once while he'd been in the process of adding flour to a bowl for the cake he was making for dessert and he'd been forced to start over. At first, I'd thought maybe he just had memory problems, but as I'd watched him more and more, I'd realized it was more complicated than that. He struggled with anything that required more in-depth thought processing. I knew he could read because I'd seen him reading recipe cards, but he seemed to struggle with things that weren't clearly spelled out. Math, especially, proved difficult for him. Father O had brought him a new recipe to add to the menu's lineup, but the recipe had been designed for a single family, so Levi had needed to quadruple the ingredients to make one of several batches of the food for the soup kitchen guests.

I'd watched him struggle through trying to figure out the new amounts, but he'd refused to ask me for help and I hadn't wanted to let him know I was aware of the issue, so I'd made an excuse about wanting to switch jobs with him since I was having trouble with getting the flavor just right for the sauce I'd been preparing.

I suspected he had some kind of learning disability, but I hadn't asked about it.

"I like when they put the tip amounts on the bottom of the check," Levi murmured as he studied the check and then looked at the money he had left in his hand. He'd already put down enough cash to cover the cost of the meal, but not the tip. I could tell from the cash he had left, he had more than enough to cover it, but from the way he was looking back and forth between the bill and the money, I knew he was having trouble figuring out how much to leave. His eyes shifted back to me briefly and I saw the shame there. I watched as he quickly took the rest of the money in his hand and dropped it down on the pile of cash he'd already left. It was almost a fifty percent tip.

"Mine was good, how was yours?" he asked, his voice a little higher than normal. I watched him flip the billfold closed, but before he could slide it to the edge of the table, I put my hand over his to stop him.

"Do you have your phone with you, Levi?" I asked.

He swallowed hard and nodded. My guess was he knew that I knew what he was struggling with.

"Does it have a calculator?"

Another nod. "I...I don't know how to calculate percentages," he said softly.

"You don't need to," I said. "Take the taxes and double them. So, if the taxes are $2.50, just add 2.5 and 2.5. When you double the taxes, the tip is usually around the fifteen or twenty percent mark. If you want to leave more or less based on the service, just add in a couple bucks or take a couple bucks away."

Levi held still for a moment. His eyes looked watery, but he didn't cry. He finally nodded and I removed my hand. He pulled the billfold back and I wasn't surprised when he had to start all over again and count out the original amount of the bill. Then he dug out his phone and carefully entered the numbers into the calculator app. When he had the amount, he slowly counted that out too and then added a couple more dollars, leaving him with several dollars in his hand.

"Thank you," he said softly, though he refused to look at me when he said it.

I reached across the small table and forced his chin up. "You're welcome," I said. "You have nothing to be ashamed of, Levi."

He pulled free of my hold, but kept his eyes on me. "We should go," he murmured.

I left the issue alone since I understood he was raw from the embarrassment of it all. We thanked our waitress as we left the diner. "See you boys tomorrow," she called and then shot us a wink.

A knowing wink.

I smiled at Levi who was blushing. Yeah, he knew exactly what that waitress was thinking. But even though I was smiling on the outside, inside I felt only guilt. Every second I was with Levi, I was lying to him. On top of that, I was lying to Ronan too.

Hell, I was lying to myself.

Thinking I could walk away from this the same man I'd been going in. Even if I was forced to do the unthinkable and take Levi's life, I wouldn't be the same. Even if he proved he was the same man he'd been seven years ago when he'd watched Seth being tortured, I'd now seen this other side of him.

The side I didn't think he was faking.

Once we reached the car, I held the door open for him like I always did, but instead of climbing in, Levi stopped next to me. Suddenly, he turned and put his hand on my shoulder and then he was reaching up to brush his mouth over my cheek in a fleeting kiss. We both hung there for the briefest of moments and I willed him to seek out my lips next. But he didn't.

Instead, he stepped back a little and sent me a small smile. "Thank you, Phoenix."

"For what?" I asked. "You paid...I should be thanking you."

He started to get in the car, but then stopped and looked at me. "For that," he said, motioning to the diner. His eyes lifted to where my hand was resting on the door. "For this." He paused. "For everything."

Fuck, I wanted to grab him and kiss him then and there, not caring who saw us or what it would do to me...or him.

But I settled for, "You're welcome, Levi."

He got into the car and buckled up while I closed the door. Even though I'd been driving him home for several days now, he still gave me directions, though I didn't need them since I'd been driving the damn route for two weeks now as part of my surveillance of him.

Two weeks of lying.

Two weeks of waiting.

Two weeks of utter hell.

I pulled the car to a stop across from his building. I was half-tempted to get out of the car and open the door for him just to delay what little time I had left with him.

"See you later?"

I nodded. "I'll pick you up at four."

I was glad when he didn't argue with me like he had the past few mornings. But unlike the other mornings, he didn't get out of the car right away. His eyes lifted to meet mine and I saw something there I hadn't expected I'd ever see.

But it was there, clear as day.

Desire.

Raw and needy.

Just like that, the air around us changed, becoming heavy with electricity. My whole body lit up in anticipation and my cock, which was always half-hard around the young man, began thickening uncomfortably in my pants.

I couldn't do this. It was just one more complication in a list of many.

"Phoenix," Levi whispered, his voice heavy with need and confusion. He knew what he wanted, but he clearly had no idea how to go about getting it. It was a reminder that, despite what I'd seen in the alley with him and T, there were certain aspects of sex that were foreign to him.

I was leaning in before I could stop myself, but with a good foot still separating us, Levi let out a strangled, "Oh my God!" and then he was out of the car like a shot.

I quickly climbed out of the car, immediately searching for danger.

And found it almost instantly.

"Henry!"

Levi's terrified shout carried across the street as he ran for the entrance to the building. But my eyes were stuck on what he'd already seen.

Because four stories up sitting dangerously close to the side of the building's fire escape was a baby, completely unaware of the peril it was in. Behind the baby was an open window, but there was no adult in sight.

I sprinted across the street as I watched the baby crawl closer to the edge of the landing it was sitting on. The bars that should have been there to protect people from stepping off the landing were gone. If the baby moved even a few more inches, it would topple over the edge.

As I reached the bottom of the fire escape, I vaulted onto a nearby dumpster and then used the extra height to make the leap to the ladder which was a good ten feet off the ground. As soon as my hands closed around the bottom rung, the ladder descended and I began scrambling up it. I kept my eyes on the baby as I climbed up to the first landing. The noise of the ladder descending had fortunately distracted the baby and it had stopped its forward crawl.

"Hey, what are you doing up so early?" I said to the baby in a cheerful voice, even though I was still two floors below it. The sound of my voice attracted the baby's attention and by the time I reached the landing, the child was watching me with wide eyes.

My whole body was shaking like crazy as I reached down to pick the baby up. Based on the name Levi had used and the blue shirt covered in trains that the baby was wearing, I was guessing it was a he. The baby, Henry, was wearing only a diaper besides the shirt. His skin was chilled so I quickly pulled him against my body and wrapped the lower part of my shirt around his lower half.

"Henry!" I heard Levi scream. I ducked into the open window to see the front door crash open and a panicked Levi tearing into the apartment.

"Henry! Oh, thank you God!" he cried when he saw the baby.

I quickly handed the baby over to him. Tears began streaming down his face unchecked as he examined the child. My guess was that the baby was somewhere between nine months and a year old. He had brown hair and huge blue eyes and he smiled happily as Levi spoke to him.

"Thank you, thank you," Levi cried as he wrapped an arm around me and cried against my chest.

"Shhh, he's okay, Levi," I murmured as I dropped a kiss on the top of his head. I put my arm around him to steady him as the panic finally began to leach from his system. When he released me to focus on the baby, I searched the small living room we were standing in and then spotted the Pack-N-Play. I grabbed a fleece blanket from it and then wrapped it around the baby before I led Levi over to the couch.

"What the fuck is going on out here?"

I looked up to see a man wearing nothing more than boxers and a plain white undershirt standing near the entrance to the living room. His dark hair was messy, like he'd just woken up, and his eyes were red-rimmed.

Levi stiffened next to me, but then he stood up.

"What the hell happened, Dad?" he nearly yelled. "Henry was out on the fire escape!"

The man seemed confused for a moment and dropped his eyes to the baby briefly. "Must have forgotten to put him back in his thing" – he waved his hand at the Pack N Play – "after I fed him."

"That's it?" Levi said in astonishment. "He could have been killed!"

"He's fine," the man said, his voice slurring a bit. I could smell the alcohol wafting off him even from where I was standing.

"Who is this?" the man said as his eyes shifted to me, his lips twisting into an ugly sneer.

"Phoenix. He's my friend," Levi murmured, though his voice had lost some of its edge. "He saved Henry."

Levi's father shifted his suddenly ice cold gaze to his son. "You dare bring *this* into my house?" he said, his voice full of disgust.

I knew that tone of voice. I'd experienced it on more than one occasion growing up. It was the voice that reminded me I wasn't equal. That even after years of serving my country, saving lives and being a good citizen, I was still defined by the color of my skin. As a black man who also happened to be gay, I routinely had to deal with an extra dose of bigotry, even from members of my own race, but to hear the disdain coming from Levi's father stung. Not because I gave a shit what the fucker thought of me, but because it made me wonder about the man I'd been spending the last several days with.

"Dad-"

"Get the fuck out!" the man snarled at me. "Your kind isn't welcome here!"

"Dad!" Levi said as he took a few steps forward, but as soon his father began heading towards him, hands fisted, Levi stepped back and I quickly put him behind me.

The move stopped Levi's father in his tracks.

"Get your nigger ass out of here before I call the cops!" the man warned.

"Levi, get Henry's things," I said. As pissed as I was, I wasn't about to leave Levi and the baby with the fucker. I'd seen enough to know where the man's rage would fall if I left them both here.

I kept my eyes on Levi's father, but saw Levi moving quickly to grab a diaper bag off the couch. "Is that it?" I asked.

"His car seat is next to the couch," Levi said. Fear was etched into his voice.

"Go, I'll grab it," I said.

I kept my body between Levi and his father as I followed him out the door, snatching the car seat on the way out.

As soon as I closed the door behind us, I put my hand against Levi's back to urge him down the stairs. "Phoenix," he began to say, but I shook my head.

"Not here," I murmured.

Once we reached the second floor, Levi said, "Just a second, okay?"

I followed him to an apartment door near the stairs. He knocked, but there was no answer.

"Okay, we can go," he said as he snuggled Henry against his chest. At some point, Levi had managed to give the child a small stuffed caterpillar and the baby was currently playing with the toy's different colored feet that also made various sounds.

As soon as we reached the sidewalk, I began crossing the street towards my car, but Levi grabbed my arm. "Thank you for what you did up there. I'll take Henry to the church until he" – Levi motioned to the building behind us – "goes to work."

I could tell Levi was tense and I suspected a lot of that had to do with his father's treatment of me.

"Get in the car, Levi," I said, keeping my voice light, despite the tension still running through my frame.

He hesitated before saying, "We need the base for the car seat. It's in my father's car…I use it sometimes when I have to take Henry to the doctor and don't want to wait for the bus."

"Which one is it?" I barely remembered to ask since I already knew which car belonged to Curtis Deming, since I'd seen the car on the video footage from the Mercer Island house.

"The blue Honda," Levi said as he motioned to the car parked a little farther down the street. Thankfully, the vehicle was unlocked and it only took me a few minutes to get the base out of the sedan and transferred to my SUV.

Once we got Henry settled in the backseat, Levi said my name again as I went around to open his door for him, but I was still too raw, so I said, "Not now, Levi."

I hated the look in his eyes, but I still had so much to fucking process that I couldn't deal with the fact that the man I was fighting an insane level of attraction for was the product of a racist.

Even though I'd grown up in an upper middle class neighborhood in the suburbs of Maryland, I hadn't been completely immune to the prejudices people of color faced in even the most benign of cases. I'd been completely clueless as to what was happening the first time I'd entered a department store as a teenager to pick out a birthday present for my mother and had been followed around by a security guard for the better part of an hour before the man had told me I needed to leave because the store was for *paying* customers. I'd been humiliated beyond words as my parents had had to explain to me what the man had meant, and even my father going down to that store with me in tow to confront the security guard as well as the store's manager hadn't made a difference. That security guard had looked at my father the same way he had me, even after he'd discovered my father was a high-ranking official for the Department of Defense. And when he'd been fired on the spot by the store's manager, I'd heard that ugly slur for the first time.

The one I'd heard in high school, boot camp and even from the occasional member of my own team in the army.

The same one Levi's father had just flung at me.

I'd learned to let that word and all the others I'd heard over the years wash right off my back. But just the thought that Levi might secretly share his father's views had me feeling sick.

"Where are we going, Phoenix?" I heard Levi ask when I headed in the opposite direction of St. Anthony's.

"My place," was all I said.

Levi didn't argue and he wisely remained silent as I made my way onto the highway. It took a mere fifteen minutes to reach my house. I saw Levi's eyes go wide as he took in the view. "You live here?" he asked.

I nodded. My house was in Alki Point, which was on a small peninsula just south of downtown Seattle. While my house wasn't huge, it had a stunning view of the Olympic Mountain range as well as the city of Seattle itself. I also had several hundred feet of private beach.

I got out of the SUV and grabbed the diaper bag as Levi got Henry's car seat out. Once inside the house, I disarmed the security system and then led Levi to the carpeted living room. I figured it was wide open enough for Henry to crawl around a bit while Levi and I talked.

"Do you want something to drink?"

Levi shook his head. "Can you...can you put some water in this?" he asked. "The formula is already in it...you just need to add water to the middle line."

I nodded and took the bottle he handed me. By the time I returned to the living room, Levi was sitting on the floor with Henry. He was helping the baby to stand and was making funny faces, which had Henry wide-eyed and showing off a toothy grin. But when the little boy saw the bottle in my hand, he began cooing in excitement.

"Look what Phoenix brought you," Levi said, a big smile on his face. He helped Henry sit down and then began clapping which had the baby clapping his hands together.

"Thank you," Levi said to me as he took the bottle and then turned Henry so he was sitting on Levi's lap and pressed up against his chest. The baby eagerly began sucking on the nipple. I marveled at the unabashed look of love in Levi's eyes as he looked down at Henry. I sat down in a chair in the corner of the living room so I could watch the pair. Within minutes, Henry's noisy sucking slowed and I could see his eyes drifting closed.

It wasn't until his eyes slid completely shut that Levi carefully removed the bottle and then looked up at me. "Phoenix-"

I could hear the apology in his voice, but I wasn't in the mood to hear it. Probably because I knew he didn't really owe me one. I was still pissed about his father's behavior, but I needed to give Levi the benefit of the doubt.

"Is he yours?" I asked as I nodded at Henry.

Levi shook his head. "He's my brother's."

"And his mother?"

"Her name is Dina. She started dating Ricky after he...after he got out of prison."

"Your brother was in prison?" I asked, feigning surprise.

Levi nodded. "He killed his girlfriend four years ago. He got out of prison a year and half ago and met Dina. She found out she was pregnant right after he died."

"So, your brother only served a few years for the murder?"

"My dad gave him an alibi, so the prosecutor decided to offer Ricky a plea deal. Ricky figured doing a few years was better than risking life."

"Your dad *gave* him an alibi?"

Levi fell silent and let his eyes drop back down to Henry who was snuggled up against his chest. The sight of them made my heart constrict with painful memories.

"Ricky wasn't a good person. I know he did it. I was home the night it happened. Ricky and I shared a room...he wasn't home that night like my dad said he was."

I wanted to ask Levi why he hadn't said anything, but I already had a pretty good idea. From his father's reaction this morning after Levi had called him out about putting Henry in danger, the man hadn't given a shit that Levi was right or that he'd been holding a baby in his arms...he'd been ready to do battle and my guess was that Levi would have come out the loser.

"Dina came to our apartment a few months after Ricky died and told my dad she was pregnant and needed money for the pregnancy. My dad told her to get an abortion, but she said it was too late. I guess...I guess she didn't realize she was pregnant right away. She and Ricky both had a drug problem," Levi murmured. "My father told her he wasn't supporting her or the kid and told her to leave. I went after her and gave her all the money I'd been saving up."

"Saving for what?" I asked.

But he shook his head. "Nothing. It's not important."

I highly doubted that, but I didn't say that. "What happened after that?"

"She kept coming back for more money. I got her to agree to lay off the drugs long enough to have the baby and in exchange, I paid her rent and medical expenses. She moved into the same building as me and my dad so I could help her with the pregnancy, and after the baby was born."

"What did your dad think of that?" I asked.

"He didn't care. Just told me not to try to shortchange him on my share of the rent for our apartment." Levi paused long enough to adjust Henry in his arms a bit. "I knew from the moment I held him, that I'd done the right thing," he said softly as he studied the baby. "I mean, have you ever seen anything so perfect in your entire life?" he whispered as he lifted his eyes to mine.

I took them both in, but didn't answer him. Because I *had* seen that kind of perfection...had held it myself. But it was too painful to think about.

"So, you've been supporting Dina and Henry this whole time?"

Levi nodded. "Dina works during the day, but she doesn't make much and she has a tendency to lose jobs not long after she starts them.

I babysit Henry at Dina's apartment from eight until I leave for St. Anthony's."

I considered what he was telling me for a moment. I knew enough about his routine to know he worked until five in the morning. If he started babysitting at eight, it meant he only got a few hours of sleep each day. Even if he wasn't babysitting Henry every day, it was still a brutal schedule.

"What happened today?" I asked.

"I called Dina while you were getting the formula ready. She dropped Henry off with my dad last night because she had a date," Levi said, the anger in his voice clear. "I've told her not to leave Henry with Dad, but if I'm even a little bit late getting to her place to babysit, she does it anyway. Dad's softened a bit towards Henry, but you saw that he's not exactly attentive."

That was an understatement if I'd ever heard one.

"Do you have a place he can sleep?" Levi asked.

I nodded and then went over to him and carefully helped him stand. I ignored the heat that sparked between us at even the minimal contact and motioned to the hallway. "The bedrooms are back here."

I contemplated where to put Henry for his nap, but the only place that made sense also wasn't acceptable to me. Mostly because it would mean I'd have to answer questions I didn't want to. So, when I reached the first door, I turned to Levi and said. "My room is at the end of the hallway. Would you mind waiting in there and I'll bring a mattress in there that we can put on the floor?"

I could see the curiosity in Levi's eyes as he nodded and turned away. I waited until his back was to me before I steeled myself and forced my hand to turn the doorknob of the one room in my house that caused me unbearable pain every time I entered it.

## CHAPTER 9

### LEVI

*I* shouldn't have paused and looked back as Phoenix entered the room, but I couldn't help myself. I didn't see much... only enough to leave me with more questions than answers.

Pink paint on the walls.

What looked like a tree with all sorts of different colored leaves stenciled on the wall.

A huge stuffed polar bear in the corner.

That was it...but it was enough. Not to mention the fact that Phoenix had looked at the door before he'd opened it like it was the gate to hell.

I walked down to the end of the hallway. The door to Phoenix's room was already open, so I was able to walk in without having to shift Henry's weight and disturb his sleep. I was still reeling from the near miss this morning. I was sure my heart had stopped in the moment I'd seen the baby sitting out on that fire escape.

Tears pricked the backs of my eyes as I relived the moment.

Henry was the only reason I was still here. There'd been so many times after I'd gotten out of prison that I'd been tempted to take the entire bottle of sleeping pills my mother had left behind years earlier, but the second I'd learned that Dina was pregnant with my nephew, I'd flushed the pills down the toilet. And as hard as things had been in the year since Dina had shown up on our doorstep, every extra hour I'd had to work, every beating I'd had to endure after I'd been forced to keep living with my father so I could give Dina the money I'd been saving up for my own place had been worth it, because I'd instantly fallen in love with the little boy who'd looked up at me with innocent, trusting eyes.

He'd needed me, though I was starting to wonder if I wasn't the one who'd ended up needing him even more.

I looked around Phoenix's room and was immediately drawn to the far side of it where there was a set of double doors leading to a balcony that overlooked the water. I noticed just one patio chair sitting on the balcony and wondered perversely if it meant Phoenix was single.

Not that it mattered. Despite having spent more time with him than I'd ever spent with anyone outside of my immediate family, Henry and my cellmate, Hank, I knew what we were…and weren't.

We absolutely hadn't been on dates. I'd reminded myself of that repeatedly every morning as I'd walked out of the grocery store that first morning to see Phoenix waiting for me.

And not just sitting in the car either.

No, he'd actually been leaning against the passenger side of the SUV so that he could open the door for me. Every time I saw him like that, I remembered one of the many movies I'd watched as a kid – chick flicks my brother had called them. I'd fallen head over heels for the guy in *Sixteen Candles* as he'd leaned against his red Porsche waiting for Molly Ringwald's character to come out of the church. I'd watched that moment over and over, dreaming the gorgeous Jake was waiting for *me*, opening that car door for *me*, stealing *me* away from the world.

I wasn't foolish enough to think I'd found my very own Jake, but I'd let myself pretend for the few seconds that it took for me to reach him that he was there for the same reason Jake had been there for Samantha.

Because he wanted to be with me.

But I knew the real reason. Phoenix was like Jake in a lot of ways –

he was good, decent, honorable and protective. He was the hero of the story, but I was just the villain pretending to be someone else.

Guys like Phoenix didn't want guys like me. Even if by some miracle I could undo that night seven years ago, I still wouldn't measure up. Phoenix had seen proof of that today.

Twice.

First with the humiliating turn of events as I'd tried to figure out something as simple as calculating a tip, a task most people could do in seconds. And second, with my father's outburst. I automatically glanced down at my arm to make sure my sleeve was still fully pulled down.

A commotion behind me had me turning around. I briefly took in the rest of Phoenix's room which was spacious and decorated with neutral shades of beige and cream. I watched the object of my quickly-growing obsession enter with a twin mattress which he laid on the floor next to the bed. The mattress already had a purple sheet covered in rainbows on it.

"I figure we can put some pillows around him to keep him from rolling off. Will that work?" Phoenix asked.

I nodded because my heart was too far up my throat to make speech possible.

"Does he need a blanket?"

"No," I said. "It's warm enough in here."

Phoenix grabbed several pillows off the bed and put them on the mattress. I carried Henry over and carefully put him down and then fitted the pillows around him to deter him from rolling off the bed if he turned over. Fortunately, he slept through everything, testament to the night he'd probably had with my father. When I'd changed him in the living room while waiting for Phoenix to return with the formula, I'd encountered a very full diaper. At best, he'd probably only been changed once the night before sometime before my father had gone to sleep.

"If we leave the door open, we should be able to hear him," Phoenix offered and I nodded. Henry was a good sleeper, so he'd likely be out for a couple of hours at least.

I followed Phoenix from the room and back down the hallway to the living room. Awkwardness settled in as he motioned to the couch. I hoped that he'd sit next to me, but instead, he sat in an armchair on the other side of the coffee table.

"Does what happened with your father this morning happen a lot?" Phoenix asked.

"No," I said as an unexpected sense of panic hit me. What if he was thinking of reporting what had happened this morning to the police? Would they make it so I couldn't see Henry anymore? "I swear, that was the first time anything like that happened. And I'll talk to Dina… I'll make sure she never leaves him alone with my father again."

"I meant what he was going to do to you," Phoenix said softly.

"What?" I asked.

Phoenix sighed. "Levi, how often does your dad hit you?"

I was ready to deny it, but the look in Phoenix's eyes stopped me. I knew he wouldn't believe the lie I'd been prepared to tell. "It's not that bad," I murmured as I dropped my eyes. "I usually just stay out of his way and things are okay." I forced my eyes up. "It's not a big deal, I promise."

"Because you deserve it?"

The question caught me off guard and I suddenly found it hard to swallow.

When I didn't answer, Phoenix asked, "Did he hit you when you were a kid too?"

I managed a nod. "He…he was worried I'd turn out like Ricky."

"What do you mean?"

I could feel the cold settling into my body and I quickly stood up. "Can I use your bathroom?"

I didn't wait for him to answer as I hurried towards the hallway where I'd seen a half-bath earlier as I'd been walking to Phoenix's room. Once inside, I closed the door and then flipped the lock. I turned the water in the sink on and began splashing my face as I willed my mind to stay in the moment.

*Ricky, stop! Please, don't!*

"Fuck," I whispered as my knees began to buckle.

"Levi?"

I was dimly aware of the sound of knocking, but I couldn't make sense of where it was coming from.

*Stop crying, you little bitch!*

"Levi, open the door."

*You gonna call out for Mommy? Do it! Let her see what her precious little boy really likes!*

Pain seared through my body and I pressed my mouth against my arm as I remembered all the times I'd imagined it was my mother's headless body I'd seen hanging from the rafter in that boiler room.

"Levi!"

The pounding in my head grew louder, but thankfully, darkness finally began to seep along the edges of my vision and the image of my mother's body receded and the pain firing up my spine began to fade. And then, blessedly, Ricky was done and I let myself slide into the blissful blackness that swallowed me whole.

## CHAPTER 10

PHOENIX

*I* was normally someone who was cool under pressure, but the longer Levi was out, the more I began to panic.

"Levi, I need you to wake up now," I murmured against his head as I pulled him even closer to my chest. After finally getting into the bathroom after Levi had ignored my requests for him to open the door, I'd found him lying on his side on the floor, his body lifeless, but his eyes open.

He'd been cold.

Frighteningly so.

I'd remembered Father O's words about needing to get Levi warm when the same thing had happened at the soup kitchen, so I'd immediately picked Levi up and carried him into my room and put him under the bedcovers. I'd gone a step further and crawled in with him in the hopes I could snap him out of his trance, because it was freaking me the fuck out. At the soup kitchen, he'd snapped out of the event within minutes. This time around, it had been almost a half an hour since I'd picked him up off that floor and he had yet to respond to me in any kind of way.

I glanced over at Henry to make sure he was still asleep. I'd been worried he'd woken up when I'd broken the bathroom door down, but he hadn't.

I lifted my hand to clasp the side of Levi's face as I held him against me. His skin felt warmer and I wondered if I should try to get him some juice like Father O had that day. But before I could move, I felt him stir against me. His arm had ended up slung across my waist when I'd pulled him against me, but he hadn't actually been holding onto me. Now, I felt his fingers press against my side.

"Thank fuck," I whispered to myself. "Levi, can you hear me?"

"Phoenix?"

"Yeah, it's me," I murmured as I began rubbing my hand up and down his back.

"Henry?" Levi suddenly blurted out and tried to move off me.

"He's fine," I said. "Still asleep."

Levi shifted enough so he could look at the mattress on the floor. He held there a moment before he relaxed in my arms again. I couldn't help but think how right it felt to have him there.

And how wrong.

"I'm sorry."

"Don't be sorry," I said as I leaned down to press a kiss against his head. "You scared the hell out of me," I admitted.

"I thought I could stop it this time."

"How often does it happen?" I asked.

"Not often," he responded. "It was bad for a while after Ricky got out of prison, but since he died…"

"What happened to him?" I asked, though I already knew.

"Not sure. Cops think it was some kind of turf war or something… said he probably pissed off a rival dealer. They said he was killed execution style and his body was found near an underpass that was popular with both dealers and users. They think whoever killed him was sending a message."

It didn't surprise me that the cops had thought that, since that had been exactly what Ronan had wanted them to think when he'd had Maverick "Mav" James terminate Ricky.

"Your brother dealt drugs?" I asked.

Levi nodded. "Before he went to prison for killing his girlfriend, he was mainly just doing drugs. He started dealing when he got out."

I felt Levi shift and I released him when he sat up. I sat up as well and then leaned back against the headboard when Levi made no effort to get out of bed. "I…I want to tell you something because I don't want you to hear it from someone else," he said.

"Okay," I said, keeping my voice as even as I could.

It took Levi an inordinate amount of time to finally say, "I was in prison too." I could tell he had to force himself to look up at me. "For drugs." He chewed on his lip for a moment and then said, "I know you have no reason to believe me, but I don't do drugs…never have. Ricky would make me go pick his drugs up for him sometimes. When the cops arrested his dealer, I'd just bought drugs for Ricky so I was arrested too. I…I was sentenced to five years but got out a year ago after serving just over three."

If I hadn't spent the past ten days interacting with the young man, I wouldn't have believed him. But I had no doubt he was telling me the truth. No, it didn't make him completely innocent, because as much as I wished it wasn't true, he *had* participated in the murders of Fred and Corinne Nichols. But his motives for going after Seth again all these years later were rapidly diminishing. I wanted to believe he wasn't a threat to Seth, but the reality was, he was struggling financially. Not just struggling, but desperate. He was killing himself trying to make enough money to pay his expenses as well as Henry's and the child's mother's, but there were only so many hours in the day. And there was still the question of his connection to T. Yeah, the brother in prison was the link, but it didn't explain what T and Levi were doing together. As much as I didn't want to admit it, Levi and T could be planning something together with Seth being the likely target.

"The police didn't believe you about the drugs being for Ricky?" I asked.

"I didn't tell them."

When he didn't expand on the statement, I leaned forward and put my hand on his back. "Why not?"

He sucked in a deep breath and I automatically placed my hand against his neck. Luckily, his skin was still warm. But his pulse was beating rapidly.

Levi shook his head and then looked at me. "Let's just say prison was the safer bet."

Despair coiled deep in my belly, because between that one statement and Levi's reactions whenever he talked about his brother, I knew that Levi's father had been the lesser of two evils in his life.

"My dad's left for work by now. Would you mind taking me and Henry home?"

I could tell Levi was on the edge and I didn't want to risk another episode, so I reached up to stroke his cheek. "Why don't you spend the day here?" I asked. "We can get some sleep and then maybe take Henry down to the beach this afternoon."

Levi dropped his eyes to the bedding and began picking at the edge of the duvet cover. "You don't know how badly I want to say yes to that," he admitted.

"What's stopping you?"

"You."

I pulled back from him a bit as his father's ugly words rang in my ear. I was surprised to see Levi cast me a sad look.

"I really wish I was your Samantha," he whispered.

If his voice hadn't been so heavy with despair, I would have laughed at the odd statement. I leaned forward again and settled my hand on his cheek once more. "I have no idea what you're talking about, but trust me when I say that I'm liking you as Levi just fine."

I'd meant the comment to lighten the mood and hopefully wipe the sadness from his pretty green eyes, but the more I held his gaze, the more things quickly changed. I told myself to release my hold on him, but the second I relaxed my hand, Levi's fingers closed around my wrist and he pressed his cheek into my hand.

"Did you mean what you said?" he asked hoarsely.

"About what?" I managed to get out, even though it felt like I'd swallowed a beach ball. My heart was pounding painfully in my chest as my dick pressed against the confines of my pants.

Levi hesitated before saying, "About sex…kissing. That it should be freely given, not taken."

I nodded even as my breath hitched because I knew there was only one reason he would be asking me that. I didn't move even an inch as Levi leaned in until our mouths were just inches apart.

"Please," I heard him whisper beneath his breath. But I knew he wasn't pleading with me to kiss him…no, he was begging me for something so much more important.

He needed me to keep my word.

Kissing Levi was a supremely bad idea. I kept telling myself that over and over as I slid my hand around the back of his neck and urged him forward that last little bit, but the second my lips touched his, I forgot everything else but the sensation of his mouth beneath mine.

In truth, it was barely a kiss because Levi pulled back almost immediately and I instantly released him. But I'd felt more with that brief contact than I had in any of the meaningless sexual encounters I'd had in the past several years. Because the sensation wasn't just lingering on my mouth. No, it was firing throughout my entire body, flooding it with heat and a clawing need unlike anything I'd ever known.

I'd expected Levi to sit back, putting distance between us. But to my surprise, he leaned in and kissed me again. Still brief, but just as intense. He again pulled back, but only for a moment and then his lips were back on mine. With every brush of his mouth, he increased the pressure and I finally realized what was happening as his kisses grew more desperate, but he didn't take the next step.

*He's never kissed anyone before.*

It was almost too unlikely to believe, but as his struggle to get more out of each contact grew, the truth became clearer.

I was his first kiss.

My stunted brain finally managed to catch up and on Levi's next pass over my mouth, I parted my lips and licked over the seam where his lips were tightly pressed together. Levi gasped and jerked back. His eyes flew to mine in surprise. I still had ahold of his neck, but I did nothing to urge him forward again. Instead, I let my eyes drop to his mouth as his tongue came out to run over his lips...tasting me.

Blood rushed to my cock at the move, but I managed to keep from grabbing him and pushing him back on the bed.

No way I was going to fuck up this opportunity.

Levi touched his mouth with his fingers for a moment and then suddenly he was leaning forward again, clasping both sides of my face with his hands. His mouth brushed mine again and this time when I licked his lower lip, he stilled instead of pulling back. I groaned when his tongue mimicked the move I'd just done to him.

Over and over he licked at my lips until I was dizzy with lust. I opened my mouth hoping he'd get the hint and take me up on my invitation.

He did.

Emphatically.

My skin burned where his hands held me. My tongue greeted his as he pushed into my mouth. The second his tongue touched mine, a switch inside of him seemed to flip because he began kissing me with fervor. The rest of his body quickly caught up and after struggling to untangle himself from the blanket, he was pushing himself onto my lap even as he continued to hold my face so he could control the kiss. I happily let him take charge and kept just a light hold on him as I wrapped my arms around his waist.

When we were finally forced to come up for air, Levi whispered, "I didn't know." That was all he said before his mouth was back on mine. As he began rubbing his body against mine, I let my hands drift down to grab his ass and instinctively began grinding my erection against him.

The effect was the same as if I'd dumped a bucket of ice water on him.

"No! Stop! Please!"

He wasn't yelling the words, but his quiet plea was no less impactful. I instantly released him and pulled back to give him space. He scrambled off my lap, but didn't leave the bed.

"I'm sorry," he said.

"No, I'm sorry," I returned. "I didn't mean to scare you."

"I...I..." He shook his head. "I didn't mean to...to..."

"It's okay, Levi. Just catch your breath, okay?" I ached to reach for him again just so I could help him calm down, but I knew my touch would end up doing the opposite.

He took several deep breaths. His gaze momentarily drifted to the baby who was still asleep since we'd managed to keep our make-out session relatively quiet. When his gaze returned to me he said, "I'm sorry, I felt your...your..."

"Erection," I supplied.

He blushed and nodded. "I didn't mean to tease you."

His words had me contemplating my own response. From his kissing alone, I would have guessed him to be a virgin. But I'd seen him with T in the alley...it wasn't the first time he'd sucked a man's cock. And his reaction after I'd almost kissed him in the kitchen the previous week was proof that he didn't view sex in a positive light, which didn't surprise me in the least since I knew what often happened to smaller, weaker men in prison.

I pushed past the pain of knowing it was extremely likely that Levi had been sexually assaulted in the past and focused on the here and now. "You didn't tease me," I said. "You turned me the hell on, but you do that every time you look at me so..."

I let my words hang as he studied me.

"You're not mad?" he asked. "That I...that I don't want to go all the way?"

"Truth?" I said.

He nodded.

"What we just did is going to fuel a lot of fantasies tonight and for the foreseeable future so no, I'm not mad." I desperately wanted to reach out and touch him again, but I held back because he looked ready to bolt. "It's a rare gift to be given something so precious," I added.

"But I didn't give you anything," he said and I nearly laughed when his eyes fell to the bulge in my pants before he jerked them back up to my face.

I finally gave in and shifted forward so I could run my thumb over his mouth. I was glad when he didn't pull away. "Yeah, you did, Levi," I murmured. "You gave me your trust." I brushed my mouth over his in the briefest of kisses and then released him. "Will you trust me just a bit longer and let me hold you while we sleep?"

It took him a long time to decide and it felt like I held my breath for every second of it. Levi cast a look at Henry before he finally shifted until he was once again lying across my chest, though this time his body was filled with tension. I settled one hand on the arm he had draped over my waist and used my other hand to play with his hair. The move seemed to relax him because I felt his body sink farther down on mine.

My own eyes began to drift closed as exhaustion began to overtake me, but just a few whispered words from Levi as he lost himself to sleep had me once again wide awake.

"You're going to be the death of me, Phoenix Jones."

## CHAPTER 11

### LEVI

"I'm just asking that you call me before you leave him with my dad, Dina," I said, trying not to lose my patience. The woman in front of me tapped her long red nails on the doorframe. Nails I highly suspected I'd paid for with money that had been intended for Henry.

Dina tossed her long red hair over her shoulder and adjusted her low-cut top. "Look, Levi, if I've got plans, I need you to step up. If you're too busy…"

"I'm busy working," I said. "If you really need to go out while I'm at work, then please, hire a sitter for Henry. Mrs. Donaldson has offered to babysit for a pretty reasonable fee."

"I'm not leaving my kid with that hag," Dina said snidely. "Bitch calls me a whore under her breath every time she sees me."

Henry began to fuss in the car seat I'd finally had to put down after Dina had neglected to take it from me or invite me into her apartment to help her get Henry settled. I'd already explained the near miss this morning, but as expected, Dina had barely reacted to the news that she'd almost lost her child. I'd spent the past eight months hoping even the smallest bit of maternal instinct would kick in, but her disinterest was further proof that she hadn't been confused any of the times she'd told me she should have just risked a late-term, illegal back-alley abortion. Even just the thought of never having had Henry in my life was enough to have tears pricking the backs of my eyes.

"You want to pay for a real sitter, fine, but it ain't coming out of my share," Dina added.

Frustration welled, but I knew any further conversation was pointless. "Did you schedule his next well-baby visit?" I asked.

"And how am I supposed to get him there?" Dina snapped.

I wanted to remind her that I'd bought her a bus pass, but when she reached down and jerked the car seat up, I kept quiet and reached for it so she wouldn't wake Henry up. He was worn out from the afternoon we'd spent at the beach at Phoenix's house. I knew that if he woke up now, he'd be cranky and that would just irritate Dina further. I pushed past her, ignoring her huff of disapproval, and carried the car seat to Henry's room. I'd managed to paint his room a pretty green color and decorate it with gently used toys and stuffed animals from thrift stores, but it was far from ideal for the little boy. The carpet was worn and stained so badly that no amount of cleaning I'd done with the carpet shampooer I'd rented from the grocery store I worked at had gotten it clean, and I cringed every time I thought of Henry crawling on it. I'd gotten Henry's crib for a decent price from a woman in the building who'd been cleaning out her storage unit in the basement, but it was old and outdated and I'd spent hours sanding and staining the wood in the hopes of giving it a cleaner look.

"Okay, Henry, I'll see you tomorrow," I whispered to the baby as I carefully removed him from the car seat, kissed his forehead and placed him in the crib. I made sure to tuck the caterpillar toy next to him since it was his favorite.

I closed the door partially since Dina tended to run the TV too loud. One of the few items I'd bought brand new was the baby monitor system. I'd learned early on that Dina was a heavy sleeper and rarely heard Henry crying without the benefit of the monitor. As I walked back out into the living room, I looked around for the receiver for the monitor to make sure it was somewhere Dina would hear it. I found it on the coffee table, but froze when I saw what was next to it.

Powder residue.

*White* powder residue.

I looked up and searched out Dina in the kitchen and saw her eyeing me as she drank what the normal person would assume was some kind of juice, but what I knew was more vodka than anything else. The woman arched her eyebrow at me and I knew she was daring me to say something about the evidence that was staring me right in the face.

Drugs.

She was fucking using again.

And there wasn't a thing I could do about it.

Maybe if she had even the tiniest bit of interest in being an actual parent to Henry, I could have played on that and threatened her with calling Children's Services, but we both knew I wouldn't do it.

Because *I* would be the one losing something, not her.

I was such a selfish son of a bitch. Despite knowing what a shitty mom Dina was, I didn't want to let go of the only real joy I had in my life. And Dina knew that and she ruthlessly used it against me. A few months after Henry's birth, I'd gotten the idea in my head that maybe I could be Henry's dad after Dina had once again lamented his existence. I'd let the idea curl around inside me for so long that it had soon become my only thought, and I'd started having dreams about watching Henry come running out of school at the end of the day and jumping into my arms and calling me *Daddy*. I'd known it wouldn't be easy, but considering all the money I put towards Henry's care as well as my own portion of the rent for my father's apartment, I'd been certain I could make it work.

I'd approached Dina with the idea a few days later, even offering to let her still be a regular part of Henry's life. I'd thought for sure she'd go for it.

She'd crushed my dreams as easily as she crushed cigarettes beneath the heel of her shoe. She'd asked me why she'd ever get rid of a cash cow as valuable as her son to a chump like me…at least for free, anyway. What had followed had been one of the sickest things I'd ever heard in my life and any pity I'd once felt for the woman who'd been foolish enough to get involved with my brother had evaporated.

She'd offered to sell me Henry like he was nothing more than a used car.

I ignored the queasiness in my belly as I left Dina's apartment and went upstairs to my own. Phoenix was waiting for me in the car, but I knew if I lingered too long, he'd come up after me. It had taken every promise I could think of plus a few passes of my mouth over his to get him to agree to give me ten minutes. It was only the reassurance that my father was working that had likely been the real reason he'd agreed.

If I hadn't been so distracted by the turn of events with Dina, I would have used the time to mull over the day Henry and I had spent with Phoenix. It had started off pretty damn rocky, but boy, had it ended well. After waking up in Phoenix's arms, I'd gotten to watch him sleep for a while until Henry had started to stir. I'd tried to get out of bed without waking Phoenix up, but I'd barely managed to shift my weight off his chest before his eyes had opened.

Then he'd smiled at me.

A sweet, soft smile that had left me feeling warm and gooey inside. I'd ended up kissing him again, though I'd promised myself I wouldn't since the man was just too damn intoxicating. Things had gotten hot and heavy very quickly, but true to his word, Phoenix had backed off as soon as I'd become overwhelmed.

While I'd gotten Henry changed and fed, Phoenix had disappeared, only to reappear with a few beach toys including a small shovel, bucket and plastic molds. They'd been geared towards a child's use, but I hadn't commented on that fact. I hoped Phoenix might tell me about the mysterious child in his life at some point, but I wasn't about to pressure him to do so.

A few kisses didn't give me that right.

Nothing I ever did would give me that right, actually. Friends told each other things like that. Lovers too. Guys whose lives were based on lies didn't get to expect something like that.

Phoenix and I had talked about unimportant things as we'd played with Henry. And we'd *both* played with the baby. Phoenix had hunkered down in the sand right next to me and we'd spent nearly two hours building up shapes in the sand for Henry to knock down. Afterwards, Phoenix had taken his shoes off and braved the cold waters of Puget Sound so he could carry Henry out into the gentle surf so he could see the small fish that were swimming around in the shallows.

It had been a perfect day.

One where I'd let myself forget who I was.

If my interaction with Dina hadn't soured it, walking into my apartment surely would have. My father wasn't home, but it didn't matter because I was instantly transported back to this morning when I'd nearly died at the sight of Henry sitting out on that fire escape. I'd never run so hard or so fast in my life. Finding the little boy safe in Phoenix's strong arms had been my undoing. And then things had gone from bad to worse with my father and his racist taunts.

After closing the window to the fire escape that my father hadn't bothered to shut even after all the morning's drama, I quickly went to my room to grab a change of clothes. My mind drifted back to Dina and pain filtered through my chest as I realized I was running out of options. I'd always told myself that Henry would be better off with Dina than in foster care, but I wasn't so sure that was true anymore. The drugs were a game changer. As was Dina's dismissal about what had happened this morning.

Henry really was just a paycheck to her.

I briefly wondered if I'd have any legal claim to Henry, but I dismissed the thought. Whoever made those kinds of decisions would take one look at my stint in prison and then ask me what the hell I'd been thinking to even ask the question. And what kind of home could I give Henry? I'd never amount to much. Yeah, I could give him as much love as he'd ever need, but even I knew that wasn't enough. No, Henry deserved that perfect nuclear family with the white picket fence and the dog in the backyard.

By the time I reached the SUV, I barely acknowledged Phoenix as he opened the door for me.

"What's wrong, Levi?"

I forced myself to focus on Phoenix and shook my head as I gave him a weak smile. "Just tired," I said. I could tell he wasn't sure I was telling the truth, so I changed the subject and said, "Thank you for today."

He smiled his beautiful smile and then reached out and clasped my fingers with his. He lifted my hand to his lips and kissed my knuckles. My belly flip-flopped wildly when he held my hand in his as he pulled the car out into traffic.

I needed to stop pretending that this thing with Phoenix was more than it was, but I was so raw from the prospect of losing Henry that I didn't care. Maybe I'd pretend for as long as Phoenix would let me. And then when he was gone and Henry was gone, I'd do what I should have done seven years earlier.

Embrace judgment day.

---

"*S*top!" I admonished when Phoenix whipped the end of the twisted hand towel at my ass for the third time in less than five minutes. I was elbow deep in soapy dishwasher and Phoenix was taking full advantage every time he passed behind me to get something from the dishrack or one of the cabinets next to me.

Phoenix chuckled and put his hands up in mock surrender. I smiled and returned to my work. The man had been trying to draw me out of my funk from the moment we'd arrived at the soup kitchen.

And I had to admit, it was working pretty damn well.

I saw Phoenix approaching in my periphery, but this time when he snapped the towel at me, I was ready and grabbed the sprayer and aimed at him. I hit him square in the chest with a spray of water. The look of shock on his face was priceless.

"Oh, it's on!" he said in a menacing voice. I nailed him again with another spray before he reached me and wrestled for control of the nozzle. Chaos ensued as water sprayed over me, him, the floor and everything else in our immediate vicinity. We were both laughing and breathing hard by the time he called for a truce.

But like the many times I'd found myself in close proximity to the man, things changed quickly and soon his mouth was on mine. I forgot all about the sprayer and dropped it so I could reach my wet, soapy arms around Phoenix's back. It wasn't until he turned me so my side was against the countertop that things changed again because my hip hit the lever of the sprayer and water shot up between our bodies like a geyser, soaking us both.

Laughing, we jumped apart. Phoenix's eyes were warm as he snagged the discarded hand towel off the counter and used it to wipe at my face. "Thanks," I said with a smile.

He held my gaze for a moment and then began wiping off the rest of me. I didn't even notice what he was doing until he said, "Oh, hey, looks like this is coming off. I'll go find you another one."

I looked down to see Phoenix carefully peeling the soaking wet large Band-Aid from the inside of my wrist.

"No, it's fine!" I yelled as I tried to stop him, but I wasn't fast enough.

The silence between us was thick as we both stared at what I'd been using the large bandage to hide.

And then Phoenix lifted his icy eyes to meet mine and I knew my days of pretending had come to an end.

# CHAPTER 12

## PHOENIX

A swastika.

He had a fucking swastika tattooed on the inside of his wrist.

The betrayal was instant and brutal.

"Phoenix," Levi whispered.

"Don't," I said quietly as I stepped away from him. I'd been such a fucking fool. My entire job depended on my ability to judge people and I'd completely missed the mark on this man. After the day I'd spent with Levi and Henry, I'd been convinced that Levi was innocent...no, not of the crime seven years ago, but of everything that had come after. He'd been trying to do good with his life. Volunteering, being a father to the little boy who needed him...

"Please, Phoenix, just let me explain," Levi begged. His eyes were pooling with tears, but for once, I didn't feel the need to comfort him.

"I get it," I bit out. "Doesn't get any clearer than that," I said, motioning to the tattoo. It was no bigger than the size of a half-dollar, but it might as well have been the size of the moon. My anger was threatening to consume me so I moved farther away from Levi. As much as he disgusted me, I didn't want to hurt him.

Why the fuck hadn't I just done my damn job?

Levi tried to grab my arm, but I jerked it from his grasp, making him let out a little whimper. I turned to leave the kitchen so I could pull myself together, but he stepped into my path.

"Please, I'm begging you-"

"Get the fuck out of my way, Levi," I snapped. "I don't want to hurt you, but I really need a goddamn minute right now."

I stormed past him, ignoring the sob that tore free from his throat. I went out to the alley and wished like hell T would be waiting out there, but the bastard hadn't shown his face since the day I'd intervened on Levi's behalf.

The day I'd chosen him over my family.

"Fuck!" I yelled and then I rammed my fist into the wall. Not hard enough to break my hand, but enough to have it hurt like a motherfucker. I'd definitely have bruises.

I was half-tempted to leave, but I couldn't do that to the people who were counting on me tonight. I might have started this whole volunteering gig to keep a closer eye on Levi, but I'd found myself putting more into it and getting more out of it than I'd anticipated. I'd started interacting with some of the people who used the soup kitchen's services and while I didn't know all their stories, I'd seen enough to know that my contribution made a difference.

I gave myself five minutes to calm down before I went back into the building. Levi wasn't in the kitchen, but I didn't really care. I kept myself busy by cleaning up the mess we'd made with the water, but all that did was cause my temper to notch up again as I remembered how eagerly Levi had kissed me back and how good he'd felt in my arms.

And how damn beautiful his laugh was.

Five minutes passed, then another five before I started to wonder if Levi had left. I hadn't seen him leave through the back entrance, but he could have gone through the church's front entrance. But I doubted he'd bail on his responsibilities. I waited a few more minutes and then began looking for him. I told myself it was because we needed to finish up the dinner preparations, but I knew that was a lie. Now that my immediate anger had started to die down, I couldn't help but remember the way he'd begged me to hear him out.

When I reached the back rooms, I noticed the door to the small bedroom was closed, so I figured that was his likely hiding spot. I knocked on the door, but there was no answer. I started to get nervous as I remembered his breakdown this morning in my bathroom.

"Levi," I called as I knocked again. Still no answer. I expected the door to be locked as I turned the knob, but it wasn't. The room was dim since only the small lamp on the nightstand was on, but there was enough light for me to see Levi sitting on the bed with his right arm balanced on his lap. It took me several long seconds to understand what I was seeing.

Because where I should have seen the black ink from the tattoo, I saw only white foam. I automatically flipped on the overhead light so I could see better. The additional light helped me see the dark ink of the tattoo, but something wasn't right. My eyes fell to a yellow bottle on the floor next to Levi's feet.

"What-" I began as I read the label from where I was standing.

Oven cleaner.

My eyes flipped back to Levi's wrist and I shook my head in disbelief.

"What the hell?" I yelled as strode forward and snatched Levi's arm so I could get a better look. The blackness I was seeing wasn't the tattoo at all. It was his fucking skin!

"What have you done?" I asked, completely horrified. The white foam on Levi's wrist was bubbling. I glanced at his face and saw that sweat had formed on his brow and his face was pale and drawn tight.

In pain.

"Jesus," I said as I snatched the bottle of oven cleaner off the floor and turned it around to read the label. I dropped it as soon as I found what I was looking for.

Lye.

One of the ingredients was lye and it was currently burning away the layers of Levi's skin. I yanked him none too gently to his feet. I knew I needed to get the shit off him, but I was afraid of the damage I'd do if I just wiped it away with my shirt or something else. I needed to get him to running water. But the second I began pulling him from the room, Levi fought back.

"No!" He tried to rip his arm free. "I need to make sure it's gone first!"

"Stop it!" I shouted and then I bodily dragged him to the kitchen.

"No!" Levi screamed again, but I ignored him and pulled him to the sink and turned the water on. But he was fighting me so much that I knew I'd only end up hurting him more if I forced his hand under the water.

"Levi, stop," I said, but he only fought me harder.

"It's not who I am!" he cried.

Guilt tore through me as I realized I'd done this to him.

Because I hadn't been willing to listen.

And because I'd been waiting for proof that he wasn't a good man. I'd condemned him to try and ease my own conscience.

"Baby, I know," I said as I released his arm and grasped his face between my hands. "I'm sorry I didn't give you a chance to explain. But please, please let me help you."

Levi began to cry. "I'm not like them!" he said brokenly.

I had a good idea of who *them* was. "Levi, I know you're not," I said quickly. My heart felt like it was going to pound out of my chest. Every second that shit remained on his skin, the more damage it did. "Baby, please, let's get it off and then we'll talk." I kissed him softly and tasted tears.

Levi finally nodded his head even as more tears fell from his eyes. I quickly adjusted the temperature of the water so it was lukewarm and then turned down the pressure so it wouldn't hit his skin with too much force. I choked back a sob when I put his wrist beneath the flow of water. The foam disappeared and immediately revealed a large oval burn that was black along the edges and an angry, splotchy mix of uneven skin that ranged from black to pink to red in color. Bile rose in my throat as I realized just how many layers and layers of skin had been burned away. I was tempted to use my hand to try to clean the wound since it seemed like not all the oven cleaner was coming off, but I didn't want to risk causing more damage. Levi was quiet as I worked, but I knew he had to be in extreme pain.

"Leave your arm under the water, okay?" I said as I began searching for a clean towel. I grabbed one from beneath the sink along with a roll of paper towels. Once I returned to Levi's side, I realized he was starting to mentally check out. "Baby, I need you to stay with me," I said as I gently put my hands on either side of his face. The move seemed to help him focus, but instead of speaking, he merely nodded.

I quickly folded several pieces of paper towel into squares and then got them wet. "Levi, I'm going to cover the burn with the paper towels and then wrap a regular towel around your arm so we can keep the area wet until we get to the hospital."

"Hospital?" Levi said and immediately began shaking his head. "No, I'm not going to the hospital." He started to pull his hand back so I carefully grabbed his arm to keep it under the water.

"The burn is really bad…bad enough that I think it will get infected if it isn't treated properly."

"We have to finish making dinner," he said quietly. I was beginning to think he might be in shock because he seemed out of it.

"I'll call Father O on the way. I'm sure he can ask Sherry or Patrick to come in early…we finished most everything anyway, remember?"

Levi managed a simple nod.

"So, you'll go?" I asked, not sure what I'd do if he said no.

Another nod. "Please don't tell Father O what I did."

"I'll just tell him you burned yourself while cooking."

"I just wanted it gone, Phoenix," he whispered suddenly.

"I know you did, baby. Let's just get you to the hospital so they can get you feeling better, okay?"

"Yeah," Levi murmured.

I got the injury wrapped as best I could and then led Levi to my car, locking the soup kitchen door behind us. Once I had Levi settled, I called Father O and told him the story I'd come up with to cover for Levi. I was certain lying to a priest had to count as some kind of sin, but since I'd been doing it from day one, I figured adding another falsehood to the list wasn't going to matter much.

The ER was a zoo when we arrived, but fortunately we didn't have to wait too long after seeing the triage nurse. But as I got up to go with Levi to be examined, Levi dealt me yet another blow when he said, "Can you stay out here?"

I nodded, but said, "You sure?"

He nodded and then followed the nurse down a hallway through a set of automatic doors. I dropped back down into a waiting room chair to begin the wait. I kept replaying the moment in my head when I'd discovered that damn tattoo. Instead of hearing Levi out, I'd turned my back on him.

So much for earning his trust.

The minutes turned into an hour and then another. I'd had enough sense to call Levi's work, since I hadn't been sure if he had his phone on him. I'd spoken to his boss, who'd merely introduced herself as Betty, and explained that Levi had had an accident. The woman had been beside herself with worry, but after promising I'd have Levi call her as soon as he was feeling up to it, she'd settled down and told me to let Levi know to take as much time off as he needed.

I suspected it would be a challenge getting him to take off even the one night.

"Mr. Jones?"

I jumped to my feet and searched out the person who'd called my name. A young man in a long white coat was standing near the double doors leading to the treatment area.

"I'm Phoenix Jones," I called as I hurried to him.

"Mr. Jones, I'm Dr. Clark. I've been treating Levi for the burn on his wrist." The man glanced at the tablet in his hand for a moment before he finally focused his attention on me. "Levi has given me permission to talk to you about his injuries and the treatment plan."

Thank fucking God!

"Okay," I said, hoping my voice sounded more in control than I was feeling at the moment. I wasn't a big fan of hospitals.

"Levi has sustained a third-degree chemical burn to the inside of his right wrist. He tells me the burn was caused by oven cleaner. As you may or may not know, some oven cleaners contain sodium hydroxide, also known as lye."

I nodded. "Yeah, I saw the bottle. It had lye in it."

"Lye doesn't instantly burn the skin; it takes time to actually cause damage. With the severity of Levi's burn, I estimate he had the oven cleaner on his skin for at least fifteen minutes. He would have been in quite a bit of pain at that point."

I wanted to throw up. I'd spent those fifteen minutes ignoring him because I'd been so pissed. "I didn't know what he was doing," I murmured.

I felt a hand on my shoulder and realized I'd dropped my eyes at some point. Worse yet, they were blurry from the tears I was trying to hold back.

"He told me why he did it," Dr. Clark said as he removed his hand. "You were right in how you treated the burn before bringing him here. The good news is that the fact that he was in so much pain means the nerves weren't permanently damaged. We've given him a mild painkiller to help take the edge off while we're cleaning and dressing the wound. It will likely become more painful as it starts to heal, especially as the skin begins to scab over."

"Do you have to do skin grafts or debridement or something?"

"Surgery is an option to try and reduce the scarring, but Levi has declined that line of treatment. He says he doesn't care if it scars or not. His biggest concern is whether or not the tattoo is gone."

I bit back the curse I wanted to let loose.

"It's too early to tell if any part of the tattoo will still be visible once the tissue begins healing, but in all likelihood, most of it will be gone or damaged to the point that you won't be able to tell what it was." The doctor paused to check his tablet. "I've contacted someone from Psych Services to do a consult with Levi since this is technically a case of self-harming, but after having spoken to Levi myself, I suspect the psychiatrist will reach the same conclusion. Levi isn't a danger to himself or others. He knew what he was doing and while his actions were not advisable under any circumstances, I don't believe he did it to actually hurt himself."

I nodded in agreement. There was only one reason Levi had done what he'd done.

And I was a big part of that reason.

"So, if the psychiatrist clears him…"

"He can go home tonight," the doctor confirmed. "We're going to send him home with some mild pain meds as well as some antibiotics. He'll need to follow up with his doctor over the next several weeks to monitor the injury for infection, but otherwise it's just going to be a long, painful process of letting his body heal itself."

"Can I see him?" I asked.

"I had to ask him that myself because he seemed pretty convinced you wouldn't even be out here when I came to look for you."

I shook my head in disbelief. I wanted to both strangle Levi and kiss the shit out of him. "You can tell him I'm not going anywhere," I said firmly.

"You can tell him yourself," he said. "It could take Psych a while to get someone down here so why don't you sit with him until then? They'll probably ask you to step out while they're talking to him."

"Thank you, Doctor," I said as I held out my hand. He shook it and then motioned towards the double doors. I followed him past several curtained-off rooms. My stomach tightened uncomfortably when I spied Levi sitting upright on a bed, the back raised to support his upper body. His heavily bandaged wrist was resting in his lap.

As soon as I reached his side, Levi said, "I'm sorry Ph-"

"Shut up," I whispered just before I bent down and sealed my mouth over his.

## CHAPTER 13

### LEVI

"Will you tell me about your family?"

I really didn't have the right to ask the question, especially since I was the one who owed Phoenix answers, but I wasn't ready to talk yet. If I had my way, I'd never have to tell him about me, my fucked-up family or the hated tattoo I was finally free of.

After I'd been discharged the previous night, I'd asked Phoenix to take me home since Betty had practically ordered me not to come into work for at least three days unless it was to stop by so she could hug the dickens out of me. Yes, she'd actually used the word *dickens*. I'd smiled when she'd said that to me, then I'd hung up the phone and cried. The very sweet nurse who'd been inserting the needle for my IV had wiped my face with tissues and told me everything would be okay.

I hadn't bothered to tell her that nothing would ever be okay again.

Because I'd figured something out while I'd been sitting in that hospital bed waiting for the doctor.

I'd been wrong when I'd told Phoenix that God had given up on me a long time ago. He hadn't given up...He'd just been biding His time. I'd never considered my time in prison or any of the events that had followed as acceptable punishment for what I'd done to the Nichols family seven years ago. My suffering had been a drop in the ocean compared to what Seth Nichols and his parents had gone through. As the years had passed, I'd kept waiting for that moment when God would pass His judgment on me, because contrary to what Father O had told me, I didn't believe my sins could be forgiven. But as hard as things had been over the years, there hadn't been that one moment where I'd felt like God had finally picked me out of the crowd and said, "Okay, it's your turn."

Turned out, Father O had been right about one thing. God *was* always watching.

And he'd finally found something that would hurt me more than a life spent behind bars or any beating or assault that T, Gun or even Ricky could have sent my way.

He'd given me someone to love.

Two someones.

I'd never understood what I'd done to deserve having Henry in my life, but I got it now. God had given me that beautiful little boy so I would know what it felt like to love someone else so much that nothing else mattered.

And now He was taking him away…no, He was forcing me to give him up. I knew I was getting off easy in a sense, because even though losing Henry would feel like my heart was being ripped out of my chest, Henry would still be alive. I'd still get to imagine him out in the world living an amazing life, even if he would never remember me and how much I'd loved him.

It was much more than Seth Nichols had been left with.

To make sure I really got the message, though, God had gone a step further and brought Phoenix into my life, and he'd waited just long enough for me to start falling in love before He'd decided it was time for lesson number two.

Because I couldn't build something with Phoenix that was based on a lie. And if I told him the truth, I'd lose him. But unlike with Henry, Phoenix *would* remember me and I'd have to live with knowing he hated me and that he would regret every moment he'd spent with me. He'd look back at every kiss he'd given me, every smile, every touch, with disgust and regret.

"What do you want to know?" Phoenix asked as he wrapped the blanket tighter around us, cocooning me in warmth. It was just after six o' clock in the morning and we'd decided to watch the sun rise from the beach at Phoenix's house. Once we'd reached the sand, Phoenix had urged me down to sit in front of him and then he'd stretched his long legs out on either side of me and pulled me back against his chest before wrapping the blanket around us both. Despite the throbbing pain I was still feeling in my wrist as well as the broken heart I was nursing, I'd never felt safer.

Phoenix hadn't argued with me the previous night when I'd asked him to drive me home after I'd been released from the hospital. No, he hadn't said a single thing as he'd helped me out of the wheelchair the staff had insisted I use to leave the building. He'd just taken my uninjured arm and led me to his waiting car and tucked me into the passenger seat, even helping me buckle my seat belt. Then he'd kissed me softly and stroked my face with his hand before he'd closed the door and gone around to the driver's side. I'd known pretty quickly that he wasn't taking me to *my* home, but I hadn't argued. After all, how could I argue with something I wanted?

Once we'd gotten to his house, he'd led me to his room. He'd helped me take my shoes, socks and pants off, but hadn't forced the issue when I'd stopped him from removing my shirt. I'd known he wasn't undressing me for sex, but I still hadn't wanted him to see my body. He'd helped me into bed and a few minutes later he'd gotten in with me. I'd been facing away from him, so he'd carefully settled himself at my back and had wrapped an arm around my waist. He hadn't been wearing a shirt, but I'd been able to tell he'd put on sweatpants.

I'd fallen asleep within a matter of minutes since the painkillers the hospital had given me had left me feeling fuzzy, but I'd woken up several times, each time in Phoenix's arms. I'd given up on going back to sleep a couple of hours ago and when Phoenix had woken up, we'd just lain there for a while, looking at each other. I hadn't had a clue what he'd been thinking, but I'd been coming to the realization that I was falling in love for the first time in my life.

And acknowledging that it wouldn't change anything.

But the more I thought about it, everything *was* going to change. Without Henry and Phoenix, I had nothing. I'd been a fool to think otherwise.

"Everything," I admitted. Even if my time with Phoenix was limited, I still wanted to know everything about the man that I could. Since I knew Phoenix had lost his mother, I asked, "Do you have any brothers or sisters?"

"A sister. Angela was a few years younger than me. My mom experienced some complications with her birth and couldn't have any more kids."

"Was?" I asked. "She's gone?"

"Yes," he said, his voice thick with pain. I had enough sense not to ask the burning question of how he'd lost her.

"And your father?" I felt Phoenix tense behind me and I knew what it meant. They were all gone. "I'm sorry, we don't have to talk about this."

He was silent for a moment before he pressed a kiss against my temple. "It's been a while since I've talked about them with anyone," he admitted. "Neither of my parents had siblings so after their parents died, it was just my parents, me and my sister. After I lost them, there wasn't anyone I could keep their memories alive with."

"There was no one special…a boyfriend or girlfriend?" I ventured, adding the girlfriend part in since I wasn't sure if Phoenix was gay or bi.

"No boyfriend," he said and then he dropped his mouth to my ear. "And definitely no girlfriend," he whispered.

I smiled. Okay, so that answered that.

"How is that possible?" I asked.

"Well, see, gay men don't generally like the girlie parts…"

I swatted at the arm he had pressed around my waist. "I meant the boyfriend part."

His chuckle rumbled through his chest and into me. I had to fight back the tears that threatened to fall.

How was I ever going to live without this?

"Not sure," Phoenix murmured. "My parents were supportive when I came out when I was a teenager so I was lucky that I never had to hide who I really was. I had a couple of boyfriends in high school, but once I joined the military, I was focused on that more than my love life. I always figured I'd have plenty of time to settle down once I was done with the army."

"Where were you stationed?"

"Texas mostly. I was an Army Ranger."

"Did you serve in Iraq or Afghanistan?" I asked.

"Both...our missions took us all over the Middle East."

"Why'd you leave?" I asked. "It sounds like you loved it."

Phoenix was quiet for a long time and I didn't rush him. "I did love it. I left after I lost my family in a car accident."

Shock reverberated through me. "All of them?" I whispered.

I felt him nod against me. "My sister was picking my parents up from the airport. They were on their way back to my sister's house when they were hit head-on by a semi. The driver had fallen asleep at the wheel. He survived."

I shook my head. "I'm so sorry, Phoenix." I pulled his hand up and pressed it to my lips. He tightened his other arm around me.

"But if you loved the army so much, why not go back to it after..." I let me words drop off because I didn't know how to phrase my question without sounding like a jerk.

"Because my sister was seven months pregnant at the time of the accident."

I stilled and then turned in his arms. There was enough light from the rising sun to see the pain in his eyes. "The baby survived?" I asked, remembering the pink room Phoenix had gone into to get the mattress for Henry.

"She did," he said with a nod. "One of the motorists stuck in the traffic jam that happened after the accident was a doctor. My sister wasn't killed instantly, but the doctor knew she wouldn't survive the trip to the ER. So, she performed a C-section right there in the ambulance. I named the baby after the doctor and my sister. Amani Angela Jones."

"Amani," I said softly. "That's beautiful."

"I left the army to take care of Amani. She was in the hospital for about a month since she was premature, but she was in perfect health when they let me take her home."

Phoenix paused and swallowed hard as he tried to collect himself and I knew in my gut that his story wouldn't have a happy ending. If it had, the door to that pink room wouldn't have been closed.

"I sued the company the driver worked for. The money they paid me to settle the case, along with the money my parents and sister left behind, was enough to ensure that Amani would never want for anything. I decided to raise Amani full-time, so I left the army and spent my days taking care of her. I adopted her when she was a few months old."

"What about her father?" I asked.

"He wasn't in the picture. He'd been dating my sister for a few months when she got pregnant, but when she told him, he didn't want anything to do with the baby. He gave up his parental rights in exchange for my sister not seeking child support. He was in the military too, so she never saw him again after that. It was just me and Amani."

His voice broke on his daughter's name and I reached up to stroke his face. "What happened to her, Phoenix?"

He shook his head and I felt my heart clench when a tear slipped down his face.

"A little over a year ago, her father showed up out of the blue. He'd left the military and after he'd heard about what had happened to Angela, he wanted to see Amani. Said he'd had a change of heart and that he wanted to be a part of his daughter's life. She was five by then and only knew me as her father…I'd been planning to tell her about her mother when she was old enough to understand it. I refused to let him see her so he took me to court. My lawyer said the guy actually had a case…that judges usually granted custody to the biological parent."

"Even after all that time?" I asked in astonishment.

He nodded. "The judge granted the guy visitation while we got ready to go to court. Amani was so confused and upset when I told her she had to spend the day with this complete stranger," Phoenix murmured. More tears began to flow unchecked down his face.

"He picked her up on a Saturday morning. He was planning to take her to the zoo. He…he wasn't a bad guy so I let her go and promised I'd see her soon. I told her how much I loved her…"

He began crying in earnest and I turned even more so I could wrap my arms around him. His arms went around me and he began sobbing, his hot tears sliding down my neck. When he settled, he clung to me for a moment before pulling back and wiping at his face. "The police showed up at my door a few hours later and told me what happened. Witnesses at the zoo said Amani had been crying outside one of the exhibits and nothing the guy did could calm her down." Phoenix's voice cracked as he said, "She was asking for me."

I couldn't stem my own tears and had to use my sleeve to wipe them away so I could focus on the man before me.

"People said the guy got more and more agitated as more people stopped to try to help with the situation. He started yelling at them to leave him alone. When a security guard tried to intervene, the man hit him. He grabbed Amani to leave, but she fought him and told him she wanted her daddy. When a Good Samaritan went to stop him, he released Amani so suddenly that she fell, and as she went down, she hit her head on a cement pillar."

Phoenix sucked in a deep breath as he tried to calm himself down. His fingers were wrapped around my own in a brutal hold, but I didn't care in the least.

"The guy left her there…just fucking left her there. The cops took me to the hospital where the doctors told me Amani had suffered a head injury. We had to wait for a few days for the swelling in her brain to go down. She finally opened her eyes about a week later. I was so fucking relieved," Phoenix said. "I thought everything was going to be okay. I…I didn't understand what the doctors were telling me at first because it didn't make sense. I mean, her eyes were open. She was able to move a little. But the doctors told me that she wasn't really awake…

not in a meaningful way. And that her movements were nothing more than reflexes."

"What…what was wrong with her?" I asked, my heart in my throat.

"They said she was in a vegetative state and that the longer she was in it, the more likely it would be permanent."

I shook my head. "No," I whispered.

"I knew they were wrong. My girl was strong…she'd come out of it and we'd go home and everything would be okay." Phoenix's eyes connected with mine. "It's been a little over a year," he said hoarsely. "I…I go to see her and she…she keeps growing up. Sometimes she'll open her eyes and she'll look right at me and I'll be so sure she's going to smile at me and say, 'Daddy, I'm back, did you miss me?'"

I couldn't bear to hear anymore and pushed myself into his arms. "I'm so fucking sorry," I whispered. I felt another sob catch in his throat and then he just held me. I pressed kisses against his temple, cheek and any other parts of him I could reach as I waited for the trembling in his body to ease. When he finally settled, I pulled back and wiped at his tears while he did the same for me. Several minutes passed before I found the strength to ask, "What happened to the guy?" I couldn't call the man Amani's father because I was looking at Amani's father.

"Cops went to his place to arrest him and found him dead. He'd shot himself. It turned out he'd been honorably discharged from the military because he was suffering from severe PTSD. The police think the altercation with the security guard set off an episode and that the guy hadn't really realized what he was doing. He left a note saying he was sorry… nothing more." Phoenix took a deep breath. "I moved Amani out here a year ago when a friend from my former unit heard about what had happened and helped set me up with a job. Amani needs round-the-clock care so she has to be in a special long-term care facility, but…I just couldn't bring myself not to set up her room, you know?"

I nodded. "I do," I said gently. As painful as hoping his daughter might someday recover had to be for Phoenix, the alternative had to be even worse.

"Do you…do you think you might want to meet her someday?" he asked.

"Yeah," I said as I shifted up enough so I could kiss him. "I would really like that."

I didn't care that it would just bind me more to this man. I'd accepted that I was going to lose him. I'd take whatever time I could get with him.

But as Phoenix drew my injured hand up to his mouth and pressed a kiss into my palm before letting his finger trail over the edge of the white bandage that was wrapped around my wrist, I knew I'd likely never even get the chance to meet his daughter.

"My turn," I whispered, more to myself than him, and then I turned around so my back was once again pressed against his chest.

Because no way in hell I could look at him while I told him the story that would make him finally realize he'd made a mistake that day in the alley when he'd come to my rescue.

## CHAPTER 14

PHOENIX

Part of me didn't want to hear Levi's story because it would be so much easier just to sit in silence and watch the sun come up as we huddled under the blanket together. It wasn't that I needed life to be easy because I wasn't that naïve. But *easier* on occasion wouldn't be a bad thing.

Between the events of the previous night and sharing my own story of loss, I was feeling pretty raw and I would have liked to pretend we were just a normal couple watching the sun rise after a night of romance and passion. But I also needed answers because I'd never been more confused in my life. None of the pieces I had about Levi made sense. How someone as sweet and kind as him could have ended up here.

In short, I needed to know who the hell it was I was quite possibly falling in love with.

Because I knew that was what was happening to me. Despite the terrible things Levi had done to Seth and his family, I could no longer judge him on that one act. But I couldn't dismiss the possibility that he might very well be guilty of what Ronan was accusing him of in terms of targeting Seth again.

"I knew there was something wrong with Ricky pretty early on," Levi murmured. "I think my parents thought it was just typical brother stuff when he broke my toys or picked on me. But there was just something about the way he'd look at me...like breaking my toys was just the opening act. I was still young when he started really acting out. He'd just turned ten when he physically attacked another boy at school for no reason whatsoever, other than he wanted to see how it felt to make the boy bleed. My father had always believed in that saying about sparing the rod, spoiling the child. My mom went the opposite way and tended to baby us. Neither way worked with Ricky," Levi said softly.

"One night at dinner a few months after he attacked the other kid, everything changed. We were eating like we normally did and my parents were talking about some troubles my dad was having at work or something...I was only five so I wasn't all that interested. Anyway, Ricky started to get up to leave the table, but my mom stopped him and told him to finish his carrots. Then she went back to talking to my dad. Ricky didn't say a thing...not one single word as he stabbed my mother through the hand with his fork. Then he calmly got up and left the table."

I tightened my grip on Levi as I felt him tremble in my arms. I moved one hand, placing it on his wrist that grasped the arm I had wrapped around his chest. Luckily, his skin was still warm, but I left my hand there so I could hopefully catch any changes in his temperature as he talked.

"My mother was afraid of Ricky after that. My father too. He'd still discipline Ricky, but he never laid a hand on him again. I wasn't so lucky."

"He beat you?" I asked.

Levi nodded. "He'd especially get mad if I tattled on Ricky for things. I think he didn't like hearing how messed up Ricky was...like he saw it as a personal failure or something."

"What kinds of things?"

"Like when he held a knife to my throat because he caught me looking through his comic books or he pushed me down the stairs for no reason at all." Levi shook his head. "I learned pretty quickly to stay out of Ricky's way. We still lived in a house then and had separate rooms, so it wasn't too hard since Ricky spent most of his time in his room. But after my dad lost his job, we had to move into an apartment...the one my dad and I still live in," Levi added.

"My parents' marriage started to suffer. Ricky got into so many fights that he got expelled from three different schools by the time he was a teenager. My dad wanted my mom to homeschool Ricky, but she was too afraid of him. The apartment only had two bedrooms so I had to share a room with Ricky," Levi murmured.

I could feel his skin starting to cool so I leaned down and pressed my mouth to his ear. "I'm right here, Levi. You're safe. He can't ever hurt you again."

Levi shuddered in my hold, but nodded. He took several deep breaths. "When Ricky was fourteen, our building's maintenance man found a whole bunch of decapitated animals hanging in the boiler room. He also found a notebook belonging to Ricky. It proved Ricky had tortured and killed the animals. When he asked my father to come down to the boiler room, I followed him, even though I wasn't supposed to."

"You saw everything?" I asked.

Levi nodded. "I threw up and passed out. When I woke up, I was in my room. I could hear my parents arguing. My dad had paid off the maintenance man along with a neighbor whose cat had been among the victims. My mom was terrified and kept begging my father to send Ricky away, but he refused. When Ricky came home and my parents confronted him, he told them he'd wanted to know what sounds an animal made when it was dying. My dad threatened to have him locked up in a mental hospital and that finally seemed to get through to Ricky because he promised he wouldn't do it again. They...they actually believed him."

As Levi's words started to drop off, I felt his skin grow more chilled and I quickly turned him around.

"Baby, look at me, I need you to focus on me, okay. Listen to my voice."

I could see that Levi was checking out so I cupped his chin and forced him to look right at me. "Levi, take a deep breath."

I was pleased when he did it. I ordered him to take several more. I felt his skin start to warm up a little bit, but it was still clammy. I tucked him beneath my chin and whispered, "We're done, Levi. You don't need to tell me anymore, okay?"

I felt him shaking his head. "Have to," he said. "You need to know who I really am."

"I know who you are," I said, though it wasn't quite the truth. I just couldn't stand to watch him suffer for even another minute.

"I asked my parents to let me sleep with them in their room that night. They said no...that everything was fine now."

I flinched as Levi continued, his voice steeped with determination.

"Ricky was listening to his headphones when I got into my bed. I was so fucking scared," Levi said hoarsely. "But I managed to fall asleep."

I felt Levi shift in my arms and I looked down to see him wiping his eyes. "I woke up face down on my bed with him on top of me. He kept punching me in the side and calling me a coward for running to Mommy and Daddy. I told him to stop and tried to call out for my parents, but he shoved my face down into my pillow."

Levi's voice broke as he dashed more tears away. "I couldn't breathe...I thought that was his plan...to kill me." He shook his head. "I wish he had."

Agony tore through me at his words and I dropped my lips to the top of his head and curled my arm around his neck so I could hold him close to my body. "It's okay, Levi, you don't need to tell me."

He let out a gut-wrenching sob, but then he barreled on. "When he pulled my pajamas down, I actually thought he was going to spank me," Levi said with an ugly laugh. "He told me to shut up and called me a coward and then said we'd see if I went running to my parents after he was done with me. I didn't understand what was happening...I thought maybe he'd stabbed me or something because it hurt so fucking bad. I was sure I was going to die because I couldn't breathe. When he finally let go of my head, I turned my head enough so I could breathe, but I didn't do anything else. I didn't scream, I didn't beg him to stop. I just cried and lay there until he finished. Then he leaned over me and told me if I told our parents, he'd string them up just like he had Mrs. Hurley's cat and then he climbed off me, went back to his bed and put his headphones on and started reading a comic book."

I could feel my own tears streaming down my face as I held Levi, but I refused to release him long enough to wipe them away. "I'm sorry," I whispered to him as I kissed his hair. I kept repeating the words over and over, even though they seemed utterly inadequate.

He'd been nine fucking years old.

"The next morning, I told my mother I was sick, but my dad said I had to go to school. My school was only a couple of blocks away so I usually walked instead of taking the bus. I left the apartment, but instead of going to school, I went to the back of our building and crawled behind one of the dumpsters and stayed there for the whole day and that night too. The building's maintenance man found me and took me home. My dad beat me for skipping school and my mom yelled at me for causing them trouble since they already had their hands full with Ricky."

"Did you ever tell them what happened?" I managed to ask.

He shook his head. "I was too afraid he'd follow through on his threat and hurt them. But when it kept happening, I started acting out. I...I was so mad at my parents for not knowing there was something wrong..." Levi murmured. "One morning when I was ten or eleven, I lashed out at my mother because she wouldn't let up on how I was letting my grades slip. I told her to shut up and called her a bitch."

Levi pulled back from me a little and wiped at his face. "I...I didn't mean it. I was just so scared and angry. I couldn't sleep anymore because I was always waiting for Ricky to come after me. I kept falling asleep in school and it had already been hard for me to keep up to begin with. My mother looked at me the same way she'd always looked at Ricky. She left a few days later."

"Left?" I asked.

"Walked out. She came back a month later to get her stuff and to tell my father she wanted a divorce...she'd met someone else. I...I was so sure she would take me with her so I ran to my room to pack, but by the time I got back to the living room, she was gone. She...she didn't even say goodbye."

"I'm sorry, baby," I said as I leaned down to wrap myself around him.

"I didn't mean what I said," he whispered.

"I know you didn't. It wasn't your fault."

We sat like that for a few minutes before Levi shifted and turned around so he could face me. "The tattoo..." he began, but then his voice faltered.

"Take your time," I said softly.

He nodded and then crossed his legs so he could sit more comfortably. I was glad he was willing to face me as he spoke.

"My father wasn't as bad as he is now, but he always talked shit about people. Black people, Hispanic, Asian...didn't matter. He blamed them for things, too. Like when he lost his job and we had to move into our apartment...he said his boss, who happened to be Hispanic, had it in for him. At another job, he lost out on a promotion because of an Indian guy. And my mother...we found out she left my father for a black man."

My insides went cold at his words.

Levi dropped his eyes. "I...I believed him when I was younger. I thought there was truth behind his words and when my mom left...I blamed the guy. I needed someone to blame," he admitted quietly. "But as I got older, I wasn't so sure. One of my teachers in school who always encouraged me and told me I wasn't dumb like the kids said I was...she was black. I didn't have a lot of friends in school, but there was this girl in my Math class who would help me out whenever I got stuck on a problem during study time. She was Hispanic. But when I tried to say something to my father, he'd get so mad..."

Levi fell silent for a moment and then fingered the bandage on his wrist. "Ricky believed everything my father said...I think he just liked having that permission, you know? To hate. It was…it was like it brought him and my father closer. I knew I couldn't change their minds, so I just stayed quiet. I didn't want the tattoo, but I knew what Ricky would do to me if I said no. I was fourteen at that time. He was still…at night…"

Levi's voice faltered, but I knew what he was trying to tell me. The sexual assaults had continued. I pulled him forward so I could press a kiss to his temple. "It's okay," I murmured.

I felt his fingers close over my arm. "He only did it when he was really mad. He had girlfriends by that age, so he didn't come after me unless he needed to punish me for something or if something set him off. He and my dad were getting along better, so he wasn't as angry all the time." Levi turned his head and stared down the length of the beach for a few minutes. My heart broke for him as a few silent tears slipped down his face.

"Something happened when I was sixteen…it was really bad," Levi said as he turned to look at me. My gut tightened as I realized what he was talking about.

"I don't want to tell you about it now, but it…" He shook his head and dropped his eyes. "It changed everything."

I wanted so badly to tell him I knew what he was talking about, but not only would telling him confirm I'd been lying to him from day one about who I was, I still didn't know for sure that he didn't have plans to go after Seth.

"I dropped out of school because it just didn't seem important anymore. I was failing a lot of my classes anyway. I tried to save up enough money to get away from Ricky and my dad, but it was hard. And then I got arrested and went to prison." Levi paused briefly before saying, "I thought I knew what to expect. I knew it wouldn't be easy, but I was so fucking clueless."

A good minute passed before he continued.

"I was raped in the showers the day after I arrived. The guy who did it decided to make me his play thing. It went on for a few weeks. I actually thought the guards would help me if I told them what was happening. I didn't realize we were no better than animals and as long as we didn't turn on them, they turned a blind eye to everything else."

I closed my hand around Levi's and watched as he played with our fingers, linking and unlinking them.

"Gun found out I went to the guards. He let a bunch of guys take turns with me and then he used the handle of a broom to..."

I didn't even bother to try and stop the tears that fell as I pulled Levi's fingers up to my mouth and pressed kisses against them.

"I thought for sure I was going to die," Levi whispered. "I was so fucking relieved," he added. "But then I woke up in the infirmary and I knew it wasn't over. I knew I deserved it for what I'd done, but I was a coward. I couldn't take it. I started making plans to hang myself when they returned me to my cell."

"Levi," I said brokenly as I cradled his hand against my chest.

"But they didn't take me back to my cell. They put me in with this guy named Hank. I was so fucking scared because the guards wouldn't let me cover up my tattoo with a Band-Aid like I always had before I'd gone to prison. Even though Gun and his guys did what they did, they also protected me because there were all these different gangs in prison. I guess they saw me as their pet and didn't want to lose me to a rival gang. The tattoo was like this neon sign that I couldn't escape. Anyway, the guy they put me in a cell with, Hank, was black."

I stilled at that and braced myself for the worst.

"I knew when they put me in there, that I wouldn't have to worry about figuring out how to hang myself. But Hank..."

Levi shook his head and then, to my surprise, he smiled. "Hank was the best thing that ever happened to me."

"How so?" I asked.

"He was the one who found me in the shower after Gun and his guys left me lying there on the floor. Hank got me help and then he convinced the warden to put me in with him."

"How?" I asked. "Inmates don't have that kind of power."

Levi shook his head. "Hank was...I don't even know how to explain it. He had a lot of respect, I guess. From the guards and the gangs alike. He wasn't an ordained priest, but he'd been studying the

Bible for a long time, so he became like a spiritual leader, I suppose. The guy who was the leader of one of the larger gangs, Jasper, respected Hank and he made sure he was always protected. The guards and warden liked that Hank could keep the peace for the most part... most of the gangs saw him as a man of the cloth, even though he wasn't officially one. I guess that's why the warden agreed to his request. Hank took pity on me and, despite the tattoo, he convinced Jasper to extend his protection to me, too. No one laid a hand on me after that. Not Jasper, not his men, not Gun."

He paused before saying, "I didn't deserve any of it, but I took it just the same. As bad as things were, I didn't really want to die and I knew that was what would happen if Gun or any of the other gangs got to me."

Levi lifted his eyes. "Hank was proof that my father was wrong. The color of a person's skin isn't the measure of who they are. I wanted the tattoo gone with a passion after that. I never wanted someone to compare me to Ricky and my father ever again. I share blood with them, but nothing else. When I got out of prison, I went to talk to a tattoo artist about removing it, but it was so expensive that I knew it would be a while before I could afford it. I searched for alternative ways to remove it on the Internet, which is where I saw the thing about oven cleaner, but I wasn't that desperate at the time since I could just keep it covered."

"But burning yourself, Levi-" I said as I shook my head.

"I wish I'd done it sooner," he cut in. I snapped my eyes up to meet his, but before I could respond, he said, "The look in your eyes, Phoenix..."

He shook his head. "I'm going to lose you," he murmured. "I know that. But I couldn't let it be because of that damn tattoo."

"You're not going to lose-" I began, but he kissed me before I could finish the statement. His hand crept around to the back of my head and he held me in place. The kiss was tame, but incredibly moving.

"Please don't make me a promise you can't keep," he whispered.

I didn't say anything because he was right. All this, his admissions, me telling him about my family and my daughter, it really didn't change things. At least not the most fundamental thing.

Not yet, anyway.

I wanted desperately to ask him about T, but I knew I couldn't. I owed it to Seth and Ronan and their children to ferret out the truth and I wasn't one hundred percent certain I'd get the truth if I just asked Levi for it.

"Are you still in touch with Hank?"

"He calls every once in a while and we write letters, but I haven't been to see him. He made me promise not to. He wants me to focus on the future." Levi was quiet for a moment before saying, "He's how I met Father O. Father O visits the prison once a month and he was the one who got Hank started on his religious studies."

"What is Hank in for?"

"He killed his father. Hank told me he found out his father sexually abused his sister for years. She committed suicide and left a note for Hank telling him what their father had done. Hank had a ten-year-old daughter…after he found his sister and the note, he asked his daughter if her grandfather had ever touched her…"

Levi's words dropping off answered the question before I could ask it. "He confronted his father and they fought. Hank shot him. He said his lawyer told him he wouldn't be able to get his sister's admission admitted as evidence and Hank refused to let his daughter testify, so he took a plea deal. He's on his fifth year of a thirty-year sentence. His wife took their daughter and moved to South America to be closer to family. He hasn't seen his daughter since the day he took the plea deal."

Levi shook his head. "I owe him so much," he murmured. "He wouldn't let me give up on myself. When Dina had Henry, she let me name him because she didn't care what he was called so I named him after Hank, whose real name is Henry." Levi lifted his gaze to meet mine. "I guess I wanted Henry to carry the name of a really good man with him for the rest of his life."

"I bet Hank really loved hearing that."

"He did, but I had to tell him over the phone. He'll probably never get the chance to meet Henry. Even if I went against his wishes and took Henry to the prison to meet him, Hank's a level two offender, so he's only allowed to have contact visits with immediate family. I just... I can't imagine going back there and only being allowed to talk to him with a pane of plastic separating us and having to use a phone. He wouldn't get to hold Henry...it just seems cruel considering everything he's lost."

I could certainly understand that. No, I had no regrets about meeting Henry or interacting with the child, but I wasn't going to lie and say it was easy to separate out my emotions. Any child I encountered was a reminder of my own loss. But I also couldn't imagine having met a girl like Nicole and not having been allowed to interact with her. And Henry was just such an incredible little boy...now that I'd had a chance to spend time with him, I wanted to do it again, despite the pain that came along with being around him.

As Levi fell silent, I let my fingers thread through his hair and I gently tilted his head up. "Thank you for sharing that with me," I said just before I kissed him. He kissed me back without hesitation and when my tongue sought entry into his mouth, he eagerly opened for me. I loved kissing him. It wasn't something I'd ever cared about much either way with other guys, but with Levi, I could easily do it for hours and not need more.

That wasn't to say I didn't want more.

But after everything he'd told me, I knew sex was something he wasn't ready for. It might not be something he'd ever be ready for.

Was I okay with that?

Yeah, I was. Because I was still trying to figure everything out and I didn't need to complicate it by adding sex to the mix.

But as Levi eagerly kissed me back, I knew it couldn't get much more complicated.

Because despite all the answers Levi had given me, I hadn't gotten the one I still needed. The one that would allow me to go to Ronan and tell him that his husband wasn't in the crosshairs.

Until I had that answer, everything was up in the air.

Well, almost everything.

Because I'd already come to one decision.

Levi would not die by my hand. As much as it killed me to do it, I'd already made the choice between Levi and the family who'd accepted me as one of their own.

And for the first time in my life, my family would not come first.

## CHAPTER 15

### LEVI

"Thank you, young man."

"You're welcome, Mrs. Spalding," I said as I closed the car's trunk. I was prepared for the tip she tried to give me since it was something she did every week when I carried her groceries out to her car for her. Closing my hand over hers, I said, "Remember how I told you that you don't have to pay me to help you with your groceries?"

The sweet old woman looked at me in confusion and then smiled and nodded. "Yes, that's right dear," she said, though from the tone of her voice, I knew she was completely confused. But just like every week, her husband came to the rescue.

"Come on, Mildred, we'll save that for the kids," he said as he came around the car and took his wife's elbow.

"The kids?" she asked.

"Remember the jar they have set up at the ice cream shop for the kids at the Children's Hospital?" he asked.

Mrs. Spalding nodded. "Oh yes, that's right."

Her husband sent me a knowing smile as he guided his wife around to the passenger seat. The couple was at least in their late eighties. But while Mrs. Spalding struggled with her memory more and more, Mr.

Spalding was as spry as ever. I loved watching them together because Mr. Spalding was always so attentive to his wife's needs while she shopped. Once he had his wife settled, Mr. Spalding walked back around the old Town Car and shook my hand. "See you next week, son," he said and then he patted my shoulder.

I nodded and watched them drive off, then grabbed the grocery cart Mrs. Spalding always insisted on taking out to the parking lot, even though she never had more than two bags in the cart. I returned the cart to the side of the building where they were stored so people could easily grab one on their way in, but when I turned around, I ran straight into T.

"Around back, now," T said as he motioned to the side of the store.

"I'm working-" I began as I tried to move past him, but stopped short when he pulled out a gun and pressed it against my belly.

"Move, Princess," he said.

Fear lurched through me as I did what he said and walked with him past the employee entrance to behind the store. The back of the store was quiet since all the deliveries were done for the day. T shoved me up against the wall and held the gun on me. "Been waiting a while to get you alone, Princess," he said snidely. "Seems you found yourself a new boyfriend. Gun did say you preferred dark meat."

Maybe if he hadn't said that last part, I could have played my role and just kept my mouth shut. But between my father and the fucking tattoo, I'd had enough. "Fuck you," I said. "He's more man than you or Gun will ever be."

My retort earned me a punch to the face and the barrel of the gun pressed against my temple.

"Listen here, you little faggot," T snapped. "We're going to get down to business and then I'm going to show you what a real man feels like."

"Do what you want to me!" I said, not caring anymore. "I'm not helping you."

The next blow left me rattled and I felt warm blood dripping down my cheek.

"The stakes have changed, Princess," T warned. "I heard something very interesting about that sweet little old lady in there," he said. I knew he was talking about Betty. "Turns out she's one rich bitch," he added. "Got me to wondering why I'm not thinking a little bigger."

Anxiety tore through me. "What do you mean?"

"You and me are going to pay her a little visit at home one night. I've seen her place…it's locked up tighter than a virgin on her wedding night. But I'm thinking she'll gladly open up for her trusted little Employee of the Month."

I began shaking my head, but T grabbed my chin and slammed me back against the wall.

"Before you try growing a set of balls and saying no, think about good ole Hank."

I froze at that.

T got right up in my face. "Don't worry, the old man's still breathing, but he's gonna be walking funny for the rest of his life. 'Course, you even think of saying no to me again, his life is going to be a whole lot shorter."

It wasn't possible. Hank had Jasper watching out for him.

But I could see from the satisfaction in T's eyes that he was telling the truth. Terror crawled through my belly. What had they done to Hank?

"You still thinking of saying no to me, Princess?"

I didn't respond. I couldn't.

"That's what I thought," T said with a smirk and then he was tucking the gun in the waistband of his pants. I didn't move as he stepped back just a little and held there for a moment, his beady eyes on me. Then his fingers went to his pants and I closed my eyes as he drew his zipper down.

*No.*

I wanted to scream the word out loud, but I couldn't. I'd been prepared to fight T on anything he wanted to do to me, including this, but that had been before he'd brought Hank into the equation.

I felt tears sting my eyes as I thought of Phoenix. It had been three days since we'd sat on the beach and talked. Afterwards, he'd kissed me for a really long time…just kissing. It had been amazing and once my mind had accepted that all he was going to do was kiss me, my body had started to react.

In more ways than one.

For the first time in years, I'd felt my dick stirring. And while I hadn't been ready to take things beyond kissing, I'd considered the possibility that maybe someday I'd be ready for more. That Phoenix would be the one who could show me that sex wasn't always about power and humiliation.

But this, with T, it would destroy all that. It would be like I was cheating on Phoenix, even though he wasn't my boyfriend.

Because in my head he was so much more than that.

And as horrifying as what was about to happen was, I did have a choice. I could run or scream or say no. I doubted he'd really kill me… at most, he'd beat me to shut me up and then take what he wanted. But if I did that, Hank's life was over. I knew that without a shadow of a doubt.

So yeah, I was choosing.

As much as I was already in love with Phoenix, I couldn't risk Hank's life.

I forced my eyes open and sucked some air in through my nose in the hopes it would clear my head and somehow give me strength to get through this. T already had his hard cock out. I started to lower myself to my knees, but stopped when T said, "No, Princess, we're going to try something a little different today."

A scream of denial pierced my brain, but I managed to quell it.

"Turn around and face the wall. Take your pants down."

I shook my head even as I did what he said. The second I turned away from him, I let the tears fall as cold numbness began to blessedly settle over my body. My fingers shook as I opened my pants. It seemed to take me forever to work the zipper down and push the pants past my hips. I couldn't bring myself to slide my underwear down. Although God and I weren't on good terms anymore, I still prayed that He'd do something, anything. But I knew my plea had gone unanswered when I felt my underwear being yanked down my body. I was wearing a smock for the store that had ties in the back. The extra fabric would have afforded me some privacy from the front, but T snapped the tie where I had it loosely knotted and then tore the smock off over my head and threw it to the ground.

I heard T spit and I knew what it meant.

A little bit of spit on his cock was the only lube I'd get. And since I hadn't heard any foil tearing, I suspected I wouldn't have the benefit of latex separating my body from his. My last line of defense crumbled and I let out a harsh sob as T pressed up against my back and said, "Let's see if this pussy is as tight as Gun said it is."

"Levi, are you out here?"

I cried out in relief at the sound of the store manager's voice. T let out a foul curse and shoved away from me. I heard his footsteps hurrying away from me as Adam, the manager, called out my name again. My limbs felt heavy as I struggled to get my pants up. I snagged my smock off the ground and bundled it up in my hand so the broken tie wouldn't be noticeable. I was shaking so bad, I was sure I wouldn't be able to stay upright.

*God had heard me.*

He'd actually heard me and he'd *helped* me.

I didn't even know what to do with that. Maybe thinking it was divine intervention was a stretch, but I didn't know how else to explain it. If T had taken that last little piece of me…

"Levi?"

"Here," I called as I wiped at the tears on my face, but when I saw the blood on my hand, I scrambled to come up with something that would explain the marks T had left on my skin. I hurried over to the dumpster and smeared the blood still on my fingers on the corner of the lid.

"Hey, you okay?" Adam said as he rounded the corner. "Betty was starting to worry about you."

"Yeah," I said as I tried to calm myself. I turned around and wasn't surprised when he gasped at the sight of me. "Had a little accident," I said as I pointed at the dumpster. "I noticed the lid was open and went to close it and it kind of got away from me."

"Wow, come on inside so we can get some ice on it," Adam said kindly.

"It's really nothing," I said as I fell in step next to him. My adrenaline rush was starting to wane and the crash was making me dizzy.

"Tell that to Betty," Adam responded with a chuckle.

I didn't bother trying to tell that to Betty as she fussed over me for a good half an hour and then insisted on me taking the night off. She even had Adam drive me home.

But home was the last place I wanted to be so as soon as Adam told me to take it easy and left, I went up to my apartment and grabbed my father's car keys, since I knew he'd be too far gone with his alcohol to even notice they were missing.

More than anything, I wanted to drive straight to Phoenix's house so I could find the safety I was craving in his arms. But I knew he couldn't help me. And now more than ever, I knew I needed to end it with him. There was something else I needed to do first.

## CHAPTER 16

PHOENIX

The second I opened the door, Levi was pushing into my arms and dragging me down for a kiss. Given that I'd brought my gun with me to answer the door since it was well after midnight, I could only wrap one arm around him as his mouth closed over mine. His body was wet from the heavy rain that was falling outside, but I didn't give a shit. I managed to put my gun on a small table near the door before wrapping my other arm around him. I kicked the door shut and backed him up against it. He'd started the kiss, but I took it over.

When we were forced to come up for air, I finally saw the bruises on his face.

"What happened?"

But Levi shook his head and put his hand at the back of my neck. "Please, I don't want to talk," he said desperately. "I just really need you, okay?"

I hesitated briefly as I took in the desperation in his expression and then nodded and kissed him again.

Him showing up at my door in the middle of the night was the last thing I expected, but it was very welcome, especially considering the shitty evening I'd had. After dropping Levi off at work, I'd gone to my daughter's rehab center to visit with her and to learn about the latest brain scan doctors had done to see if there'd been any improvement in her condition.

There hadn't been.

They'd reminded me that she also hadn't deteriorated, so that was something, but every time they did one of these scans, I always still kept up hope for some small sign that she'd find her way back to me someday. It was getting harder and harder to keep that hope going.

"Tell me what you need," I said as I let my hands skim up and down Levi's back. I really wanted to know who the hell had put the bruises on his face, but I could force myself to wait.

Especially if it meant I could give Levi something he so clearly needed.

"Would you...would you touch me?" he asked.

I nodded. "How about we go to my room?" I asked as I gently brushed my mouth over his.

"Yeah," Levi whispered.

I kissed him deeply and let my hands slide down to his ass. He whimpered deep in his throat, but he didn't pull away from me. I moved my hands down and gripped the backs of his thighs and then lifted him. He squeaked in surprise, but then his mouth was back on mine, hungrier than ever and his legs went around me. I had no clue what had driven this change in him, but as badly as I wanted to know what he'd feel like wrapped around my dick, I knew he wasn't ready for that. So once I reached my room and laid him down on the bed, I kept up the kissing while making sure to keep my weight off his body.

As I let my hand skim up underneath his shirt, I thought about removing it, but I remembered how hesitant he'd been after the night he'd burned his wrist. He'd been okay with me taking his pants off, but he'd wanted the shirt to stay on. I suspected it might have something to do with the large scar running up his side.

"Can I take this off?" I asked as I brushed soft kisses against his lips. His desperation had eased and while I couldn't exactly say he was relaxed, he didn't seem on the brink of bolting either.

Levi managed a nod. His right hand was resting on my forearm, but I forced myself not to focus on his bandage, which was also wet.

I levered up on the bed long enough to work the shirt off over his head. I'd already known he was lean, but he looked a bit on the thin side…presumably because he was running himself ragged every day between work and caring for Henry. I sealed my mouth over his and licked over his tongue when he opened for me. I kept him focused on my mouth as I trailed my hand back and forth over his chest. I didn't do much more than that, but I could tell he was enjoying the contact because he kept pushing up into my hand whenever I eased off on the pressure. His skin was chilled and damp.

"Baby," I murmured against his mouth. He kept trying to kiss me which had me chuckling. I gave him a few more pecks before I backed off and said, "Will you come take a shower with me?"

It took him an inordinate amount of time to nod. If I hadn't felt how cold he was, I would have backed off the request.

I took his hand and pulled him to his feet and then held onto him as I led him to my bathroom. I got the shower going and then turned to face him. He was absently rubbing one of his arms and his shoulders were slumped as if he was trying to make himself smaller.

I slid my hand around his waist and dropped my forehead to his. "Levi, I just want you to get warm…if you want to take the shower by yourself-"

"No," he interjected. "I…I want to take it with you. It's just…"

"What?" I asked when he didn't continue.

"It's been a while since I've been able to get…"

Color flooded his cheeks and it hit me what he was saying. "An erection?" I asked.

He nodded. "I mean, I wake up with one sometimes, but when I touch myself…" He let out a rough laugh. "God, I can't even get this part right!"

"What part?" I asked as I stroked his biceps in the hopes I could get a jumpstart on warming him up.

"Seducing you," he said in exasperation. "Turning you on."

I smiled at that. "You came here to seduce me?" I asked.

He nodded miserably.

"Baby," I said as I used my hands to tilt his head up. "You don't even have to be in the same room as me to turn me on." I kissed him until he was moaning. "And you can practice your seduction skills on me any damn time you want."

Levi pushed into my arms without another word. I let him take control of the kiss even as steam from the shower began to envelop us in damp heat. I forced myself to step back from him and then pushed my sleep pants off my hips. I wasn't wearing a shirt, so once the pants were off, I didn't give Levi time to obsess over my size. With my build, I was proportionally sized, but to someone like Levi with his history, I knew I was likely intimidating, especially considering how hard he'd made me.

I let the water rain down over me as I watched Levi struggle with what to do next. I could tell he was nervous about revealing the rest of his body, but that didn't surprise me after what he'd told me. I kept my eyes on his in the hopes he'd understand my silent message that he didn't need to do this. A full minute passed before he finally went for the button on his jeans. As he undressed, I held his gaze and once he was naked, I extended my hand to him. I felt rather than saw that, true to his word, he wasn't hard, but I didn't care since he felt so good pressed up against my body.

"So perfect," I murmured against his mouth. His arms went around my neck and I carefully pulled him against me until we were flush from thigh to chest. He tensed briefly when my cock came into contact with his, but he didn't pull away.

"If I do anything you don't want, tell me. You're in control here, Levi," I said as I pressed kisses to his jawline and neck. The sight of the fresh bruises threatened to stir my anger, but I managed to quell the urge to go hunt down both his father and T and beat the ever-loving hell out of them just because I could.

"I'm scared," he said. I could tell the admission had been a hard one, because he had trouble looking at me even when I urged his chin up. I waited until he finally raised his eyes.

"I know you are," I whispered. "But nothing happens that you don't want. I'd cut off my own arm before I ever raised it against you."

He nodded and then he stretched up so he could get his arms all the way around my neck. He pressed his head against my chest. I held him for a long time before I began letting my hands roam over his back, steering clear of his ass. I waited until he initiated another kiss before I began exploring his front. I stroked up and down his sides, making sure not to linger on his scarred skin. I caressed his thighs, but didn't touch his cock. All the while, I plied him with deep kisses that kept him on the edge. It didn't take long until his desperation returned, and with it, I finally felt his cock stir against mine. But I still refused to focus any attention on it. I risked gripping his ass now and again, but I never held him for more than a few seconds before my hands moved on.

Within minutes, his erection had grown and he began grinding his pelvis against mine. I wondered if he even realized he was doing it. It was hard to tell because he'd become so desperate that he was clinging to me like he'd never let go.

"Phoenix," he finally called out. His eyes had gone dark, the light green giving way to his dilating pupils.

"I've got you," I reassured him. I let my hand skate down his belly to his groin, but I didn't touch his hardness. It wasn't until he pressed his cock against my hand that I finally gave him what he wanted and let my palm briefly cup his shaft.

"Oh, God," he cried. His fingers bit into my shoulders even as he pulled back so he could watch my hand.

I took my time tracing the larger veins and the ridge beneath the perfectly shaped mushroom head. Levi wasn't big, which wasn't a surprise given his size, but he had a gorgeous cock and I wanted so badly to sink to my knees to taste him. But I wasn't sure if he was ready.

I closed my hand around his dick and began stroking and was rewarded with throaty moans of pleasure. There was only the slightest hesitation before Levi began fucking my hand.

"That's it," I whispered as I dropped my mouth to his ear. "Fuck my hand, baby. Pretend it's my ass…hungry for you to fill it up."

The dirty talk had Levi whimpering and pumping his dick into my hand. I wondered if he'd ever actually fucked another guy. My guess was no, since he seemed completely overwhelmed by everything that was happening to him.

I let my mouth trail along his cheek until I reached his lips. I kissed him hard and said, "I want to taste you. Can I?"

His breath was seesawing in and out of him. His eyes met mine and I saw the mix of passion and confusion in them.

Yeah, he definitely had no clue what was happening to his body. If he'd orgasmed before, it was nothing compared to what he was about to experience.

And I really wanted to have his dick shoved down my throat when he did.

"You want…you want…"

"I want to suck your beautiful cock," I supplied since I could tell he was too embarrassed to voice the thought.

I eased my stroking of his dick so he could come down enough to think. But the second I loosened my hand, he yelled, "No!"

I thought he was talking about me blowing him, but then he shook his head and said, "Yes! I mean, don't stop. Please...taste me like you said. I…I got tested after T…after he…"

I nodded in understanding. "Everything was negative?" I asked gently.

"Yeah. Sorry, I didn't mean to ruin…this," he said awkwardly.

"Talking about being safe is always a good thing, Levi." I rewarded him with a kiss before dropping to my knees. I ignored the water cascading down my head and reached out to run my tongue up Levi's cock and he let out a harsh shout. I could tell he was close because I could taste the pre-cum leaking down the side of his shaft. Its sweet flavor mixed with the water, and that spurred me on to suck his entire cock into my mouth. Levi screamed and grabbed my head. I swallowed around him and then sucked hard. My intention had been to drag this out, but his pulsing shaft had me guessing he wouldn't last long. I reached down to stroke my own cock as I worked Levi's in my mouth.

"Phoenix, oh God, I think…I think I'm gonna-"

That was all he got out before a burst of semen hit the back of my throat. Levi's cries of delight had my own orgasm rushing to the surface and I groaned around his dick as my climax tore through me. I swallowed over and over as Levi continued to shoot. His cock pulsed in my mouth as the last bit of his seed slipped over the back of my tongue. I gently sucked on him to bring him down. He was leaning heavily on me, his hands resting on my shoulders. When I released his spent dick, he sank to the floor. I expected him to kiss me, but I was caught off guard by the tears in his eyes. I knew they were tears because small sobs were bubbling up from his throat. He put his arms around my neck and buried his face against my shoulder.

Since I knew I hadn't hurt him, I just held him. My guess that he was just completely overwhelmed proved to be right when he finally lifted his head long enough to whisper a quiet, "Thank you" in my ear.

And I knew without a shadow of a doubt that he wasn't just thanking me for the pleasure I'd brought him.

# CHAPTER 17

## LEVI

"What the fuck are you doing?"

I flinched at the anger in Jed's voice as he watched Ricky yank the woman to her feet.

"The missus and me are going to go check things out upstairs. Maybe someone" – Ricky viciously kicked the man kneeling before him – "will start remembering better if he ain't got his pretty little wife around to distract him!"

"No!" the man screamed as he lunged to his feet. Jed kicked the back of his knee and the man went down hard. The boy was sobbing as he tried to get closer to his father.

"Fred!" the woman shouted as my brother dragged her from the room.

My stomach rolled violently since I knew what was coming. My eyes darted around the room in desperation. There had to be something I could do.

"Hey!" Jed snapped as he hit me upside the head. "Get the tape!"

I stood there and stared at him because I had no idea what he was talking about.

"In the bag, you idiot!"

My eyes shifted to the small green duffle bag a few feet away. I'd assumed Jed had brought it to carry the money, since it looked practically empty.

Why the hell did he need tape? He'd already tied all three people's hands with plastic zip ties.

Another smack had me moving forward. The gun in my hand felt like it weighed a ton, even though it had no bullets in it. As I neared the bag, my eyes fell on the cordless telephone sitting on a side table. I desperately wanted to grab it, but I knew Jed would probably shoot me if I did.

I searched the bag for the tape, but between my shaking hands and tear-filled eyes, it took me a while to locate it. I could hear Jed yelling at the guy behind me, along with the teenager's muffled cries, but I purposefully tuned out as much as I could.

But I couldn't tune out the female scream that rattled through the house. I let out a guttural sob and felt the vomit crawling up my throat.

"Hurry the fuck up!"

I returned to Jed and handed him the tape.

"No, cover his mouth," he said as he waved his gun at the kid.

"What?" I asked.

"Cover. His. Mouth."

I shook my head. "No," I said automatically.

Jed didn't hesitate in the least as he stepped past the guy and pressed his gun to my head. "Cover his fucking mouth."

I stifled a choked cry and forced myself to walk around the boy's body so I was facing him. He was on his knees, his hands bound behind his back. His wet eyes were on his father.

He flinched when another muffled scream came from upstairs.

"Corinne!" the man shouted just before Jed hit him with his gun.

"Shut up or I'll start putting bullets in your kid!"

The man instantly fell silent, except for the sound of his crying.

I so badly didn't want to look at the young man as I tore off a piece of tape and leaned down to put it over his mouth. But his terror-filled eyes lifted to mine and I saw the silent plea.

I can't help you. I can't even fucking help myself.

*I didn't say the words to him, of course. I did as I was told and put the tape on his mouth.*

"Good, now that that's out of the way," Jed said as he turned his attention to the man. "Where's the safe?"

"Safe?" the man asked as he shook his head. "I don't know what you're talking about—"

"Wrong answer!" Jed snarled and he hit the guy again.

*The man seemed physically stunned from the force of the blow. But when Jed asked him the question again, he said, "We don't have a safe."*

*Jed went from pissed to lethal just like that. I watched in horror as he pulled a knife from a holster on his belt. He yanked the roll of tape from my hand and slapped a piece over the guy's mouth.*

*I was frozen with fear as I realized what was about to happen. But instead of stabbing the guy, Jed moved towards the boy. He rolled up his sleeves, exposing a long snake tattoo on his arm.*

"No!" *I said as I pushed between him and the kid when I realized what he was doing.*

"Step the fuck off or you'll be first."

*He didn't yell the words at me. I probably would have been less afraid if he had. But I didn't move. I couldn't.*

*But I also wasn't any kind of match for Jed and he easily shoved me out of the way.*

*I scrambled to my feet and grabbed Jed's arm, but he hit me hard, knocking me on my ass. I was too physically stunned to move, but what I saw Jed do had me rolling onto my side and covering my ears with my hands as I closed my eyes. The kid moaned as Jed began cutting him right through his T-shirt. Even though I wasn't watching, I knew exactly every time Jed slid the knife across his skin because the kid cried and the father screamed through the tape. I heard Jed curse and opened my eyes long enough to see Jed kick the father in the head, knocking him to the ground before he could reach his son. The boy's stomach was covered in blood and he was sobbing uncontrollably. With the next slice, he screamed, but the tape muffled the sound.*

*The father's agonized cries had me backing away from the horrible* scene. I barely registered the sound of the woman's screams from upstairs. They too, sounded muffled. I remembered how Ricky had always shoved my face into the bed or my pillow to keep me quiet. On the occasions when he hadn't fucked me in my bed, he'd used his hand to cover my mouth if my father happened to be home.

Jed ripped the tape from the father's mouth.

"Seth! Oh God, stop. Please, I swear, I'm telling you the truth!" the man cried. I was having trouble seeing anything because of the tears in my eyes. I wanted to run, but I knew if I did, the man and his son would have no chance whatsoever.

"Where's the fucking safe?" Jed yelled as he yanked the guy's head back by the hair.

"I swear to God, we don't have a safe!" the man cried. Broken sobs bubbled up from his throat. "Please, please don't hurt my son. Take me...take me with you. I'll take you to an ATM. You can have my car, anything. Just please let my wife and son go!"

"If I want your fucking car, I'll take it!" Jed shouted. "Last chance...where's the safe?"

The man cried, but didn't answer and I knew it was because he was afraid to.

"He's telling the truth!" I yelled as I stumbled to my feet. "Look at him!" I said. "He wouldn't trade his kid for money!"

Jed seemed to get lost in thought for a moment. "You're right," he murmured.

Thank God!

"Let's just go!" I implored.

I was certain my words had gotten through to him, so I wasn't prepared for what happened next.

Of course, nothing could have prepared me for it.

I was dimly aware of the kid screaming, but I didn't make a sound. I knew what I was seeing couldn't be real.

Because shit like that only happened in the cheesiest of horror movies.

The movies I hated.

But the blood that gushed from the gaping wound across the man's throat was very real. I began retching, but there was nothing in my stomach, so I was really just dry heaving. My stomach cramped as my body tried to expel something that wasn't there.

I was dimly aware of my brother reappearing in the room, his gloved hands covered in blood. There were blood splatters on his face, but he either didn't notice or didn't care.

"Where is it?" Ricky asked as his eyes dispassionately roamed over the scene before him.

"Not here," Jed snapped as he dropped the man's body to the floor.

"What do you mean, not here?" Ricky asked.

"It means there's no safe here."

"You said your source was good!"

"Well, obviously, he got it wrong!"

"Fuck!" Ricky snapped. I watched as he walked towards the back of the house. Jed eyed the boy whose head was hung. He was crying softly.

I'd cried like that once.

The night Ricky had taken my innocence.

I didn't give my actions any thought because I didn't care anymore what Jed or Ricky did to me. I kept my gaze on Jed as I reached behind me and searched out the cordless phone. It seemed to take forever to remove it from its cradle, though I knew it was likely only seconds. I froze when Ricky reappeared with a bottle of bleach in his hand.

"What the hell are you doing?" Jed asked.

"This little bitch puked all over the fucking floor up there!" Ricky snapped as he jerked his head towards me and pointed towards the ceiling. "I saw a show where cops can track DNA or some shit like that!"

I dropped my eyes when Ricky passed me. The second he was out of the room, I maneuvered the phone carefully behind my back. I squeezed my eyes shut as I hit the button. I waited for Jed to ask me what the hell I was doing, but he seemed preoccupied with destroying what was left of the room. The first thing he and Ricky had done when we'd gotten everyone tied up had been to rip the paintings off the wall. I hadn't realized until Jed had started asking the father about a safe that that's what they'd been looking for. Now, he was tearing up the rest of the room, though I had no clue why. All I knew was that he was giving me the time I desperately needed.

The sound also helped drown out the sound of the dial tone. I couldn't see the phone so I had to feel around the keypad and hope like hell I got the numbers right because I was only going to get one chance at this. As soon as I dialed, I pressed the phone against my back to muffle the sound I knew the operator would make when they answered. I could only hope and pray that they wouldn't think the call was a hoax or wrong number and disconnect it.

A good minute passed before Jed finished trashing the place. I whispered silent pleas in my head as I listened for the sound of sirens. But there was nothing. I was so busy trying to listen for the 911 operator on the other end of the phone, that I didn't notice Jed returning to the boy.

The boy's quiet sob caught my attention and I finally snapped out of my daze long enough to see that Jed had pulled the boy to his feet. As soon as Jed pulled his arm back and the sheen of the knife reflected the light from the only lamp that hadn't been shattered into a million pieces, I shouted "No!"

But Jed ignored me as he thrust his knife into the boy's body.

I stepped forward, not remembering the phone in my hand. I also didn't see my brother as he returned to the room.

He saw me, though. He saw me and then he was on me, snatching the phone from my grasp and hanging it up without saying even a single word to me. I heard the sickening sound of Jed stabbing the helpless kid, but I couldn't do anything for him.

Because I was too busy staring into my brother's eyes as I watched him pull his own knife from his waistband.

"Levi, wake up, damn it!"

As I jerked upright at the sound of Phoenix's voice, I bumped my injured wrist. Between the searing pain and the remnants of my nightmare, I promptly lost it and began sobbing.

"Shhh, it's okay," Phoenix whispered in my ear as he pulled me against his bare chest.

Reality slowly returned as I remembered where I was and what had happened the night before.

After I'd taken my father's car, I'd driven to St. Anthony's in the hopes I'd be able to talk to Father O before he locked up for the night. I'd caught a break because he'd been in the process of locking the front door. While I hadn't been able to tell him how I knew something had happened to Hank, he'd agreed to contact the prison, since they wouldn't give information on an inmate to anyone but family. My hope was that as a member of the clergy, they might tell him something, anything about Hank's condition.

I'd been lost after that. My fear for Hank and the close call with T had sent me right to the edge. I'd wanted more than anything to go to Phoenix right then and beg him to help me, but I'd known that wasn't an option.

So I'd gone to the one place I'd never wanted to go near again, but that kept drawing me back like a lure. I'd sat in front of the Nichols house for hours, reliving that night and pretending things I had no business pretending.

Like that Fred and Corinne Nichols still lived in that house and their greatest joy was when their son came home from college for visits.

Or that they were spending a sleepless night in the home as they prepared for their child's wedding the next day.

"Talk to me, Levi," Phoenix urged as he stroked my back.

My naked back.

After we'd gotten out of the shower, Phoenix had taken his time drying me off with a towel as he'd kissed me softly over and over again. Then he'd carefully changed the soaking wet bandage on my wrist. I'd spent the entire time still reeling from what he done to me.

What he'd made me feel.

Never in a million years had I expected someone like him to bring me any kind of pleasure, let alone what he'd actually done. And when he'd talked about me being inside of him...

Even now, my body reacted to the thought.

"Just a bad dream," I murmured, knowing the answer wouldn't be enough for him. I forced myself to sit up and glanced at the clock. It was just after six in the morning.

"A bad dream didn't bring you to my door last night," Phoenix said as he brushed my temple with his fingers. "It didn't put those bruises on your face, either."

God, I didn't want to lie to him.

"Some boxes fell off a pallet at work…they sent me home early."

Phoenix pulled me against him so that his forehead was pressed to my temple. "I wish you would trust me," he whispered. "I can help you."

I choked back a sob and closed my eyes. God, he felt so good…so warm. What I wouldn't give to wake up in his arms every day.

"I promise I'll tell you everything soon," I finally said as I pulled away. "But I need to take care of some things first."

He pressed a kiss against my skin. "I'm holding you to that," he said.

I nodded.

I *would* tell him. But it would be from the other side of a sheet of plexiglass and through a phone. Because T had sealed the deal for me.

I couldn't fight anymore.

I'd get Henry situated and pray that the State found him a good situation, assuming they took him from Dina at all. Then I'd do what I should have done seven years ago. I'd walk through the nearest police station's doors and tell them about T and his threat against Betty. Then I'd tell them about Seth and his family.

I didn't care where they sent me this time, because I wouldn't survive it. It was the coward's way out, but I'd find a way to end my life once I was back behind bars.

"I should go," I said. "I need to get my father's car back before he realizes I took it," I said. "And Dina will be leaving for work in a couple of hours."

"I'll come with you," Phoenix said. "You can bring Henry back here and we can spend the day together."

I began to shake my head, but I was surprised when Phoenix

murmured, "Please, Levi." I turned to look at him and finally noticed his features etched with tension.

"What happened?" I asked as I turned to face him.

"Amani's doctors did another brain scan yesterday. They check it every few months to see if there's been any change."

"Is...is everything okay?" I asked, my heart in my throat.

"There's been no change," he said softly. "None whatsoever."

I understood what he was telling me. While some might take that as good news, he wasn't looking at it the same way. I knew he didn't want to lose his child, but I couldn't even fathom the torture he went through every time he saw her, knowing she was just beyond his reach...would likely always be.

"I'm sorry," I said as I put my arms around him and hugged him.

"I...I was hoping you might come meet her today and then we could take Henry to the park or something."

I nodded, though I knew it was a terrible idea. Every second I spent with him, the harder it would be to give him up. "Henry and I would love that," I said.

He nodded and then he kissed me.

I watched him get out of bed and head towards the bathroom. He hadn't gotten dressed again after our shower so his perfect body was on full display for me. My eyes fell to his ass and I once again wondered if he'd meant what he'd said about me fucking him. It just didn't seem possible.

"You coming?" Phoenix asked once he reached the doorway. From the smirk on his mouth, I knew he'd caught me ogling his ass.

I forced myself out of bed and tried not to stress over how scrawny and pale I looked compared to him. The man could literally have any guy he wanted...

Once I reached him, I went to move past him and into the bathroom, but his arm came out to prevent me from moving forward and then his other arm came up to cage me in against the door frame. If he'd been anyone but him, I would have been scared. But all I was was incredibly turned on. Especially when his dick brushed against mine.

"You see something you like?" he asked as a playful smile spread across his beautiful lips

I knew I was probably blushing to the roots of my hair, but I nodded anyway.

"Maybe you should take a closer look…get a feel for the goods," he said.

I smiled at that, mainly because he was having so much fun with the play on words. The night before had been so intense and heavy, but this…this was different. But no less intriguing.

I hadn't gotten a chance to touch him in the shower. It wasn't because I hadn't wanted to, I'd just been too overwhelmed by my own body's responses to everything he'd done to me.

I lifted my hand to stroke over one bicep, tracing the arcs of heavy black ink. His muscles were rock solid beneath my touch, but his skin was soft. He wasn't a particularly hairy guy, though he did have the happy trail thing going on that had me curling my toes as I fought the need to explore it.

I slid my hand up to his neck, pausing briefly at his pulse point which was thrumming rapidly.

Was I doing that to him?

It seemed odd that something as simple as a touch to his arm would get him going, but I realized my own heart was racing in my chest and I'd barely done anything yet. I lifted my other hand, ignoring the stinging in my wrist, and caressed his chest. His nipples hardened when I touched them and before I could think too much on it, I leaned forward and swiped my tongue over one of them. Phoenix gasped and I felt his fingers curl in my hair. But he didn't try to hold me in place. I did the same thing to the other nipple and was rewarded with another gasp.

The idea that I had any kind of power over him was mind-boggling. But when he murmured my name, I knew it might actually be true.

And for the first time in my life, I wondered if there was a chance this pleasure I was feeling would linger if I touched him in the ways other men had always forced me to touch them. Would he feel the way I'd felt last night when he'd had my dick down his throat? He'd acted like he'd wanted it...enjoyed it. And I hadn't missed the fact that he'd found his own release shortly after I'd taken mine.

I ran my hands up and down his sides and then slipped them around to his back.

"Kiss me," I whispered. "Please."

His mouth swooped down on mine, but he didn't take complete control. He consumed my mouth, yes, but I still felt like I was in the driver's seat. I let my hands settle on his ass, marveling at the firm flesh. I could feel moisture dripping onto my sensitive cock and I released Phoenix's mouth long enough to confirm it was mine *and* his.

"I meant what I said," Phoenix said as he reached behind himself and took one of my hands in his. But instead of pulling my fingers away, he urged them down into his crease. I let out a sharp breath when I felt his hole. He dropped his mouth to my ear and murmured, "I can't wait to feel you inside of me." Then he pulled my fingers from his ass and stuck them in his mouth to get them wet. I had no clue what he was doing until he urged my hand back to his crease.

"I...I've never-"

That was all I got out because I let out a groan as soon he used his thick fingers to force one of mine into his body. The grip, the heat...I could have come in that moment alone. As it was, I was grinding my dick against his, but I couldn't get the pressure I needed.

"Fuck! Yes..." Phoenix said harshly as he pushed back onto my finger until it disappeared completely inside of his body.

"Fuck me with it," he urged.

I felt like the top of my head was going to blow right off. I was both terrified and intrigued. Granted, I'd only ever had a dick up my ass, but I couldn't fathom that a finger would bring this much pleasure to someone. But based on the throaty moans falling from Phoenix's throat and the contorted look of passion in his eyes, I knew he was loving it.

I kept my moves slow, but the more he pressed back on my hand, the more secure I felt and I increased the pace. I also began twisting my finger just to test what he felt like. When I found something that felt different than the rest of him, I pressed against it and stilled when Phoenix let out a vicious curse.

"Right there! Again!" he demanded.

I did as he asked and measured his intense reaction. Phoenix's mouth sought out mine and he kissed me hard before breathing against my lips, "So good, baby. More, please."

Was he actually begging me?

I gave him what he wanted as heat swamped my body, much like it had the night before in the shower. God, I was so fucking turned on.

I was about to reach for my own dick when I felt Phoenix's hand wrap around it. But it wasn't just his hand against my sensitive flesh. The velvety skin of his cock was rubbing against mine. He was gripping us both in his huge hand.

I'd watched a little bit of gay porn as a teenager, but nothing I'd seen compared to this moment. Phoenix's body was pressing me back against the doorjamb and he had one hand above my head, supporting his weight. His other hand was jerking us both off as I plunged my finger inside of him over and over again, pressing against that spot he seemed to like so much now and again.

"Oh God," I said as I felt what I'd felt the night before. The pressure in my balls, the tingling in my spine.

Phoenix kissed me. "Come for me, Levi. I want to watch you go over again."

It started as soon as he said my name. I shoved my finger inside of him as far as it would go and held there as I gripped his ass with my other hand. The climax tore violently through me and I shouted against his mouth. Tears stung the backs of my eyes from how good it felt. And not just the climax, but all of it. His body, his smell, his heat...I could have stayed there forever.

"Fuck," Phoenix growled and then I felt his entire body shudder as his ass clamped down on my finger. God, what would it feel like on my dick?

"Damn," Phoenix murmured once he'd relaxed against me and I'd gently pulled my finger out of him. "Guess we'll need another shower," he observed as he looked down at our spent dicks, covered in cum.

"I'm good with that," I said and then we were both laughing.

Sex and pleasure?

Humor too?

What fucking alternate universe was I living in?

And what did I have to do to stay here forever?

~

"Peaches, I brought some people I'd like you to meet."

I wanted to smile at the nickname Phoenix had told me about. He'd given it to his daughter when she was a baby. He'd told me that for months, the little girl had refused to eat anything but peaches and even as she'd grown older, the sweet fruit had remained her favorite. But as endearing as I found the story, I was too tense to dwell on it or imagine Phoenix and his daughter together before the accident.

I hadn't been sure what to expect as we walked into the spacious room, but it wouldn't have mattered because nothing could have prepared me for any of it. Starting with how Phoenix spoke to his daughter.

Like she could hear every word he said.

And I wondered if maybe she could.

The girl looked tiny in the big bed. Phoenix had warned me that it was likely her eyes would be open, but that she wouldn't actually be seeing me. I hadn't been prepared for what it would be like for her to look directly at me, though. It broke my heart because she looked so… normal. I couldn't even imagine the pain it must be causing Phoenix.

I'd thought the little girl's room would be a basic utilitarian hospital room, but it wasn't. Yes, the walls were the standard off-white color, but someone, Phoenix presumably, had put wall stickers on them including a large one that formed a tree that looked much like the one I'd seen a glimpse of in Amani's room at Phoenix's house. Her bed had pretty yellow sheets with princesses and castles on them and she was wearing a pink nightgown. Framed pictures sat on one of the nightstands. I recognized Phoenix in a couple of the pictures…the rest I suspected were of Amani's mother and grandparents.

"Amani, this is my friend Levi and this is Henry," Phoenix said as he motioned to both of us. He held his daughter's hand as he spoke.

"Hi, Amani," I said as I went to Phoenix's side. I had Henry in my arms. He looked at the girl curiously, but luckily, he didn't get upset by the strange environment. Even though the girl's room looked as much like a child's as it probably could, it still had a lot of the standard hospital equipment in it and there were several machines hooked up to the little girl including what I assumed was the feeding tube Phoenix had told me about.

Amani's eyes moved around the room, occasionally settling on her father, but never staying there for long. The fingers he held in his occasionally twitched, but never closed around the big hand holding hers like it was made of glass.

I listened as Phoenix talked about nonsensical things like the weather and the ducks and ducklings we'd seen out in the pond in front of the rehab center. I tried not to dwell on the possibility that the girl was somehow trapped in her own body and could hear and feel everything but not respond, but it was tough. And I felt completely helpless to support Phoenix in any way. So, I did the only thing I could think of and put my free hand on his back and rubbed circles against it. When it came time for the visit to end, I watched Phoenix kiss his daughter goodbye and whisper something in her ear. I cuddled Henry against my chest because I was just so damn grateful to feel his warm, squirming body against mine.

When Phoenix stepped away from the bed, I covered Amani's hand with my own, but didn't say anything. I just gave her fingers a squeeze and then left the room to where Phoenix was waiting in the hallway. I could see it killed him to have to walk out of there without her. I rubbed his arm and his eyes met mine. Then he did something that surprised me. He reached for Henry.

Without hesitation, I handed the baby to him. I had no doubt it probably hurt to see another child so full of life, but I didn't see anything in Phoenix's gaze that said he begrudged the baby in any way.

He settled Henry in one arm and smiled when the little boy gave him a huge grin. Then Phoenix put his hand at my back to urge me down the hallway.

On the way towards the exit, he did something I'd been dreaming of from almost the first day I'd met him.

He reached down and grabbed my hand in his.

And held it all the way to the car.

## CHAPTER 18

PHOENIX

"Do you know where the salt is?"

I glanced at Levi and motioned to the container of salt next to the big pot of water that was just starting to boil on the stove. "Next to you," I said.

To say he was distracted was an understatement. In the two weeks since I'd been working with him in the soup kitchen each night, I'd never seen him so scattered...not since that first night when I'd intervened between him and T.

"Oh, right."

He reached for it, but then hesitated.

"You already added it to the water," I offered, since I knew that was what he was struggling to remember.

His gaze shifted to mine, but he didn't say anything. He looked tired...and dejected.

Despite the great day we'd had at a local petting zoo with Henry, Levi had been distracted all day. He'd checked his phone several times throughout the day, though he'd tried to be discreet about it. I suspected it had something to do with how he'd gotten the bruises, but since he wasn't talking about it, I was at a loss.

I hadn't believed his story about it being an accident at work. I knew it was likely another run-in with T, but I couldn't discount that it could have just as easily been his father as well. I cursed myself for not having been around to intercede, but I'd needed to be at the rehab center to discuss the result of Amani's brain scan and I'd thought Levi was safe at work.

I knew Levi was on the cusp of trying to get out of whatever tentative relationship we seemed to be forming, because every time he looked at me, he seemed to grow even more despondent. I was on the verge of telling him the truth about who I was, but I needed to reach out to Ronan first. I was certain that if I showed Ronan that Levi was no threat to Seth and that he hadn't gotten off scot-free after the attacks, that the other man would back off. But the big sticking point was, I had absolutely no proof he wasn't a threat.

I believed it in my heart, but Ronan wouldn't accept anything but concrete proof...not when his husband's life was at stake.

I didn't know what the fuck I'd do if I couldn't convince Ronan. The logical answer was to take Levi and run, but I couldn't leave my daughter. I wouldn't. As much as I loved Levi, and I'd come to accept that I was, in fact, in love with him, I knew that just wasn't an option for me.

The alternative was to help Levi go into hiding, but then I wouldn't be able to protect him. If Ronan sent someone else after him, he wouldn't last five minutes on his own.

As I finished rinsing the dish I'd been cleaning and set it in the dishrack to dry, my gaze shifted back to Levi who was still standing in front of the pot of water, which was now rapidly boiling. The salt was still in his hands. He was staring at the water, but not really seeing it. I went over to him and put my arms around his waist. I used one hand to free the salt from his iron grip.

"No, I need to add that," he said half-heartedly as he reached for the salt.

"You already added it," I murmured and then I kissed his neck.

"Fuck," he whispered before he shut his eyes.

I was about to plead with him to tell me what the hell was going on, but a discreet cough had me pulling back a little and both of us turned to see Father O standing a few feet away. His face was drawn tight and my initial thought was that he wasn't happy to see Levi in my arms. The Catholic faith wasn't exactly accepting of people like Levi and me and as much as I liked Father O, it wouldn't surprise me if he'd put his religion's antiquated beliefs first. I half-expected Levi to panic about being caught in an intimate embrace with me, but he didn't seem concerned.

Neither man spoke, but Father O made a slight motion to the left with his head and then walked away.

Levi turned to face me. "Can you add the noodles?"

I nodded and then looked in the direction Father O had gone. "Everything okay? Is he going to have a problem with this?" I asked as I motioned between us.

"No," Levi shook his head. "I told him I was gay back in prison... Father O doesn't think the same way a lot of priests do," was all he said. "I'll be right back."

I liked that he brushed a brief kiss over my mouth before leaving the room. I tried to focus on getting the spaghetti going, but I couldn't help but glance at my watch every few minutes. When Levi returned, his face was pale and I could tell he'd been crying. But as soon as I reached for him, he skirted out of my grasp and hurried to the freezer to search out the dinner rolls.

"Levi-"

"Can you get the oven going?"

"Levi-"

"I'll be right back. I'm going to go check the other freezer for more rolls."

I knew he was talking about the larger freezer located in a back room. But I also knew we had plenty of rolls in the main freezer. It was an excuse to escape my questions.

It went on like that for the rest of the night, but when Levi tried to insist on walking by himself to the grocery store, I put my foot down and practically dragged him to my car. When we reached the store and he tried to get out of the SUV, I clamped my hand around his uninjured wrist.

"What's going on?" I asked, trying to keep the frustration out of my voice.

He refused to look at me as he said, "Nothing...just tired."

"Cut the shit, Levi," I snapped. He flinched and I instantly regretted my harshness. I leaned across the console and put my hand around the back of his neck. "Don't do this," I whispered as I pressed a kiss to his temple.

"It was never going to work," he said, his voice uneven...like he was on the verge of tears.

"Why not?" I asked, though I knew the answer.

The kicker was, he was absolutely right. We were building something based on lies. Only, he thought he was the only one lying. With that thought rattling around in my head, I released him when he pulled his hand free. Pain tore through me when he turned his face and brushed his mouth over mine.

"Please don't be here waiting for me tomorrow morning," he whispered. I was about to tell him no, that I would most definitely be waiting for him, but when he clasped the side of my face with his hand, he croaked out another "Please." I couldn't ignore the pain in his voice, but I couldn't force myself to say the word, so I merely nodded.

He kissed me one more time and then he got out of the SUV. I didn't wait for him to look back because I knew he wouldn't. As soon as he entered the building through the employee entrance, I moved my car to the part of the lot where Levi wasn't likely to notice it, but that would still afford me good views of both the front and side entrances.

It was about an hour before closing time when my phone buzzed and I looked down to see a text from Ronan.

*Where are you?*

I typed out a brief message telling him I was outside the mark's work, but cringed at the use of the word 'mark'.

Because Levi was anything but.

And I most certainly wasn't there to keep an eye on him on Ronan's behalf.

Not anymore.

Ronan didn't respond, but twenty minutes later, his luxury SUV pulled in the spot next to mine.

Fuck, this couldn't be good.

The man looked cool as a cucumber as he strode around his car, but I saw the familiar tick in his jaw.

He got in the passenger seat, but didn't say a word as he handed me a file folder. I flipped it open and felt my gut clench.

In the folder was a single picture.

Of Curtis Deming's car sitting in front of the old Nichols house.

And it was dated the night before.

I swallowed hard as I realized the picture had been taken a couple hours before Levi had shown up at my door.

"I want you to take him out."

I closed my eyes and flipped the file shut. "Ronan, there are things about him-"

"I don't give a shit!" he snapped. "I don't care about this" – he motioned to the store – "and I don't care that he's trying to look legit by volunteering at that damn soup kitchen!" Ronan paused, seemingly to pull himself together. I'd never seen him so enraged before. Of course, I hadn't been around when Seth's life had been in danger a year earlier either.

"I let him live because it was what Seth wanted. But this shit ends now," he bit out and then he was out of the car before I could even respond.

While I understood his fury, he also wasn't the Ronan I knew. Not the emotionless killer, anyway. The one who believed in serving justice, not vengeance. And while I couldn't condemn him for the fear that was driving his rage, I also knew nothing I said would get through to him.

Which meant my options were growing more and more limited by the second.

I glanced at the picture again and then looked up at the store in frustration. Why the hell had he gone to that house again? As I pondered the question, my eyes settled on the security camera pointing at the front entrance. There was a second one pointing towards the short drive leading to the side where the employee entrance was. I reached for my phone. I dialed and waited until Daisy answered. I'd only met the group's tech girl once, but I'd spoken to her often enough to know she was capable of getting to even some of the most difficult of information.

"Hi, Phoenix," she said happily. I could hear the clicking of a keyboard.

"I need you to do something for me…stat."

The clicking stopped. "Go," was all she said, her voice all business now.

"I need you to check some security footage. Carlisle's Food Market, Rainer Avenue."

"Timeframe?"

"Yesterday between 7:30 pm and" – I glanced at the timestamp on the photo – "10:00."

"Subject?" she asked.

I hesitated before saying, "Levi Deming or Hugo Larson."

Daisy was silent for a moment before she said, "It will take a little time."

"Send me any footage you find."

I said my goodbyes and then hung up. I knew I might possibly be putting the nails in Levi's coffin when it came to Ronan, since Daisy would be forced to tell Ronan what she found, but I was desperate enough to hope I'd get some much-needed answers from the footage.

I settled back in my seat to wait and let my thoughts drift to this morning. It had taken several minutes to rouse Levi from the nightmare that had held him in its grip and my heart had broken all over for him in those minutes. He'd actually spoken a couple of sentences during the dream, as if he were living that moment all over again. I'd heard the name Jed a few times as well as Ricky…proof that the memory had most likely been about the attack on Seth and his parents rather than the brutal rapes he'd suffered at the hands of his brother and the inmates in the prison shower.

I wanted to curse the whole situation. I'd finally fallen in love for the first time in my life and I'd also managed to become a part of a family after losing mine, but the two things were incongruent. I could have one or the other, but not both.

Though, in truth, I'd already lost my new family because I couldn't keep my unspoken promise to them.

I'd always believed in the strength of family. It was something that had been instilled upon me even as a small child. Although it had just been me, my parents and my sister, we'd been an extremely tight-knit family and losing them all at once had been something that had changed my entire outlook on life. I'd been so focused on my career in the military, that I hadn't always considered life beyond serving my country. But Amani had been my second chance and I'd never loved anything or anyone the way I loved that child. I'd been terrified at the prospect of being a father, but I'd muddled my way through the nighttime feedings, lack of sleep and constant fear that I'd miss something vital in her development. I'd been fortunate that I'd had the financial resources to be a full-time parent to my daughter, because even without a job to worry about, I'd still struggled to keep up with the responsibility.

But I'd been paid back in spades.

Events like the first time Amani had called me Daddy and catching her when she'd taken her first tentative steps had made every change in my life worth it. But in the blink of an eye, it had been snatched away. I'd railed at God for the cruel twist of fate He'd thrown into my path for the second time in my life. Although I was grateful I still had my child, deep down in a part of my soul that I refused to even consider, lingered that question that I would never to give voice to. My focus was on the here and now and I still had my daughter with me. Cruel twist of fate or not, I knew I wouldn't wish for anything different, except maybe that the man upstairs hadn't brought Amani's birth father back into the picture.

I'd never been a religious guy, but I was starting to wonder if God liked his little moments of fuckery. Because he apparently hadn't found enough entertainment in torturing me with my daughter's uncertain fate; no, he'd gone and added Levi to the mix.

Sweet, tormented Levi who'd suffered more in his life than anyone I'd ever known.

It was shitty enough that God had decided my loyalty to my new family needed to be tested, but to let me fall in love with someone I could never be with was the ultimate cruelty, second only to the half-loss of my child.

My phone buzzed, jerking me from my pity party. I checked the text from Daisy.

*Four external cameras. North, south and east cameras working, west camera offline. Footage attached from east and north cameras.*

The east camera was the one facing the entrance to the store, the north faced the employee entrance. Which meant the one offline was at the back of the store where the dumpsters were kept and deliveries occurred.

I hit the first video attachment. The picture wasn't as clear as I would have liked, but I could make out Levi when he came into the frame as he returned a grocery cart to the long line of carts outside the store's entrance. Someone approached him from behind and while I couldn't be sure it was T, he had the right build and hair color. Levi turned and ran into the man and they exchanged words. I couldn't tell if there were bruises on Levi's face. The image also wasn't good enough to see his expression, but Levi's body language showed his tension as he turned and walked with T towards the side of the store. It looked like T was holding his arm, but I couldn't be sure.

I switched to the next video and saw T and Levi walking past the employee entrance and out of the view of the camera. Frustration coursed through me as I realized they were going to the back of the store where there'd be no video footage.

The last video showed Levi walking back towards the front of the store with a guy I didn't recognize. Again, I didn't have a good view of Levi's face so I didn't know if there were bruises or not.

I texted Daisy a quick thank-you and then tossed my phone in the cup holder. I'd hoped the video would offer proof that T had assaulted Levi, but all it had done was make him look guiltier. At least, that's how Ronan would see it. I knew in my bones that T had done something to Levi at the back of that store, but I was in the same position I'd been an hour ago.

With orders to kill a man who didn't deserve it, but no way to prove it.

The ironic part was that Ronan wasn't behaving any differently than me. I, too, was going on emotion and instinct when it came to protecting the man I loved.

As darkness fell, the store closed and all of the employees left. I was tempted to go knock on the employee entrance and force Levi to talk to me, but I knew it wouldn't get me anywhere. Not while I was still struggling with how to proceed with everything. Since my car was now one of the only ones left in the parking lot, I moved it to the street where it wouldn't stand out as much, but where I could still have a good view of anyone coming or going.

My phone rang and I saw Ronan's second-in-command's name come up on the screen.

"Hey, Memphis."

"Hey. I need to see you."

My gut tightened. This couldn't be good.

"I'm on a job," I said.

"I'm sending someone to cover for you."

I wanted to tell him no…that I wanted to keep an eye on Levi myself, but I knew that wasn't an option. "Who are you sending?"

"Dante."

"Okay. I'll head over to your place as soon as he gets here."

I hung up and contemplated the turn of events. There was only one reason that I could think of that Memphis would want to talk to me.

It didn't bode well for me…or Levi.

Headlights appeared in my rearview mirror about fifteen minutes later. I got out of my car and walked to the plain navy blue sedan. For all his flash off the job, Dante was the consummate professional on it. He lowered his window and brushed back the dark curls that had a tendency to fall in his face. We bumped fists.

"Memphis give you background info?" I asked.

"Yeah. Levi Deming, 24." Dante motioned to a file folder sitting on the passenger seat. I wondered how much he really knew. Fear curdled through me as something occurred to me.

"Can you step out for a second?" I asked, since I didn't want to have this conversation through a car window.

Dante did as I asked.

"How much do you really know?"

The other man studied me for a moment and then leaned back against his car, folding his arms.

"I know that whoever this guy is, he's important enough that I had to leave my fiancé alone in bed on the one night we've had together in weeks," he said coolly.

I ignored his comment and strode around to the car's passenger side. I opened the door and grabbed the file folder and flipped through it, the light from the interior dome light enough to let me see the contents. It was just Levi's arrest record and his picture. Nothing more. But that didn't really mean anything. I tossed the folder back on the seat and shut the door before going back to the driver's side.

I stepped close to Dante and said, "You and I have always gotten along, Dante. But you go near him," – I motioned to the store – "and that won't be the case anymore. Do you understand me?"

Threatening Dante wasn't the smartest thing I'd ever done, but if my hunch was right and Ronan had lost faith in me, I needed to be sure Dante understood the stakes.

Dante's jaw tightened for the briefest of moments, proof that he didn't like the warning I'd issued, but then, to my surprise, he relaxed his posture.

"Look, Memphis just told me to sit on the guy until you get back. I don't know what the fuck is going on or who this guy is to Memphis... to you." Dante paused before saying, "I just want to get this done so I can get home to my man, so get out of here. He," – he jerked his head towards the store – "is in good hands. I promise."

I searched Dante's eyes for any kind of lie, but didn't see any sign of deception.

I nodded and forced myself to go to my car. The drive to

Memphis's house took about twenty minutes. I was greeted at the door by one of his lovers, young Tristan Barretti.

"Hey, Phoenix," he said as he gave me a hug. He held me for a long time and I knew why. I'd been tasked with guarding him when he, Memphis, and their other lover, Brennan Devereaux had been struggling to figure out their relationship. I'd grown particularly close to Tristan, had even told him things about Amani that I hadn't told anyone else.

"Hey," I said. "How are things?" I asked as I followed him into the house.

"Good," he said with a broad smile. "How's Amani?"

I nodded. "She's good."

Tristan brushed his hand up and down my arm, but didn't say anything. It was one of my favorite things about Tristan. He was good at giving a person just what they needed.

"Memphis is in the office," Tristan said as he led me to the living room where I saw Brennan sitting on the couch in front of a big screen TV, a white cat curled on his lap.

"Hi, Phoenix," Brennan said with a wave.

"Hey." To Tristan I said, "Thanks," and started walking towards the back of the house. I saw Tristan go sit down next to Brennan who immediately put his arm around his shoulders while Tristan laid his head on Brennan's chest. I wondered if I'd ever have that. That need to always be touching another...like you'd become part of them and they you. Even when you were doing something as simple as watching television.

I made my way to the office where Memphis was sitting behind a desk, his eyes on a piece of paper in front of him.

"Come on in," he said. "Close the door."

I did as he said, but when he motioned to the chair, I didn't move. His dark eyes lifted to meet mine and then he leaned back in his chair.

"I was thinking Ronan might be mistaken, but now I'm guessing not," he said.

"Ronan's wrong about this," I said, not bothering to dance around the subject. "We don't have all the information yet."

"Phoenix," Memphis said with a sigh. "Sit...please." He motioned again to the chair on the other side of the desk. I reluctantly sat down.

"Ronan has concerns that you may be compromised. That you feel pity for the mark."

"His name is Levi," I said, trying to keep my anger in check.

"Levi," Memphis conceded. "Ronan's shared his notes with me. Why don't you tell me what you've discovered?"

"Does it matter?" I asked. "You've made your decision. Ronan's made his."

"Think about it for a moment, Phoenix. Ronan could have called any one of his guys tonight and given his order. He could have easily had a dozen guys detain you while one followed through on his termination order. But he called me."

"Why?" I asked.

Memphis shook his head. "Because I think he's scared shitless. I think he came close to losing Seth a year ago and that's not something you can just come back from."

I watched as Memphis dropped his eyes. I knew he was remembering the moment when he'd learned both his lovers had been abducted by his vengeful ex. Brennan, in particular, had suffered terrible things at the man's hands.

"He gave that order and I believe he meant it, but I think there's that part of him that isn't so certain. That's the part that called me and told me to find someone else to handle the job."

Memphis leaned forward and folded his arms on the desk. "So let's start with you telling me all you know about Levi Deming," he said. "And then you can tell me why this job is no longer a job for you."

It didn't really surprise me that he'd figured out the truth about me. I could deny it, but I found that I didn't want to. So I told him everything I knew, including the things Levi had told me in confidence about his brother's sexual assaults as well as what had happened to him in prison. When I was finished, Memphis was frowning. He was quiet for a long time before he said, "So, you don't know for sure that Levi isn't colluding with this T guy to try to get to Seth again...besides the gut feeling anyway."

"No," I said. "I just need more time. I think Levi's on the verge of telling me everything. If I can just get him to trust me, I can find out about him and T and their plans. Even if it's true, T is forcing him into it. I know it. I just don't know what he has on Levi."

Memphis nodded. "I'll buy you time with Ronan...but it will probably only be a day or two. If you can't get Levi to open up, we'll need to force the issue."

As much as I hated the sound of that, I knew he was right. Confronting Levi head on might be the only way to save his life. But that was also assuming his answers were enough to prove to Ronan that if he was in fact targeting Seth, it was because he had no choice. Hopefully, we'd be able to convince Ronan that if we removed T from the equation, Seth would once again be safe.

Fuck, that was a lot of *ifs*.

My phone rang before I could respond and I felt my insides tighten at the sight of Dante's name on the caller ID.

"What happened?" I asked as soon as I answered it.

"Relax," Dante said with a sigh. "I just wanted to let you know the mark is on the move."

I ground my teeth together to keep from yelling through the phone that his fucking name was Levi. "That's impossible," I said. "He's scheduled to work until five tomorrow morning."

"Okay, fine, but his doppelganger just left the store and got into a cab. From the direction it's headed, I'm guessing he's on his way to your house."

"Stay with him," I said as I jumped to my feet.

For Levi to leave work to come see me, it had to be something big.

I hung up the phone. "I have to go," I said.

"Keep me posted."

"Yeah," I muttered, only half-listening as I hurried to the door.

"And Phoenix?"

I turned to face Memphis.

"Make sure he doesn't go near that house again. Even if you have to tell him who you are. It won't take much to push Ronan over the edge to where he'll deal with it himself."

I nodded in understanding. I wasn't as confident as Memphis that he could get me a little more time, but I really had no choice. I barely managed to say my goodbyes to Brennan and Tristan as I rushed from the house.

The drive home seemingly took forever, but in truth, traffic was light and with my foot heavy on the gas pedal, I made it in fifteen minutes. I saw Dante's car sitting by the curb and as soon as I pulled into my driveway, his headlights turned on and he drove away.

Leaving me with Levi.

I didn't bother to put my car in the garage since I could see Levi sitting on my front stoop. His arms were wrapped around his legs and his forehead was pressed to his knees.

"Levi," I said softly as I hurried to him. I dropped down in front of him when he didn't raise his eyes. "Baby, can you look at me, please?"

He shook his head and I heard him choke back a sob. But then he lifted his face. Tears were running down his cheeks.

"Did something happen at work?" I asked. I wondered if maybe T had called and threatened him or something.

Levi dashed at his tears. "No…I called Betty and told her I wasn't feeling well and that I needed to go home." More tears fell as he whispered, "I'm falling in love with you."

The admission was the last thing I expected to hear. My heart leapt to life in my chest. "That's good, because I'm already completely in love with you."

He began sobbing as he pushed into my arms. I held him close as his body shuddered against mine and I knew, just knew, he hadn't come here just to tell me he loved me.

Though I wished he had. As badly as I needed to get the truth out of him about Seth, I needed this moment more. This moment where it was just him and me and nothing else existed.

"I need to tell you something," Levi murmured against my ear when he'd calmed down a little.

"Do you want to go inside?" I asked.

He nodded. I forced myself to release him, but took his hand in mine and then went to the door to unlock it. Once inside, I led him to the living room and sat down on the couch. But instead of sitting down next to me, he moved to the farthest end of the couch. I didn't like that he felt the need to put so much distance between us, but I was glad when he shifted his body so that he was facing me.

"I told myself I would wait to tell you the truth, but I can't. I need to let you go now because I may not be strong enough to do what I need to do otherwise…"

Before I could respond to his comment about letting me go, he lifted his eyes to meet mine and said, "It happened seven years ago and it was the worst night of my life."

# CHAPTER 19

## LEVI

*I* hadn't expected him to tell me he loved me.

I wished he hadn't.

It was going to make this all the harder to do.

My night had gone from bad to worse from the moment Phoenix had dropped me off at work. I'd been so distracted at work that I'd done just about everything wrong. I hadn't been able to keep up with which register to bag for and I'd arranged the groceries in the bags so poorly that two bags had ripped, causing the contents to hit the floor and break. I'd offered to pay Betty to replace the things I'd broken, but she'd told me not to worry about it and then she'd given me a hug and told me how proud of me she was.

I'd lost it at that point and escaped to the back of the building to start going through the items that would need to be priced and put on the shelves after the store closed. But after I'd ended up pricing every single item the exact same price, I'd known I was a lost cause and I'd called Betty to tell her I wasn't feeling good. Luckily, my earlier behavior had supported my cause and she'd told me without hesitation to go home and rest and that she'd have someone take care of everything in the morning.

It was only the second time I'd ever bailed on work, the first time being the night before after T had attacked me behind the store.

I'd known what the problem was, of course.

And it was a reminder of how selfish I was.

Because I didn't want to let Phoenix go.

Or Henry.

Even after Father O had told me about Hank, I'd still wanted to find a way where I could have everything I wanted, instead of following through on my plan to go to the cops about T and that night seven years ago.

Father O had been able to get information on Hank's condition. He'd been attacked in the laundry after some of Gun's men had started a fight with some of Jasper's crew in another area of the prison. Hank hadn't told the guards who'd attacked him, but I already knew it was Gun. Without Jasper and his men to protect him, Hank had been at Gun's mercy for those precious few minutes. He'd been severely beaten to the point he was almost unrecognizable and one of his knees had been shattered, so he'd likely never be able to walk normally again. Father O had said they'd taken Hank to the hospital, but once his knee was surgically repaired, they'd return him to prison. I knew that meant I only had a day or two to get my shit together, because even in the infirmary, which was where they'd likely keep Hank for a while, he was vulnerable to another attack.

And T had made it clear that there would be another one if I didn't cooperate.

So, as I'd contemplated what would happen in the coming days, I'd wanted just a little more time.

With Phoenix.

And with Henry.

I needed something I could hang onto through everything that was about to come my way. There wouldn't be a trial because I'd plead guilty to the murders of Seth's parents. I'd thought about trying to end my life in jail, before they transferred me back to prison, but things would likely move pretty quickly once I was sentenced. Of course, I could try to do it before sentencing, but that would rob Seth Nichols of the chance to confront me in the safety of a courtroom. I was terrified of what he might say to me, but he deserved that closure.

I forced my attention back to Phoenix and sucked in a breath. "I was still in school at the time. I hated going home afterwards, so I'd go to this park most afternoons and work on this comic book I was writing. It was about this kid who saves the world with his pen." At Phoenix's confused look, I shook my head and said, "Everything he draws, happens in real life. So if someone's robbing a bank, he draws the police showing up and that's what really happens. It was stupid."

"No, it isn't," Phoenix said softly. "Did you like to draw?"

I nodded. "I wasn't any good at it, but I liked it. Anyway, I'd stay at the park until it got dark and I was forced to go home. That night when I got home, my dad was already off on one of his benders at his favorite bar, but Ricky was waiting for me. He told me I was going with him, but he didn't say where. Sometimes he'd force me to do things, like buying drugs for him, but he didn't usually take me along for his bigger jobs...said I'd fuck things up. Which was fine by me." I paused before saying, "I thought he just wanted me to get him drugs. I don't know why that night was different."

I got lost in thought and Phoenix had to prod me to continue by saying, "What happened?"

"I knew better than to argue with Ricky, so I went with him. We met up with this guy named Jed. Ricky told me to get in the car, but when I saw a black ski mask sitting on the back seat, I knew it wasn't about drugs. I tried to get away, but Ricky grabbed me and said he had a job for me. When I told him no, he hit me and forced me into the back seat." Even the memory of that moment had me wanting to curl in on myself.

"We drove around for a while as Jed and Ricky talked. They were talking about this safe and Ricky kept asking Jed if he was sure the guy who told him about the safe was right about it being full of money. We stopped at this abandoned gas station and Ricky explained to me that we were going to rob some rich guy. I didn't say anything, because I knew just by looking at Ricky that I wouldn't be able to talk him out of it. He was so...excited."

My stomach rolled violently and I felt my body start to get cold. I shook my head because I needed to get this done. I willed myself to relax and waited until the chill passed. "On the way to the house, Ricky gave me an unloaded gun. Just the sight of it scared the hell out of me, but when I told him I didn't want it, he hit me again. When we got to the house, I realized something was wrong. The way Jed and Ricky had been talking, it was just supposed to be the guy. But when we got inside the garage, they started arguing about the guy not being alone. I thought that would stop them...that we'd turn around and get out of there."

"But it didn't," Phoenix observed.

I shook my head. "The man's wife and son were home too. The kid...he was only fourteen. I found that out when I saw the story on the news the next day. He was so fucking scared, Phoenix," I whispered.

The couch shifted slightly as Phoenix moved closer to me and settled his hand on my leg. "Finish your story, Levi. So it's no longer between us."

"Jed and Ricky got all three of them out of bed and we took them downstairs. We tied them up with zip-ties and then Ricky and Jed started ripping the paintings off the wall. I didn't realize it at the time, but I guess it was a wall safe that they'd been looking for. They kept asking the father where it was, but he wouldn't answer them...I think he was in shock or something. That's when...when Ricky took the mom upstairs."

Bile suddenly crawled up my throat and I jumped to my feet. "I'm going to be sick," I managed to choke out and then I darted to Phoenix's bathroom. I barely made it to the toilet in time. Humiliation washed through me as I felt a hand settle on my back. My stomach cramped painfully as my body tried to expel something that wasn't there. Tears flowed from my eyes as the dry heaving continued. Once my insides relaxed, I dropped to my knees and immediately felt a cool washcloth being pressed against my forehead before it was used to wipe my face clean.

"Here," Phoenix said softly as he handed me a toothpaste-covered toothbrush he'd just worked free from its packaging. I scrubbed my teeth until the rancid taste in my mouth finally disappeared. Phoenix helped me to my feet so I could rinse and spit and then he handed me mouthwash. When I was finished, he pressed a kiss to my forehead before he took my hand in his. But he didn't lead me back to the living room. Instead, we went to his bedroom and he urged me up onto the bed. I was glad when he didn't force me into his arms as he leaned back against the headboard, though that was exactly where I would have liked to have been. But I needed to see his reactions as I told the rest of my story. I was looking for that moment where his pity would turn to disgust. It was coming, I just wasn't sure when.

"What happened after he took her upstairs?" Phoenix asked.

"Jed had me get the tape from his bag - to cover the kid's mouth. I didn't know why he wanted his mouth covered because the kid wasn't making any noise...all he was doing was crying. I didn't want to do it, but Jed put the gun to my head so I did. The way the kid looked at me," I whispered. I wiped away the tears that began to fall again. "But I couldn't help him. I...I didn't know how to tell him that. I was such a fucking coward."

"You were a kid-"

"Yeah, but so was he!" I said angrily. "I knew what Ricky was like, but I got into that car anyway. I did everything he told me to do because I was more afraid of him than anything else. Even when he wasn't in the fucking room, I was still scared shitless." I tried to calm myself down so I could finish my story and get the hell out of there.

"When the father didn't tell Jed where the safe was, he pulled out his knife and put some tape over the father's mouth. I thought he was going to stab him. But then he went after the kid. I tried to stop him, but he pushed me aside and when I grabbed his arm, he knocked me down. I was too out of it to do anything after that. He started slicing the kid up...to make the father talk."

I felt rather than saw Phoenix's hand on my knee as he pushed some tissues into my hand.

"The father was screaming, even with the tape. And I could hear the woman upstairs...it was a fucking nightmare. When Jed finally stopped and let the father talk again, he started begging Jed not to hurt his wife and kid anymore. That he'd do anything. That was when I knew there was no safe…there never had been. Jed actually agreed with me when I told him that. I thought it was over…"

"But it wasn't," Phoenix ventured.

I shook my head. "He slit the guy's throat," I whispered hoarsely. "Like it was nothing…like it was something he'd done a thousand times. The kid started screaming, but he still had the tape on his mouth. I threw up, but there was nothing in my stomach anymore. My brother came downstairs…he was covered in blood. The woman had stopped screaming."

I stopped because I couldn't seem to catch my breath. Everything hurt. My eyes, my nose, my wrist, my stomach. "My brother and Jed started arguing. I still couldn't process what was happening. My only thought was to get help. So when Jed and Ricky weren't looking, I picked up a cordless phone from the table behind me. Ricky went back upstairs to deal with some evidence he was worried about. Once he was gone, Jed started tearing up the rest of the room…I don't know why."

"Probably so the cops wouldn't zero in on just the paintings and realize a wall safe had been the target."

"Why would that matter?" I asked.

"Because a wall safe isn't a common thing. It would have led the cops to believe it was an inside job…that someone who knew the family and knew they had a wall safe had told Jed and Ricky about it. By trashing the room, Jed was making it look like a regular robbery."

I nodded in understanding. I hadn't even considered that. "While Jed was doing that, I dialed 911, but kept the phone pressed against my back so he wouldn't hear the operator talking. I was hoping they'd be able to trace the call or something, like they do on TV. To this day, I don't know if it worked. I wasn't paying attention to Jed, so I didn't see what was happening until it was too late."

"He went after the boy," Phoenix murmured.

"Yeah. He began stabbing him. I forgot all about the phone, but before I could try to stop him, Ricky came back into the room."

"He saw you with the phone."

I nodded. "He didn't say anything," I said softly. "He didn't even look pissed...he looked almost glad. Like when he'd been talking about all the money we were going to steal. He walked over to me, not even looking at what Jed was doing to the kid once. He just took the phone from my hand, hung it up and then he stabbed me."

I could feel the scar on my side tingling, though I knew it was likely just my imagination.

"If Jed hadn't stopped him, he would have killed me for sure. Jed told Ricky there'd be too much evidence to cover up. Ricky told Jed to take me out of the house while he cleaned up the evidence...I was still conscious and able to walk, but I was bleeding pretty bad. I saw Ricky grab the bottle of bleach he'd taken upstairs with him, so I assume he used that to get rid of my blood."

"What happened once you guys got out of there?"

"I'm not sure. I heard Jed and Ricky arguing about getting rid of their knives. Jed wanted to throw them in the lake. I passed out after that. When I came to, I was in the hospital. My dad was in the room with me. He warned me to keep my mouth shut and to let him do the talking. I found out later that he'd told the people in the ER that I'd fallen through a glass window and that was how I'd gotten hurt. Everyone seemed to believe him and I was too scared to tell the truth. I saw the news the next morning about the kid and his parents. The kid made it, but the parents didn't."

I allowed myself to look at Phoenix. "You want to hear the most fucked up part?" I didn't wait for him to answer because I didn't expect him to. "They brought the kid to the same hospital as me...he was on the same floor."

Phoenix stiffened and his eyes went wide. I let out a choked laugh. "Yeah, he was three rooms down. I heard the nurses talking about him. They'd had to put him into a coma or something...to let his body heal. I was terrified Ricky would find out, but luckily my dad didn't make the connection and I knew Ricky wouldn't be coming to see me in the hospital. But even with him right there, on his fucking deathbed, I still didn't do anything. No Ricky around, no Jed. Hell, my father didn't even stay past the time it took him to make sure I wouldn't rat on

Ricky...I had dozens of opportunities to tell someone. But I didn't, and you want to know why?"

"Why?" Phoenix managed to ask, though from the expression on his face, I knew I'd managed to shock him.

"Because I knew Ricky would kill me. It didn't even occur to me that if I told, I'd spend the rest of my life in prison or that Ricky would too. All I could think was that Ricky would string me up like he had Mrs. Hurley's cat."

I shook my head and dropped my eyes again. I'd hoped I'd feel some measure of relief after finally telling someone the truth about that night, but all I felt was cold and empty. I waited for Phoenix to say something, anything, but I heard nothing.

And the longer the silence lasted, I knew the pipe dream I'd had that he might somehow forgive my sins, even when I couldn't, had been yet another one of God's punishments.

"I know you don't owe me anything, but I need a favor," I murmured. "I need 24 hours to get Henry situated. I'll go to the cops then. You have my word." I kept my eyes averted as I climbed off the opposite side of the bed, the side Phoenix wasn't sitting on, in the hopes that I wouldn't see that look of disgust I'd been waiting for. I knew he had no reason to let me go since my word meant shit to him after everything I'd just told him, so I held my breath as I walked around the bed and towards the door. But when I didn't hear anything behind me, no shifting on the bed, no footsteps, I quickened my pace.

I'd just made it to the bedroom door when fingers closed around my upper arm and dragged me backwards. Phoenix's hand slid around the back of my head.

"So that's it?" he asked as he pressed his forehead to mine. His arm went around my waist. It felt so good having him touch me, that I had to bite back the tears that were threatening to fall.

"I mean so little to you that I don't even warrant a final look?"

"No, I-"

"Do you think me telling you I loved you came with conditions?"

His question caught me off guard. "Finding out you're in love with a murderer is a pretty damn good condition," I said.

"You're not a murderer," he bit out. "You were a kid, Levi. You got caught up in an impossible situation and you did the best you could."

"I had so many chances to stop it!"

"And instead of two victims, there would have been four! That kid is alive because of you. I listened to your story, Levi. I didn't hear one thing you could have done differently that would have changed the outcome!"

I shook my head, but Phoenix snagged me by the chin and forced my head up so he could look me in the eyes. "Look at me. I'm still here! I'm not walking away. Nothing you said, nothing you did or will do changes how I feel. I love you. I've never said that to another person outside my family, because I don't take those words lightly. But if you aren't sure-"

"I'm sure," I cut in and then I was lifting up to kiss him. "I love you," I breathed against his mouth. I knew it was a mistake, but I didn't care. It wouldn't change anything, but I needed to be allowed to love him…to have him love me back, even if it was just for tonight. Maybe I could survive the hell of prison if I could carry this moment with me.

Phoenix's mouth covered mine and then his tongue was seeking entry. I opened for him and moaned when his tongue swept over mine.

Yes, I was going to take this moment.

Because it would need to last me forever.

## CHAPTER 20

### PHOENIX

*I* was pissed, shell-shocked and turned on all at the same time.

Pissed that Levi had thought he could just walk away and I'd actually *let* him.

Shell-shocked to learn the lengths Levi had gone to try to stop what had happened to Seth. I'd never thought to ask Ronan about how help had gotten to Seth in time, but if Levi's call had gone through, I had my answer.

And the turned-on part was pretty obvious because Levi was trying to climb me like a tree as his need grew. I knew I needed to stop all this and talk to him about T, but my body wasn't cooperating.

Neither was Levi because his hands were all over me as his tongue dueled with mine. When we were finally forced to come up for air, he whispered, "I want to know what it's supposed to feel like."

"What?" I asked.

"Making love," he murmured. He began pressing soft kisses against my mouth. "I want...I want to know what having a man inside of me is supposed to feel like."

I stilled at that because it was the last thing I'd expected to hear. "Levi-"

He put his finger over my lips to stop me from talking. "You said sex is something that should be freely given, not taken. I know you said I could be inside of you, and I want that – I really do. But I want to give you more than my body. Ricky, the men in prison…they took something else from me. I want it back."

I knew exactly what he was talking about. The violations he'd endured hadn't been about stealing sex from him. No, it had been about taking away his power, his control, his ability to choose. Fucking me might give him some of those things back, but it wouldn't be the same.

Because he needed to *choose* to give himself to me. And he needed to know that he could change his mind at any point.

His trust in me was humbling, but it also frightened me. I had this one opportunity to undo some of the damage that had been done to him…to make him see that he had worth…that he was worth fighting for. He wasn't that terrified little boy whose voice no one had heard when he was being tortured by the brother who should have protected him. And he wasn't the broken man the fuckers in prison had left humiliated and bleeding on a dirty shower floor.

He was my Levi.

My beautiful, brave, kind-hearted Levi who continued to get up no matter how many times he was knocked down.

I used my hands to caress his face, mindful of the bruises. "You can say no. Anytime, no matter what. This isn't something I need in order to be with you."

"I know. And I know you'll stop if I can't find the words to tell you myself."

I nodded and then leaned down to kiss him. His mouth moved hungrily over mine, so I used that to gauge his reactions as I ran my hands all over his body. The only time he wavered was when my hands roamed over his ass, but his tension was a fleeting thing. But I knew I'd have to go slow, because it would take just one wrong touch or word to send him right back to the past.

I lifted him up and was pleased when he instantly wrapped his legs around me. It was a short walk to the bed and when I laid him on it, I let some of my weight press down on him. Levi kept his legs wrapped tight around me, but when I straightened so I could remove my shirt, he released me and levered up on his elbows to watch me. I'd always kept my body in prime condition because it was a requirement of the job, but knowing how much Levi enjoyed it was an added benefit. After tossing the shirt aside, I put my hands around Levi's hips and gently pulled him towards me so his ass was closer to the edge of the bed. The position would come in handy shortly.

I helped him sit up and then reached down to lift his shirt off. He tensed briefly, but didn't try to stop me. His eyes were bright with desire, so I knew he was still with me. As I drew the shirt over his shoulders, his hands came to rest on my hips and then slid down to explore my outer thighs. His gaze went to the bulge in my jeans before he lifted his questioning eyes to mine. I nodded, since it seemed like he wanted permission to touch me.

His fingers were shaking as he worked my button free and then carefully pulled the zipper down. I helped him push my jeans past my hips, but didn't reach for my underwear since I wanted to see what he would do. His hand came up to tentatively stroke me through the briefs. I willed my body to relax, but it was an impossible request with Levi's fingers exploring my length and thickness. When he removed his hand, I thought maybe he was finished, but then his hands slid around to my ass and he pressed his nose right up against my crotch. He nuzzled my cock through the fabric and then, without warning, closed his mouth around the shaft. I couldn't stifle the groan that spilled out of me.

Levi's eyes lifted to mine. "I…I never liked this part, but I want to see if it's different with you. I don't want you to be disappointed if I can't-"

I leaned down to stop his words with a kiss. "Nothing you do will ever disappoint me," I said and then I lifted again.

Levi's fingertips grazed my skin as he reached for the waistband of the briefs. He took his time sliding them down my hips, carefully working the material over my hardness. He studied me for a long time before he put his hand around the base of my dick and stroked up towards the tip. I knew it would be an impossible thing to be silent for his explorations because just the sensation of his hand on my highly-sensitized cock was enough to have me moaning deep in my throat. I watched pre-cum well up from the tip and slide down the shaft until it hit Levi's hand. The contrast of his pale skin against my dark flesh was mesmerizing, as was the sight of his mouth parting when my juices continued to gather at the juncture where his thumb met his finger. I watched in fascination as Levi released me and lifted his hand to his mouth. His pink tongue darted out to taste the nearly clear fluid.

'Fuck," I whispered before I could stop myself.

Levi's eyes returned to mine as he considered my taste. It wasn't until he leaned forward and let his tongue flick against the head of my dick that I had the answer to the question of whether or not what he'd tasted had turned him off.

Every time more pre-cum bubbled up, Levi licked it away. I was already struggling to control my raging lust when he closed his mouth over my tip and sucked gently. A ragged moan tore free of my throat which had Levi looking up at me, even as his mouth remained wrapped around my cock.

"Jesus," I whispered as I took in the sight of his lips stretched around me. No fucking way I was going to last.

I let him pull me a little deeper down his throat, but when the base of my spine began to tingle and the pressure in my balls mounted, I gently pulled Levi to his feet and kissed him. "Not going to last if you keep doing that," I murmured against his mouth.

"You taste good," he said with a sigh.

"God, you're killing me here," I said with a groan. He smiled against my mouth.

"I'll behave, I promise."

I chuckled and kissed him again. I was glad that he was feeling good enough to joke with me. I kissed him long and deep as I began working his pants open. When he didn't protest, I pushed his pants and underwear down and then urged him to sit on the bed so I could get them all the way off. As soon as he was naked, I settled my weight on top of him. From what he'd told me about what his brother had done to him, I'd surmised that he'd been raped from behind, so I most definitely wanted to keep us face to face.

Though that wasn't the only reason.

Not by a long shot.

Levi's hands roamed over my back as we made out, but it wasn't until they gripped my ass that my lust shot to a whole new level. I began humping against him so our cocks were rubbing back and forth over one another. Levi let out a little whimper as he began thrusting his hips upwards.

"Phoenix," he croaked.

I knew what the desperation in his voice meant and while I was eager to get inside of his tight little body, I knew he wasn't anywhere near mentally ready. So, I lifted off him enough so that there was some much-needed space between our bodies and then I trailed my lips down his neck. I nipped at him gently before I sucked on his skin hard enough to leave a mark.

A mark he'd see for days to come and remember this moment.

Now I just needed to make it memorable in a really good way.

I braced myself with my arms as I worked my way down Levi's body, nipping, sucking and licking as I went. I left practically no part of him untouched.

Except his cock.

I bypassed that altogether and slid to the floor so I could lift his legs up and drape them over my shoulder one at a time so I could give them equal attention. Even his toes weren't ignored. By the time I'd released his leg and lowered his foot back to the floor, Levi had taken his cock in hand and was stroking it swiftly as his eyes remained glued on me. I enjoyed the show for a while.

"Are you thinking about my mouth on you, baby?" I asked smoothly as I ran my palms back and forth along his thighs.

He nodded and then licked his lips.

I leaned forward and pressed a kiss against his thigh as I watched him work himself. Then I pushed his legs open. Levi tensed briefly and his hands stilled on his dick, but when I didn't just dive right into his hole like he was probably worried I would, he relaxed and began fucking his hand again.

"Keep doing that," I urged as I pressed kisses along his inner thigh and worked my way upwards, inhaling the scent of man, musk and arousal as I went. When I reached his dick, I ignored his pulsing flesh and pressed kisses against his hand instead. Then I slid my tongue down until I reached his balls. He jumped when I licked over one, but I pressed on and sucked one into my mouth.

"Fuck!" he shouted and his hand began pumping his dick more frantically. I sucked on him for a few seconds and then switched to the other one and gave it the same attention. Only when I'd enjoyed the taste of him there did I move my mouth.

But not up towards his dick.

Which was certainly what Levi had been expecting.

With the position he was in, my first tentative lick over his hole was limited, but his reaction was no less intense. He bucked off the bed and sat upright and put a hand on my shoulder to stop me.

"What...what are you doing?" he asked. "It's..."

He shook his head, at a loss for words.

It didn't surprise me in the least that he'd never been rimmed before. He likely hadn't been fingered before either. Guys had just shoved their dicks into him, so he was clearly expecting me to do the same.

"Does it scare you?" I asked, not willing to give up on giving this to him just yet.

"No, but it's..."

"Wrong?" I asked. "Dirty? Forbidden?"

He nodded, but I was glad that he didn't seem entirely certain. I straightened enough so I could reach his mouth. I was glad that he let me kiss him, considering how freaked out he was by where my mouth had just been.

"Nothing we do together is ever wrong," I said. "Or dirty." I kissed him again. "I want to make you feel good, that's it. If you don't like it, I'll stop."

"Has someone done it to you?" he asked.

I nodded. "A couple of times, but the best time was the first guy who did it to me…my first boyfriend in high school."

"I'm sorry, I know I'm being ridiculous."

"No, you're not," I murmured. "I like knowing that I'm the first one to show you that nothing about sex between two consenting adults is wrong…and that when it's between two people who love each other…well, there's just no way to explain that. You'll have to trust me just a little longer to show you."

"I do," he said without hesitation. "I trust you."

"Good, then will you lie back? Give me a minute, that's all I ask."

Levi didn't even hesitate for a moment. He just laid back down on the bed and spread his legs wide again. And when I reached for each leg and moved it until his feet were flat on the edge of the bed, exposing his hole completely to me, he didn't protest.

I leaned in and pressed a kiss against his puckered flesh and hoped like hell I didn't screw this up.

## CHAPTER 21

### LEVI

I nearly jumped off the bed again when Phoenix's mouth closed over the entrance to my body and he kissed me much like he'd kissed me on the mouth moments earlier. My inner voice once again reminded me how wrong this had to be, but the argument was falling on deaf ears. Because the second Phoenix's lips touched my skin, electricity shot up my spine and out to my limbs. My toes involuntarily curled and my dick jumped against my stomach. Heat pooled in my belly as I waited for what he would do next. Another kiss, then another. Phoenix's hand moved up to rest on my stomach, bypassing my dick. I waited for him to close his hand around my flesh, but instead, he pressed his hand down on my abdomen with a small amount of force a split second before the flat of his tongue brushed over my hole.

"Jesus, God!" I shouted as I slapped my hand over Phoenix's where it was resting on my skin. Another lick had me fisting my other hand into the bedding. By the third lick, I was pressing my ass against his face, not caring how it might look. I just wanted more.

I lost all sense of time and space as he continued to lick me. I reached for my dick, but was surprised when Phoenix grabbed my hand and pressed it to the bed. He did the same with my other hand...it wasn't enough to actually restrain me and if I wanted to get my hand free, I could. But the message was clear. He wanted to continue the sensual torture, but he didn't want me to come yet.

I wasn't sure how long I'd last because the need to come was wreaking havoc with my senses. I felt too hot and too tight all over. Like I wanted to bust out of my own skin. I dug my fingers into Phoenix's hands, not caring about anything else but hanging onto him…like I was afraid if I let him go, I'd drift away from him, from this moment.

Phoenix continued the licks and kisses, but when I felt his tongue probing the entrance to my body, I froze.

No way! He couldn't be planning to…

But that was exactly what he did.

I didn't move for all of five seconds as Phoenix's tongue thrust into my body and then pulled back out before pushing in again. But as soon as his tongue entered me again and he licked my insides, I lost it and spewed cum all over myself as my orgasm wrenched through me without any kind of warning. I instinctively jammed my hips up, even though there was nothing to fuck but air. My dick didn't care, though, because seed kept shooting from it, hitting me on the chest, the chin and God only knew where else. And the whole time, Phoenix kept fucking me with his tongue.

When my body was spent, I let my weight sink into the bedding as the euphoria covered me like a warm, soft blanket. I was staring at Phoenix's ceiling, but for all I knew, it was a soft white cloud.

Because I had to be floating.

It was the only way to explain the weightlessness.

I was dimly aware of Phoenix shifting his weight as he released my hands, but I couldn't move. A warm, wet tongue slid up my dick and then closed around the tip and sucked gently. I moaned at how sensitive my cock felt, but luckily Phoenix knew to keep the pressure light. His mouth moved up my body, licking me as he went.

Collecting every drop of evidence that my body hadn't had any issue with what Phoenix had just done to me.

And truthfully, my mind no longer did either.

He'd been right...the pleasure two people who loved one another could bring to each other's bodies could never be wrong.

Because nothing had ever felt more right in that moment.

"You okay?" Phoenix asked when he got to my mouth.

I nodded. "More than," I murmured drowsily.

He kissed me gently and I tasted myself. I could have fallen asleep then and there, but the more he kissed me, the more my body began to come alive again. No, my dick wasn't joining the party just yet, but all thoughts of sleep drifted away as I wrapped my arms around Phoenix's neck and kissed him back. His cock was still hard where it was pressed against my hip. I hadn't even given one thought to his pleasure. It was a testament to how well he'd loved me...how well he'd used the trust I'd given him.

And he'd given me exactly what I'd wanted in return.

I'd chosen to let him pleasure me. I'd given him the power to do to my body what he had. I'd gotten to feel. There'd been no fear of what was coming next or whether he would hurt me or not. Because I'd already had those answers going into this.

He wouldn't hurt me.

It was like he'd said...he'd cut off his arm before he raised it against me.

I brought my hands up to hold Phoenix's face so I could have his complete attention. When his dark eyes met mine, I whispered, "What did I do to deserve you?"

"You were you," he answered. His mouth moved over mine and I knew that even with everything he'd given me, I wanted more.

I wanted it all.

"Make love to me, Phoenix."

He stilled and then leaned back enough so he could brace himself on his elbow. His fingers skirted through my damp hair, pushing it off my forehead. "We don't have to do anything else tonight," he said. "We have plenty of time."

Time was one thing we most definitely did *not* have, but I didn't tell him that. Even if I could have changed things so that there was a way I could spend the rest of my life with him, I'd still want him right now just as badly. It wasn't an issue of time at all. It was much simpler than that.

I just wanted every part of him.

"I want tonight to be about us," I said. "Just us. Nothing else exists outside this room, okay?"

Luckily, Phoenix seemed to understand what I was saying because he kissed me gently and then he started making love to me all over again. But it wasn't just him loving me. At one point, Phoenix rolled us so he was on his back and I took complete advantage and explored his body the way he had mine. When I reached his cock, I didn't hesitate to suck it to the back of my throat. Even when he began fucking my mouth, I took pleasure in the act. With T and Gun, my goal had been to get them off as soon as possible. With Phoenix, I wanted to draw out the pleasure, so I purposefully kept him on edge. And instead of cursing me or trying to force me to suck him harder or longer or faster, he praised me and told me how good it felt and how he just wanted more.

It was a heady experience and I was on cloud nine.

Until Phoenix rolled me on my back and his cock brushed over my hole.

And then I locked up tight and squeaked out a muffled protest as I waited for him to shove into me.

"Baby, open your eyes," Phoenix said as his fingers skimmed my cheek.

I did as he told me, though I didn't remember closing them.

"I'm sorry," I said as I realized what I'd done. For whatever reason, that simple act of his dick touching my hole had made me forget where I was.

And who I was with.

"It's okay, you didn't do anything wrong."

"I don't want to stop," I blurted, because I could see from the way he was looking at me that he was going to suggest just that. "I just got a little lost."

"I know, baby, and it's okay. We can keep going if that's what you really want."

I nodded, because that was exactly what I wanted. I tried to push past the embarrassment, but it wasn't easy. But Phoenix seemed to be in no rush as he began kissing me again. Whenever he shifted his hips, I tensed up, but as soon as he reminded me to open my eyes, I relaxed. At one point, he levered off me and said, "Are you sure? You can still stop me whenever you want, but I just want to make sure you're still with me, one hundred percent."

"I am," I said. Yes, I was scared. I wouldn't lie to myself about that. But I was also eager to take this final step with him.

Phoenix climbed off me long enough to get a condom and a bottle of lube from his nightstand drawer.

"Move up here," he said as he motioned to the head of the bed. He sweetly made sure my head was comfortably supported by a couple of pillows before he settled back down on top of me. As before, he kissed me to get my body back to the edge and then kept me there by grinding our dicks together. I tensed when he got the bottle of lube open and put some on his fingers, but I kept it together as his hand moved between my legs. If he hadn't been kissing me, it would have been harder for me to not react when his finger began probing my entrance. But with every stroke of his lush tongue over mine, my fear over what was coming began to diminish. It stung when his finger pushed into me just a little bit, but instead of ignoring my discomfort, he settled his arm around my shoulders and waited for my body to adjust. And the entire time, he nuzzled my ear and kept telling me he loved me and how beautiful I was.

When my body would relax around the digit, he'd slide more of it into me. He never did anything that caught me off guard and he constantly reminded me to look at him. The intensity in his eyes was overwhelming. I didn't think it possible, but I fell in love with him even more when I saw the effort he was making to make this good for me. While I'd had the benefit of having had one orgasm already, he hadn't.

By the time his finger was completely inside of me, my need had grown again and I was eager to get his mouth back on mine. When I tugged Phoenix down, he happily covered my mouth with his and kissed me hungrily. He captured my moan as his finger pulled out of me before carefully easing back in. It still stung, but there was something else too. Something more than just the sparks of electricity licking at my balls.

It was a hunger of some kind.

But not like what I'd been experiencing since the moment he'd kissed me earlier tonight. No, it was different. A need. I was too empty. Even with his finger inside of me, it didn't feel like enough. And while I knew his cock would cause me at least some pain – there was just no avoiding it – I still wanted it.

"More," I murmured, hoping he'd know what I wanted.

Because I certainly couldn't form the words.

The finger inside of me began to pump in and out with more frequency. The burn faded and something else took over. I was just starting to enjoy the sensation and began bucking my hips up to meet Phoenix's finger when he twisted inside of me and hit something that sent shockwaves through my entire body. It had to be akin to being struck by lightning. The difference in sensation was that intense.

"Oh, God, please!" I wailed, even though I had no clue what I was asking for. But whatever it was, Phoenix gave it to me again.

And again.

Over and over until all I could do was cling to him, eyes closed, tears trailing down my cheeks.

Phoenix kissed me and whispered, "Levi," and then stopped whatever it was he was doing to me. I wanted to beg him to continue, but I forced my eyes open when he ordered me to.

"I can make you come just like this," Phoenix said as he pressed against that spot again.

I let out another shout. My body felt strung so tight, I was sure it would cleave in two when my orgasm hit me.

If it hit me.

Because at this rate, I had no clue what was happening.

I was about to tell him yes, anything to make him finish what he'd started, but then I felt his dick pressed against me and I remembered what I really wanted out of all this.

Not just to experience pleasure.

But to experience it with him.

"No...no, I want you inside me," I managed to say, though I was having trouble catching my breath.

Phoenix nodded and then kissed me. "I'm going to use a second finger to open you up a little more, okay?"

I nodded.

There was little pain and only a slight burn as he pushed another finger into me. He fucked me a few times with both digits, then he hit that magic spot again and I arched my back. I felt Phoenix shift away from me, but he somehow managed to keep his fingers inside of me, gently tickling that place that had me hovering right on the edge of perfection. I'd finally come to realize it was my prostate.

Phoenix continued to massage my inner walls with his fingers even as he tore the condom package open. I felt bereft when he finally pulled his fingers free of me so he could work the condom and some lube over his length. As on edge as my nerves felt as they waited for the imminent orgasm, I was starting to feel tense again as I took in the size of Phoenix's cock. He was definitely bigger than anyone I'd ever been with, but I reminded myself that even the guys in prison who'd had smaller cocks, had still made me feel only pain.

Because that was what they'd wanted me to feel.

I forced the memory away because it had no business here.

Phoenix settled between my legs, but didn't shove into me. He just kissed me gently, sipping at my lips like I was a fine glass of wine or something.

"I want you to keep your eyes open," he said. "I want you to see me, the man who loves you. Only me."

It was almost an order and one I would gladly follow. Because I knew he was right. If I closed my eyes, my mind would play tricks on me.

"I promise," I said.

It wasn't a hardship to keep my eyes fastened on Phoenix's. Because he was just so beautiful and perfect...I didn't want to miss any of the expressions that flashed through his eyes as he positioned his cock at my entrance and began to push into me. Yeah, it hurt. I couldn't pretend it didn't. But the pain was a drop in the bucket compared to what I'd known in the past. And I still had the lingering pleasure from everything he'd already done to me to hang on to.

Once his crown breached me, he hung there, letting me adjust. The pain dissipated, leaving behind an intense burn.

"Good?" Phoenix asked.

I sucked in a breath and nodded. I had my hands on his biceps. The muscles rippling beneath my fingers were a constant reminder of how strong this man was, but how gentle he was being. He took his time working his length into me. He'd occasionally pull back a little, causing an intense tugging sensation that didn't feel at all bad, before he rocked back into me. By the time he was fully seated inside of me, I felt stuffed full.

And I loved it.

The mix of pain, burning and pleasure had my whole body trying to adjust to the mix of sensations.

But the best part was the way Phoenix was wrapped around me.

Around me.

In me.

He was a part of me.

And I him.

I'd never felt more complete in my whole life. Everything was right in my world.

"So beautiful," Phoenix whispered against my lips.

"I love you so much," I said with a shake of my head, because I knew the words weren't enough to convey what I was feeling. And I knew it wasn't just the high that came along with the pleasure. It was more than that.

"I know, baby. I love you. And I promise you, we're going to figure all this out and then we'll be together. You're mine, do you understand me?"

I nodded.

I *was* his.

No matter what any man did to me after this, I would always belong to Phoenix.

"Yours," I said softly. He kissed me hard and then he began moving.

The result was powerful.

My dick, which had gone soft when Phoenix had begun his entry, sparked to life. My whole body lit up with need, excitement and anticipation. I wrapped my arms around Phoenix's broad shoulders and my legs went around the backs of his. There was no space between us whatsoever, but I'd never felt freer.

I clung to him as he began to shuttle in and out of me with more speed and intensity.

"Keep your eyes on me," Phoenix reminded me. I did, but not because I had any fear about seeing someone else if I closed them. There was just no mistaking who I was with.

Every time Phoenix rocked into me, his tight abdominal muscles brushed my cock, causing me to moan because of the sweet, agonizing pleasure of it all. My orgasm was just beneath the surface, but unlike the first one which had snuck up on me, this one was building infinitely slower.

And I knew it was because Phoenix wanted it that way.

His power over me, himself, us, was absolute. His body worked mine expertly. Each time the climax built on itself, I sucked in more of Phoenix's sounds, smells and flavors. The heat wafting off his body, his powerful muscles flexing beneath my fingers, his sweat mingling with mine...it all just drove me higher and higher. It got to the point that I was afraid of the climax that was coming. I wouldn't be able to control it. Not it, not myself. On the one hand, it was what I wanted. But now that it was here, I was scared.

"I'm right here," Phoenix reminded me, his voice hoarse and gruff as he pounded into me. There was no longer any pain or burn. Just pressure and friction and heat. And that coil winding tighter and tighter inside of me.

"I'm afraid of it," I admitted between ragged breaths.

"I know you are, baby, but you don't need to be. This is what love really is."

And I knew that was what I was afraid of. Not the actual fall, but knowing it was the beginning of the end. Knowing what I'd have to do once it was over.

I wanted to resist as long as I could, but when Phoenix shifted his hips and hit that spot deep inside of me, I was helpless to stop the release that shattered me into million pieces.

I screamed as the pleasure rolled over me with the strength of a hundred freight trains. Blackness threatened my vision, but the sound of Phoenix's guttural cry and the feeling of his cock pulsing inside of me kept me grounded and I forced my eyes open to watch the man in my arms fly apart.

I had no words to describe him in that moment. But I'd remember it forever.

I welcomed Phoenix's weight as he crashed down on me. I was hot, sweaty and exhausted, but I couldn't think of any place I'd rather be in that moment. The feeling lasted long after Phoenix withdrew from my body.

And after he gently pulled me from the bed.

And as he lovingly washed me in the shower.

And even as I fell asleep in his arms.

But by the time I opened my eyes just as the sun's rays began filtering into the room, the feeling was long gone and I was once again cold and empty. And while it didn't make it any easier to carefully extricate myself from Phoenix's arms, it was a good reminder the night before had been just that

A night.

A perfect night that I'd take with me and that would rest beside that other night I'd been carrying around in my mind for seven years.

As I got dressed and walked out of Phoenix's room, I allowed myself one long last look at him and hoped it would be enough to see me through the coming days.

## CHAPTER 22

PHOENIX

*I* disliked Henry's mother on sight.

Partly because when she answered the door, she was wearing just a bra and barely-there boy shorts panties. But it was the way she was wiping at the white powder on her nose that really had me wanting to reach out and shake the woman. Of course, with the way she kept eying me as she leaned seductively against the door, I suspected she wouldn't have a problem if I did just that.

"Is Levi here?" I asked.

"Levi?" she asked with a wobbly smile. Yeah, she was definitely high.

"Yeah, Levi. Is he here? He babysits for you, right?"

"Oh, yeah," she said with a big grin. "Nah, he took Henry with him."

"Do you know where he took him?"

Dina had to think about it for a long time before she shook her head. "If you see him, tell him I need some money. You a friend of his or something?"

"Or something," I muttered in irritation. I didn't bother telling her to have Levi call me if she saw him, because I doubted she'd remember the request. I turned away from her and debated what to do next.

I'd woken up to find Levi gone, though I had no clue when he'd left. It was almost nine in the morning so Dina had been the first logical stop. I had to wonder why the woman was even home, though with Levi's comments about the woman tending to lose jobs, I had a pretty good guess. The fact that she *was* home hadn't stopped Levi from taking Henry for the day, though that wasn't a surprise either considering what I had just witnessed.

I'd tried calling Levi, but his phone had gone straight to voicemail, which had me wondering if he'd turned it off. As worried as I was about him, I was hesitant to ask Daisy to trace the phone because my request could get back to Ronan. And if he found out I didn't have eyes on Levi…well, it just wouldn't be a good thing.

I was pissed that he'd disappeared on me. I'd thought for sure we'd reached a new point in our relationship…that we were actually *in* a relationship. But the fact that he'd snuck out and was ignoring my calls and texts was a pretty clear sign that last night hadn't meant to him what it had to me.

As much as I hated what I was about to do, I trotted up the stairs and stopped outside Levi's apartment. I'd seen his father's car out front, so I doubted Levi was actually home, since he avoided his father whenever possible. But I couldn't risk missing him on the off chance he'd changed his routine.

My first knock went unanswered. After the second, I heard a crash in the apartment and a loud curse. I was about to knock again and call Levi's name when the door was yanked open.

By his father.

The man was dressed in a dirty undershirt, sweatpants and a ragged-looking robe that was open at the waist. He smelled of alcohol, cigarettes and body odor.

"What do you want?" the man snapped, his words heavily slurred.

"Is Levi here?"

"You stay away from my boy," was the reply.

"Your boy?" I asked in disbelief. "He hasn't been your boy from the moment you let that monster you call a son lay his hands on Levi!"

"Don't you get all uppity with me, nigger," he bristled.

It took everything in me not to grab him. "Listen to me, you worthless piece of shit. You ever lay another finger on Levi, it will be the last thing you do, do you hear me?"

He tried to slam the door in my face, but I easily caught it and shoved it back, knocking him backwards into the apartment. He fell on his ass.

"I'm calling the cops!"

"You do that," I snarled as I leaned over him and grabbed the lapels of his robe and yanked him upright until he was once again standing. But I didn't release him right away. "Now, do I need to repeat myself, you disrespectful son of a bitch?"

The man finally had the sense to look afraid and he quickly shook his head. He was a fucking bully, through and through.

"I'll know if you touch him," I warned as I held his gaze. "You believe me?"

He nodded. "Yes."

"Yes what?" I asked, just because I could. Because I needed to find a bit of pleasure in this moment.

"Yes, sir," Levi's father murmured, though I knew it killed him to say it.

"Good," I said and then released him. I patted the lapels of his robe to straighten them, making sure I used more force than necessary. The man stiffened, but kept quiet. I turned and left the apartment, but as soon as I did, my satisfaction drifted away because I was back at square one.

I hurried down the stairs and to my car and hoped like hell my next stop would prove to be more fruitful.

## CHAPTER 23

### LEVI

As I began the walk from the parking lot of the rehab center to the front entrance, I asked myself again what the hell I was doing. I'd spent the morning avoiding Phoenix, going so far as to turn off my phone so I wouldn't be tempted to answer his calls, yet here I was, rushing to his side.

After leaving him in bed, I'd walked to the nearest bus stop and had begun the journey of making my way back to my apartment. It had taken over an hour and several transfers. But I hadn't actually gone to my apartment. No, I'd stopped at Dina's and pounded on her door until she'd woken up and answered it. I hadn't even gotten her permission before I'd strode into the apartment to get Henry from his crib. I'd merely told Dina I was taking him and that I'd bring him back later. She'd spouted some shit about having plans with a friend, but I'd ignored her. The fact that she'd made plans for a work day had me guessing she'd lost yet another job. Normally, that fact would have pissed me off, but I was kind of glad because when I called Children's Services, it would go a long way in proving Dina wasn't fit to care for Henry.

My plan was to make the call the following day, so I'd decided to spend today saying my goodbyes.

To Henry.

To Father O.

But my visit to Father O had changed things.

I'd still had Henry with me when I'd entered the church and found Father O replacing candles. He'd been relieved to see me, though I hadn't understood why until he'd mentioned that Phoenix had stopped by looking for me. I'd made up some excuse about Phoenix probably wanting to talk to me about our shift that afternoon and had prepared myself to tell Father O that I wouldn't be able to volunteer anymore. I hadn't planned on telling him why, since I'd known he'd find out soon enough when he saw the news about me admitting to the Nichols family home invasion.

But before I could say anything, Father O had mentioned how worried he was about Phoenix because of the phone call Phoenix had gotten while they were talking.

The phone call about his daughter.

I'd been surprised to learn that Phoenix had told Father O about Amani, but all of that had disappeared as soon as Father O had explained that the call Phoenix had received had been about some kind of emergency with the little girl. Phoenix had left right after that, but not before asking Father O to give me a message.

*Tell him to trust me just one more time.*

One more time. I didn't know what that meant, but it was a request that was hard to ignore. If I hadn't heard about Amani, I might have managed it. But concern for Phoenix had overshadowed my judgment.

What if something had happened with Amani's condition? What if she'd taken a turn for the worse? Phoenix was alone. He had no family to lean on if the worst did happen.

It was that thought that'd had me saying my goodbyes to Father O and hurrying back to Dina's place to drop Henry off. As much as I hated taking Henry back to Dina, I needed to be able to focus on Phoenix while I was at the rehab center. I had to hope that Henry would be okay for one more day.

Once I'd dropped Henry off, I'd gone to my own apartment to get my father's car keys. I'd seen his car out front and had known what it'd meant. He'd called in sick to work...that, or he'd gotten fired. I didn't care either way because starting tomorrow, he was on his own. And I found that I didn't care.

He'd been passed out on the couch when I'd walked in the door. In the past, I'd always looked at him through the fearful eyes of a child, but all I'd seen this afternoon was a pathetic old man who'd never been my father.

Because my father would have protected me.

The walk to the rehab center took longer than it had last time I'd been here with Phoenix, because I had to park in the lot on the farthest side of the building due to construction that was happening near the entrance. A large pond separated the parking lot from the building, so I cut through the grass and walked alongside the pond rather than on the walkway. As I got closer to the entrance, I could see a little girl standing several feet back from the water. She was feeding the ducks from a bag of bread. A young man and little boy were several hundred feet away playing on a small playset that was part of a little playground. I guessed the girl to be maybe eight or nine and the boy only three or so. I could see the little boy smiling as he and the young man played, but I couldn't hear them over the sound of the construction work happening just up the hill from the pond.

As I got closer to the girl, I heard someone yelling and glanced up to see a construction worker waving his hands frantically at something. I couldn't hear what he was saying over the sound of the machinery, but suddenly he jumped out of the way and there was more yelling. I quickened my pace to see what was happening. A large bulldozer came speeding out of nowhere. It had two huge cement culvert pipes attached with chains to the front of it. From the way the driver was jerking the steering wheel and the levers that I assumed controlled the machine's speed, there was clearly some kind of problem.

Someone screamed as the bulldozer veered to the left to avoid a huge dump truck. It hit the curb hard and I watched in stunned disbelief as the chains holding the cement pipes broke and the pipes tumbled to the ground.

But they didn't stop there.

No, they began rolling down the hill towards the pond.

And straight for the little girl feeding the ducks.

I yelled at her to run, but she didn't even look up. I saw the young man with the little boy realize what was happening. He too yelled and waved his arms for a split second before he began running towards the girl, leaving the boy behind in the swing, since he was in no immediate danger.

I began running towards the girl because I was closer and I knew the other guy wouldn't make it in time. My lungs burned as I saw the pipes pick up speed. Panic curdled in my belly because I knew they had to weigh at least a thousand pounds. They would crush the girl to death.

"Move!" I screamed, but the little girl still didn't look up.

Terror ripped through me as I got within feet of her and looked up to see the first pipe less than a dozen feet away. I wrapped my arm around the little girl's waist just as the ducks took flight. I heard her let out a little cry and prayed I'd hadn't hurt her. I flung myself forward as I saw the first pipe in my periphery and knew I wouldn't outrun it. I hit the ground hard, but managed not to crush the child beneath me. I felt a searing pain across the back of my shoulder as I curled myself around the little girl in the hopes I could protect her body from the impact. Seconds passed as I waited for darkness to claim me, but it never came. I could hear yelling and the splashing of water. I looked up to see both pipes had missed us and had landed in the water.

"Nicole!"

The young man's frantic voice had me shifting off the little girl who was crying beneath me. I quickly sat up, ignoring the pain in my shoulder and skimmed my hands over her, searching for any signs of blood. Thankfully, she looked okay.

"Oh my God, Nicole!" the man shouted as he reached us. He dragged her into his arms and held onto her as she cried. "It's okay, honey," he said as he gently pushed her back and began moving his fingers in front of her. It hit me then why she hadn't heard me telling her to run and hadn't reacted to the crash at all.

Because she was deaf.

"Are you okay? Are you hurt?" the man said out loud as his fingers flew.

The girl watched his fingers and then shook her head as she signed something back to him. He dragged her back into his arms.

"Thank you!" he said to me and then he reached out to touch my arm. "Thank you so much!"

"You're welcome," I said with a nod.

"Are you guys all right?" one of the construction workers yelled as he came tearing down the hill. Several more men followed. One of them helped me to my feet as another helped the young man and girl up. The girl clung to him and he picked her up. She wrapped herself around him and continued to cry.

"We're okay," he said. "Can someone go inside and find their father? He's with Phoenix Jones. Room 127."

"I will," one of the construction workers said as he turned to run back up the hill.

He knew Phoenix? I was about to ask him how he knew Phoenix when he said, "Jamie" and turned to make sure the little boy was still okay.

"I'll get him," I offered, since it looked like the boy was on the verge of tears.

"Thank you," he said

I moved out of the circle of men surrounding us and hurried up to the little boy who'd managed to climb off the swing.

"Hi, my name's Levi. What's yours?" I asked, though I already knew.

"I want Daddy," he whispered.

"I know you do," I said softly. My shoulder hurt like a son of a bitch, but I ignored it and leaned down to pick him up. He put his arms around my neck and I quickly turned and started walking back to the young man who was still standing in the same spot, reassuring the lingering construction workers that the girl was okay.

As I neared him, I heard someone yell, "Tristan?"

I saw two men at the top of the hill, one blond and a little shorter, the other one older with brown hair.

"She's okay, Seth! They're both okay," the young man holding the little girl called.

I froze when I heard the name Seth. My heart leapt into my throat as I watched the blond run down the hill towards us.

"What happened?" the man, Seth, asked as he reached us and took the little girl into his arms. I felt bile creep up the back of my throat as I took in his features.

It couldn't be.

But it was. I'd never forget those eyes. Even if I hadn't seen a recent picture of Seth Nichols, now known as Seth Grisham, I would have recognized those eyes anywhere. The ones who'd pleaded with me for help.

The ones I'd had to look into as I'd done nothing.

"Daddy Seth," the little boy called, his voice heavy with tears.

"Come here, buddy," Seth said as he held out one arm for his son.

He had kids.

I was too shell-shocked at first to move, but when the little boy began squirming in my hold, I quickly carried him over to Seth and put him on his feet. The girl, Nicole, had calmed and was leaning against Seth's chest. He was kneeling in the grass so when Jamie reached him, he tucked him up against his body and asked him if he was okay.

My eyes fell on a man standing just behind Seth. He was muscular with cropped, light brown hair. He was wearing what looked like black military pants and a black T-shirt. But what unnerved me were his eyes.

Because they were fixed on me and it looked a lot like he either recognized me or was trying to figure out if he did.

But that wasn't possible, was it?

Then I remembered the other young man, Tristan, talking about Phoenix. That Seth had been with Phoenix.

As I put two and two together, I shook my head in disbelief.

Phoenix and Seth knew each other. What did that even mean?

"He saved Nicole, Seth...I couldn't get to her in time. Sorry, I don't even know your name."

I realized the young man, Tristan, was talking to me and I glanced at him. But I couldn't speak. I couldn't do anything but stand there and try to make sense of things. But as soon as I looked back at Seth, everything fell into place.

Because he most definitely recognized me. I saw it in his stunned expression. And I saw the way he hugged his kids tighter.

And if he knew who I was, it meant Phoenix did too.

Fear speared through me and I took several steps back. "I have to go," I said and then I turned and began walking towards my car. Within a few steps, I was running.

"Reese, don't," I heard someone, Seth probably, say, "Let him go."

I no longer felt the pain in my shoulder as I sprinted to my car. All I could think about was one thing.

And it wasn't that Seth Nichols knew who I was.

It was that Phoenix had lied to me.

~

*I*'d only been sitting in the church for about twenty minutes before I heard the door behind me open. I knew it wasn't Father O, since he'd mentioned going to the hospice this afternoon to visit patients there and wouldn't be back for a while yet. Since I'd told him I was going to the rehab center to check on Phoenix, he'd said he'd have Patrick and Sherry come in early to prepare the meal so Phoenix could focus on his daughter and I could focus on Phoenix.

Phoenix, who'd lied to me.

From day one.

Though I had no idea why.

And in truth, I didn't care why. I wanted to know how.

After everything he'd said to me…after last night…

My eyes burned, even though I hadn't shed a single tear since leaving the rehab center. Probably because my body had nothing left to give. *I* had nothing left to give. Which was why when I turned around and saw a dark-haired man standing just inside the church doors, I felt only relief.

Not because he wasn't Phoenix.

But because I knew who he was. His picture had been right next to Seth's in the article I'd read about Seth's wedding to a trauma surgeon named Ronan Grisham.

The gun hanging loosely in the man's hand at his side had me guessing he wasn't just a trauma surgeon. Another piece clicked into place for me as I remembered Phoenix telling me he worked in security. Perhaps that was his link to Seth.

It didn't matter.

I stood and turned around, but didn't step out of the pew, mostly because I didn't know how these things were done. Would he shoot me right here? Was he going to take me somewhere and get rid of me so my body would never be found?

Not that anyone would look too hard.

"Do you know who I am?" Ronan asked as he stepped forward.

I nodded. "You're Seth's husband."

Ronan's jaw tightened and I wondered how my simple statement could have caused the reaction.

"Are you going to do it here? Or someplace else?" I asked. "Father O doesn't deserve to have it happen in his church," I said, though I knew this man wouldn't give a shit about that.

"So you know why I'm here?"

I nodded.

"You don't deny it?"

"No," I said. "I did it."

"I knew giving you a second chance was a mistake," Ronan murmured. "I told Seth as much, but he was adamant that people can change…that you could change."

His comment confused me, but I kept quiet. What did he expect me to say? Did he expect me to defend myself? Beg for mercy?

"There's an alley outside…can you do it…do it out there?" I asked. I knew my priorities were fucked up that I was more worried about messing up Father O's church, but I wasn't exactly at my best.

"Ronan."

The sound of Phoenix's voice had me closing my eyes. I forced myself to open them and saw Phoenix standing in the doorway to the right of the altar that led to the back of the church where the soup kitchen was housed. The sight of him had my heart swelling with love and that feeling was instantly followed by a cruel, sharp pain at the reminder that this man had betrayed me. Like Ronan, Phoenix was armed, but his gun was also at his side as he moved farther into the room. By the time he was standing at the other end of the aisle, I felt like I was caught in some fucked up O.K. Corral showdown.

The men stared each other down. Phoenix never took his eyes off Ronan as he said, "Levi, get behind me."

I wanted to laugh and cry at the same time.

"You know each other?" I asked.

"I work for him," Phoenix said.

I shook my head. "So that day in the alley, you weren't going to your car, were you?"

"No," he responded quietly. He still wouldn't look at me. "I was hired to follow you…and to eliminate you if you stepped out of line."

He was a hitman.

I did laugh then, but it was because my emotions were so far beyond my control that I could do nothing else. I'd been played for a fool and I'd fallen for every line he'd fed me.

"So it was all a lie?" I whispered, though I hadn't meant to ask that. Because it changed absolutely nothing.

"No," he said and then he did look at me. "It wasn't. Please get behind me, Levi."

I finally saw the fear in his eyes and I looked back and forth between the two men. I let the sting of betrayal fade away for the moment as I realized what was happening.

Phoenix was choosing me.

For whatever reason, he was going against his boss. Even knowing everything I'd done to the man's husband, he was still siding with me.

I stepped forward out of the pew, but I didn't go to him. I backed away from him so he couldn't easily reach forward and grab me. "I don't want to run anymore, Phoenix. I'm tired," I said softly. "So fucking tired."

"I know you are, baby, but we can figure this out."

I shook my head as he stepped forward and I took several more steps back, putting myself closer to the man behind me. His eyes went from me to Ronan.

"Ronan, don't do this! He's no threat to Seth anymore."

I turned to face Ronan and saw his cold eyes shift between me and Phoenix. "If you knew that for a fact, you would have proved it to me," he said.

"I do know it! But I knew you wouldn't listen. I knew you wouldn't see reason-"

Ronan suddenly lifted his gun and pointed it at me. "You come talk to me about seeing reason when the man you love's life is at stake!" he snapped.

"I am!" Phoenix retorted and a glance over my shoulder showed Phoenix had raised his gun too and he'd shifted enough so that he could shoot around me if he had to.

Fuck, this was getting out of control.

Before I could say anything, the church door opened and I stiffened at the sight of Seth entering the church, followed by a tall, dark-haired man. It wasn't the same man from the rehab center.

"Ronan?"

Ronan flinched at the sound of his husband's voice.

"What are you doing here, Seth?"

Seth walked to his husband's side and then stepped in front of his raised arm without any kind of hesitation. Ronan instantly lowered the weapon, but kept his eyes on me.

"I called Memphis after I recognized Levi. Reese called you, didn't he?"

Ronan nodded. "He told me *he*" – Ronan motioned towards me with the gun, but kept it lowered – "was there."

"And did he tell you that he saved our daughter's life?"

Ronan's eyes snapped to his husband. "What?" His gaze came back to me for a moment. "I...I hung up on Reese after he told me about Levi. I didn't answer when he tried to call me back. Is Nicole-"

"She's fine. She and Jamie are with Tristan and Reese. I asked Reese what he was doing there and he told me you've been having him shadow me for weeks. When you wouldn't answer your phone, I called Memphis and told him what had happened. He knew what you were planning and tracked your phone."

Ronan glanced over his shoulder at the dark-haired man before looking back at Seth. "What happened?" he asked.

"There was an accident with some construction equipment near the spot the kids were waiting with Tristan for me. The chain holding some culvert pipes snapped and the pipes rolled down the hill towards the pond. Nicole was feeding the ducks so she didn't see what was happening."

I heard Seth's voice crack and Ronan's free hand immediately came up to grab one of Seth's.

"Tristan was too far away to reach her. If Levi hadn't...if he hadn't gotten to her in time, we would have lost her, Ronan," Seth whispered.

Ronan swallowed hard and then he pulled his husband against his chest. They held on to each other for a long time before Seth stepped back.

"He's still a threat to you, Seth," Ronan said. "I saw the footage of him and his friend from a couple of days ago. Right before he went back to your old house."

I stiffened at that. They knew I'd gone back to the Nichols house?

"Levi," I heard Phoenix say and I was surprised to find him just a couple of feet behind me. I hadn't even heard him move. "Tell us what you and T talked about at the store the other night...the night you got the bruises."

I was so confused that I nodded and said, "T's been trying to get me to help him. First he wanted me to help him steal prescription drugs from the pharmacy of the store I work at. A couple of days ago, he told me he wanted me to help him steal money from Betty. She owns the store and a lot of other ones just like it. He wanted me to go to her house and get her to let us inside. She's got a lot of money so he wanted to rob her."

My throat felt tight as I realized what I was saying. I shot Seth a glance and saw how pale he'd gone.

I dropped my eyes and said, "He had his brother, Gun, hurt my friend Hank in prison to blackmail me into helping him. He said...he said if I didn't help him, Hank would be killed."

"So he never talked to you about going after Seth?" Phoenix asked.

"What? No!" I said, completely stunned. Was *that* what they'd thought? "No! Why would you think that?" I asked as I turned to look at Seth and Ronan.

"You've returned to the house on Mercer Island four times," Ronan said, his voice carrying an accusatory edge to it. "The house Seth grew up in. The house you and your brother and Jed broke into seven years ago."

I felt like I was going to be sick. I shook my head in disbelief. "You thought I was going there to...to case the place or something? So I could try again?"

"Why else would you return?" the dark-haired man asked. Seth had called him Memphis. I had no fucking clue who he was or how he fit into any of this.

"Because I..."

I realized what I'd been about to blurt out and snapped my mouth shut.

"Because you what?" Ronan asked.

I felt Phoenix's hand on my back. I wanted to shrug it off because I felt too raw inside to deal with it. To deal with any of this.

"Because I wanted to go back, okay?" I admitted as tears stung my eyes. "I wanted to go back to that night and try to find something, anything, I could have done different. I wanted to pretend that you" – my eyes fell on Seth – "and your parents were asleep in your beds and that everything was fine and that fucking night had never happened." I dashed at the tears that fell. "I imagined you graduating from high school and your parents throwing you a party. I imagined you getting ready to leave for college and your mom..." My voice broke as Corinne Nichols's screams rang in my ear.

My knees buckled. Phoenix caught me as I sank to the floor. "I imagined your mom hugging you goodbye over and over again and crying and then watching you drive off." I was dimly aware of

Phoenix's arm going around my shoulders, but it did nothing to ease the cold that was starting to seep through my veins.

"Why did you leave this morning without talking to me?" Phoenix asked.

"Because I knew you'd try to stop me."

"Stop you from what?"

But I shook my head. "I just wanted one last day with Henry. I went to see Father O to tell him I wouldn't be able to volunteer at the soup kitchen anymore, but he told me you got a call about Amani." I lifted my eyes to his. "Is she okay?" I asked.

He nodded. "She's fine. There was an issue with her feeding tube, but they got it sorted out by the time I got there."

Thank God.

"Levi, why did you need one more day with Henry? Why can't you volunteer here anymore?"

I shook my head again, but when Phoenix kissed my temple and whispered, "Please tell me," I caved.

"Because I don't want to live like this anymore. I knew T wouldn't stop and I didn't want Betty to get hurt so I knew I had to go to the cops. T…T and Gun hurt Hank. Because of me…to get to me. I knew it was never going to stop so I was going to tell the cops about T and what he wanted to do to Betty and then I was going to tell them what happened that night. I just needed time to say goodbye to Henry and call Children's Services. .I wanted them to take him away from Dina so she and my father couldn't do to him what he and Ricky did to me."

I felt Phoenix's hand rubbing my back, but when he rubbed over my shoulder, I winced. His hand stilled. "Are you hurt?" he asked.

I shook him off and climbed to my feet.

I didn't dare approach Seth, but I made sure to face him when I said, "You deserve justice for everything that happened that night. I don't know where Jed is, but my brother, Ricky, is dead. He's the one who hurt your mom," I managed to say. "I wanted to give you the chance to confront me in a courtroom, but you can do it here too. I don't care. I'll listen to anything you want to say to me and then you can decide my punishment. Whether it's prison or death, it doesn't matter. I deserve it. All of it."

Seth still had ahold of Ronan's hand, but he didn't say anything at first. When he went to open his mouth, Phoenix cut him off.

"Seth, I need to ask you a question before you say anything."

Seth's eyes shifted to Phoenix before he nodded.

"That night...do you remember anything that happened after you were stabbed?"

"Bits and pieces," Seth said softly. "The man with the snake tattoo coming at me, someone screaming the word no, the paramedics telling me to hang on."

"After you were stabbed, did you move at all?"

"No," he said with a shake of his head. "I don't think so."

"He didn't," Ronan said. "I saw the crime scene. The paramedics worked on him in the same spot he was stabbed...I could tell from the amount of blood on the floor. Most of it was limited to the spot where Seth and his father were attacked."

I was certain I was going to be sick again as an image of Fred Nichols went through my head.

"Seth, if you didn't move, who called 911?"

"What?" he asked as his brow furrowed in confusion.

"Who notified the paramedics?"

Seth turned to glance at his husband, but Ronan shook his head. "Your mother?" he asked.

"No, my parents didn't keep a phone in the bedroom...not even their cell phones. My mom didn't like how many calls my dad would get, even at night, so they left their phones downstairs when they went to bed."

"Seth, while Jed was attacking you, Levi managed to call 911 from your house's landline. He wasn't sure if the call got through or not because he had to hide it from Jed. I had Daisy check the 911 records. The call *did* come from your house and not a neighbor who might have heard something. And that voice you heard saying no was Levi's. He said it right before Ricky discovered him making that call...and then stabbed him."

Seth's eyes shifted to me.

"It doesn't matter," I said. "It doesn't change anything."

"Yes, it does," Seth said.

"No! It doesn't! I saw the way you looked at me when I put that tape on your mouth. You were begging me to help you! And I did nothing!"

"Damn it, Levi!" Phoenix shouted. "There was nothing you could do! Your gun wasn't loaded, your brother and Jed were armed with guns and knives! You were a scared sixteen-year-old kid dealing with two psychopaths bent on murder!"

When Phoenix tried to grab me, I twisted free of his hold. "It doesn't matter!"

"Levi."

The sound of Seth's voice had me quieting and I turned to face him.

"I remember that moment too…when you put the tape on my mouth. Yes, I was terrified, but I saw the same thing in your eyes. Not that you didn't *want* to help me, but that you *couldn't* help me."

I hung my head and shook my head.

"I also remember you trying to stop Jed more than once."

"It wasn't enough," I murmured.

"It was," I heard Ronan say. "Seth's still here. He survived that night because of you. If you hadn't made that call…"

Disbelief tore through me at the way the man's voice cracked. Seth reached out to link their fingers together. Their eyes connected, but even without words, I knew what they were saying.

This was wrong. It had to be.

"You deserve justice," I whispered. "Your parents deserve it."

"We got it, Levi," Seth said softly as his damp eyes met mine. He smiled slightly as he continued. "And if my parents were here right now, my mom would be hugging you and my dad would be patting you on the back and inviting you over for dinner. Because that's what kind of people they were. You saved my life, Levi. And you saved my daughter's life. If I didn't think it would freak you out, I'd hug you myself."

I wanted to cry. Both because none of this made any sense to me and because deep down, I'd wanted him to forgive me. It wasn't something I'd ever admitted to myself though, because I didn't believe in wishing for the impossible.

"Levi?"

The sound of Father O's voice got my attention and I saw him standing in the doorway leading to the soup kitchen. His eyes scanned the room. Neither Phoenix nor Ronan had put their guns away. I didn't even know where to start with explaining to him what was happening. I was about to try when my eyes fell on what he was holding in his hand.

I moved past Phoenix and hurried to him.

"Is that...is that Henry's toy?" I asked as I took in the sight of Henry's stuffed caterpillar. I finally noticed how pale Father O looked.

"I...I just got back from the hospice. This" – he held the toy up – "was taped to the soup kitchen door. There was...there was a note attached to it."

He held up a small, folded piece of paper. I met his eyes and knew by the panicked look in them that he'd read it. I took it from him and forced myself to open it, though in my gut I knew what it was.

*The game's changed.*
*Call me or you'll never see the brat again.*
*206-555-2100*

"No," I whispered to no one in particular. But this time when my knees gave out, Phoenix wasn't there to catch me.

## CHAPTER 24

PHOENIX

*I* reached Levi seconds after he crumpled and fell to his knees. I'd already noticed the toy in Father O's hand, but I hadn't understood its importance until I'd seen Levi read the piece of paper Father O had handed him. I took the crumpled note from Levi's fingers and scanned it.

"Ronan!" I called as my heart threatened to punch through my chest.

I felt Ronan take the note from my hand. I got Levi upright and then led him to the first pew and sat him down.

"Father, when was the last time you used the door this was taped to?" I heard Ronan ask.

"When I left ..a couple of hours ago."

"Levi, look at me," I whispered. His skin was cold and I was worried he was going to have one of his episodes. Luckily, his eyes focused on mine "We'll get him back."

"He's just a baby," Levi murmured. "T wouldn't hurt a baby, would he?" he asked. But I knew he was asking me because he wanted me to lie to him.

Because he already knew enough about T to know the man likely wouldn't have any issue with hurting a child to get what he wanted.

"He needs him alive to get what he wants," I hedged. I looked up to see Ronan, Seth and Memphis surrounding us. "Memphis, can you go to Levi's apartment and see if you can find Henry's mother? Apartment 220."

"Seth, I need you to go with Memphis, okay?" Ronan said. His eyes shifted to Memphis. "Call Reese for backup."

Memphis nodded. Ronan gave Seth a quick kiss and then the pair were leaving the church.

"Levi, do you have your phone with you?" I asked.

He nodded. He was still clearly in a state of shock because his moves seemed sluggish. I listened as Ronan called Daisy and told her to prepare a trace.

"Baby, I need you to listen to me, okay?" I said. "I need your help to get Henry back."

My words seemed to snap Levi out of it and he quickly nodded. "Yes, okay."

"The good news is that T has no idea about us or what we're capable of. Ronan is going to have T's phone traced. But we can also hack the phone to see who he's called. So even if he doesn't have Henry with him, we'll have a good chance of finding where he stashed him."

"He's at an apartment near the airport," Ronan said as he handed me the note. "Daisy's hacking his phone now. It will be a few minutes before we see who he's called recently."

I nodded and then took Levi's phone and dialed the number. Before I hit send I said, "Levi, we just need to find out what he wants and then you need to agree to it, whatever it is. We're just buying time, nothing more."

"Okay," he said with a quick nod. He took the phone from me and when I nodded, he hit send.

"Put it on speaker."

He did as I asked and then we waited in utter silence.

T picked up on the fourth ring.

"Hello, Princess," he said. "You got my present, I see."

"Where's Henry, T?" Levi asked.

"Now, is that really how you want to start this conversation?" T asked.

"Please, T, I just need to know he's okay. I'll…I'll do anything you want."

"The little shit's fine. He's in good hands…it's a step up if you ask me. That bitch mother of his probably would have sold him to me for the coke if she hadn't been so busy offering me her pussy instead."

"Do you have Dina?" Levi asked.

"Princess, you really do need to focus. Unless you don't want the little squealer back."

Levi pulled in a breath and covered his mouth briefly as if trying to get control of himself. "Tell me what you want me to do."

"I want you to go to your little old lady friend and convince her to help you buy the kid back. I'm thinking she can afford a hundred grand."

I hit the mute button on the phone. "Don't give in right away or he'll get suspicious."

Levi nodded so I unmuted the phone.

"T, she's not going to give me that kind of money."

"Well, you better bat them pretty little eyes at her or whatever it is you faggots do to get what you want, because the clock's ticking for that kid."

"Okay, okay," Levi quickly said. "I'll get the money, I swear. Can you…can you send me a picture of Henry? She might want proof or something."

"Fuck, you're one stupid shit," T snapped. "Get the money, Levi. And next time I see you, keep in mind there won't be anyone to interrupt me this time around when that pussy of yours is wrapped around my dick."

My eyes shifted to Levi and I saw his cheeks fill with color.

"Call me when you've got the money," T bit out and then he hung up.

Levi shuddered and I took the phone from him. "What was he talking about, Levi?"

"Nothing."

"Levi-"

"It's nothing, Phoenix! It's not important."

Understanding dawned. "That day at the store. When he gave you the bruises. Did he…"

I couldn't even finish the thought because even the possibility made me violently ill.

"No," Levi murmured. "He tried, but Adam, the store manager, interrupted him."

I settled my hand on his shoulder and then kissed his temple. "I'm sorry, baby. I should have been there."

He shook his head, but didn't pull away from my touch. His phone beeped. I saw the text from T and opened the picture attachment. I felt the same relief as Levi when I saw a picture of Henry, unharmed and seemingly asleep in his car seat.

Ronan's phone rang and he stepped away to answer it. Levi didn't speak to me, nor would he make eye contact with me. He'd pulled his feet up onto the pew so he could wrap his arms around his legs and rest his forehead on his knees.

"T's only made one call today," Ronan said as he returned. "To a woman named Jalissa. Her apartment is at the same location where T's phone call came from."

"Henry's with T," Levi said, his voice heavy with fear.

"He'll be okay, Levi. Trust me."

I saw the flash of anger in his eyes before he could mask it. I hadn't allowed myself much time to think about the damage I'd done to our relationship with my lies, but I hoped like hell he'd give me a chance to make it up to him when this was all over.

"We need to go," Ronan said.

"Levi, I need you to stay here with Father O."

"No!" he said as he jumped up. "I'm coming."

"No," I said, but Levi ignored me and pushed past me. I shot Father O a glance. "We'll call you as soon as we can, Father."

The man nodded. "I'll pray for you."

I nodded because I wasn't above receiving some divine intervention. Not when Henry's life was at stake.

I followed Ronan to his car. Levi got into the back seat without hesitation. As we drove, I took Ronan's phone when Memphis called. I put it on speaker.

"Did you find her?"

"Yeah," Memphis said, his voice heavy. "Not in her apartment though. We saw a stroller sitting by the alley when we got here. I had Seth stay in the car while I checked it out."

I glanced over my shoulder at Levi who was listening attentively.

"I found her behind a dumpster at the back of the building. Strangled."

I heard Levi gasp and turned to see him with his hand over his mouth.

"Did you call it in?" Ronan asked.

"Yeah, I called Declan."

"Good," Ronan said. "Tell him what's going on, but make sure he knows we don't need backup. If T sees even a single patrol car, he might panic and do something stupid."

"Okay. Seth and I will wait here for Declan and his guys. Keep us posted."

"We will," I said and then I hung up. I looked at Levi again and saw he was barely holding it together.

"She...she was a shitty mom, but she didn't deserve that," Levi whispered.

"I know," I responded, because what else could I say?

Once we reached the apartment, we parked a street over where T wouldn't be able to see us. I was torn with what to do next because I didn't want to leave Levi in the car, but I knew Ronan and I would both need to go to the apartment to get Henry. I got out of the car and opened Levi's door. I extended my hand into the backseat and waited until he took it. I urged him out of the car and then leaned him against it, caging him in with my body.

"I know you hate me right now, and I can't say I blame you, but I need you to do what I tell you. And not just because I don't want to put you or Henry at risk, but because if I have to worry about you for even a second, it could get me or Ronan killed. And I don't think you want that."

"No," he quickly said. "And I don't hate you," he whispered.

I leaned down and kissed him. "I need you to stay in the car and lock the doors. If you hear gunshots, I need you to stay in the car. If you see T, I want you to duck down so he can't see you. If you are at risk of getting hurt at any time, you take the keys and drive away." I caught the car keys when Ronan tossed them to me.

"Please, promise me you'll do that for me."

"I promise," Levi said solemnly.

I kissed him again, but when I went to pull away, he grabbed my arm. "Promise you'll come back. All three of you," he said as he glanced over at Ronan.

"Promise," I whispered and then I pressed a soft kiss against his lips.

"I love you," I said, but I didn't wait to see if he'd say it back. I was afraid he wouldn't. "Get in the car and lock it," I urged as I left his side and strode around the car.

As Ronan and I approached the building, I glanced at him and said, "Thank you for this."

He nodded. "I think we both have some things we need to say to each other when this is over," he murmured. "I fucked up. I put my fear for one family member above my trust of another."

His words warmed me and gave me hope that maybe my friendship with this man wasn't beyond repair.

"I'm not sure I would have behaved any differently. I understand that now," I said. "I wouldn't have before Levi."

Ronan nodded and then he gave me a slap on the back. "Let's do this."

The apartment building wasn't big and the neighborhood was even worse than Levi's. The few people on the streets sent glances our way, but didn't do anything more than quicken their strides when they saw us pulling our guns out. I suspected guns weren't anything new for the residents around here.

"Fire escape," I said. Daisy had given Ronan enough information to confirm there were only six apartments in the building and that Jalissa's was on the top floor facing the street. Like Levi's apartment, there was a fire escape in front of the window. But unlike the day I'd climbed up from the bottom of it to get to Henry, I needed to be quieter this time around so I wanted to climb down from the roof. Ronan and I entered the building and took our time clearing the stairwell as we made our way to the third floor. Ronan waited as I went to the door leading to the roof and quickly picked the lock. It took just minutes to get to the fire escape. I'd put in the earpiece for the communications system that would allow me to interface with Ronan through an identical earpiece he was using while I'd been in the car.

"I'm at the fire escape," I said.

"Copy."

I carefully climbed over the edge and tested the fire escape to make sure it would hold my weight. Fortunately, it was more solidly put together than it looked. It also didn't make as much noise as I'd expected.

"I'm in place."

Since I didn't know where in the apartment T was, I waited until I heard Ronan knock on the door and announce himself as an employee for the utility company. I hoped his ploy about investigating a gas leak would work. I gave him a couple seconds, then dropped down to the landing just outside the window. The glass was dirty and scratched, but I could make out T sitting on the couch in front of a TV. A woman was heading for the door.

As soon as she opened it, T jumped up and pulled a gun out of his waistband. But instead of pointing it at Ronan, he ran down a hallway. I rushed to the next window and saw T storm into an almost empty bedroom.

Empty except for the car seat sitting in the middle of it. I didn't hesitate at all to fire right through the window. I saw T go down before he was able to get off a shot and as I kicked in the window, Ronan appeared, the woman following.

"He's okay," Ronan called as he approached the car seat. I kicked in what was left of the glass and stepped into the apartment and then went around the car seat. Relief flooded my system at the sight of Henry's scrunched up face. He let out a loud wail.

It was the best sound I'd ever heard.

I knelt down and unbuckled him from his seat and lifted him to my shoulder. "I've got you, Henry," I murmured as I patted his back. I reached into my pocket and pulled out the caterpillar toy and handed it to him. He settled quickly as his fingers closed around it.

"Come on, let's go find your daddy," I said. Even though Levi wasn't Henry's biological father, he'd most certainly earned the title and then some.

Ronan grabbed the car seat and, with the woman in tow, followed me from the apartment. I heard him talking on his phone, presumably to Declan Barretti, a captain in the Seattle Police Department. The man and his extended family had become close to Ronan and several of his men over the past year.

When we exited the apartment, I was glad to see that Levi wasn't just outside the apartment building. He'd kept his word because as we rounded the building, he was still sitting in the car. As soon as he saw us, he jumped out and ran to us. I gladly handed him the baby as he cried and thanked me and when he put his arm around me, I hugged him back.

I just hoped it wasn't for the last time.

## CHAPTER 25

### LEVI

I didn't hear the knocking on the front door at first because I was too busy staring at the spot where my brother's bed had once been. After his death, I'd taken every one of my brother's possessions, along with the twin bed, and carried them down to the dumpsters. I'd done it on the day the garbage was being picked up and I'd waited until after my father had gone to work to do it. He'd beaten the shit out of me for it when he'd gotten home that night, but I hadn't cared.

It had been worth it.

Because nothing of my brother had remained after that.

I'd even gone through the family albums my mother had left behind and found every single picture of Ricky and removed them. I hadn't even once considered saving any of the pictures for Henry because I hadn't wanted him to know anything about his father. I hadn't really planned how I'd handle it when he grew up, but now it didn't matter.

Because Henry was gone.

I'd thought I'd been prepared to let him go, but it had nearly killed me. Maybe because I hadn't expected it to happen so quickly after getting him back. I'd still been reeling from the fact that T had taken him in the first place. Then Phoenix had carried him out of that apartment, unharmed, and I'd lost it. Less than an hour later, a woman from Children's Services had shown up at my apartment to take Henry away.

She'd said it was until things could be straightened out with custody since Dina was dead.

But I knew there'd been nothing to straighten out.

Henry was gone and it was for the best.

Phoenix was gone too, but only because I'd pushed him away.

As we'd gotten back to my apartment building after the cops had arrived at T's place, I'd taken Henry into my apartment and answered the questions the police officer who seemed to be friends with Phoenix and Ronan had asked me. Both men had stayed with me throughout it all, but when I'd told the cop that I had a confession to make about something, Ronan had stepped in and asked his friend to give us a minute alone. When the cop had stepped out, Ronan had told me that neither he nor his husband wished to see me go to prison for something I hadn't done.

I'd tried arguing with him, but the man was even more stubborn than Phoenix. He told me that if I confessed, Seth wouldn't back up my story at all. He was fully prepared to say only two people had been involved in his parents' deaths.

None of it had made sense to me, but I couldn't deny that I was secretly relieved.

Because I really didn't want to go back to prison. And if Seth didn't benefit from me being punished, it almost made the whole thing moot. In effect, Ronan and Seth had taken the wind out of my sails.

And now I had no idea what to do with myself.

After the cops had left and Henry had been taken away, it had just been Phoenix and me since my father hadn't been around. But I hadn't been ready to talk to Phoenix and I'd told him as much. When he'd pressed the issue, I'd told him a half-truth...that I no longer trusted him.

I'd never forget the look of hurt in his eyes for as long as I lived. He'd left after that and I hadn't heard from him again.

My words had been partially true. Because that was how I'd felt at the time. Now, I wasn't so sure. Yes, he'd lied to me. But the more I'd thought about things from his side, I'd started to understand the position he'd been in. And I hadn't exactly been forthcoming about my relationship with T. Through his eyes, my actions *had* looked suspicious. And while it was too late to do anything about it now, I realized if I'd told him about T and what he'd been doing, Phoenix would have believed me.

I'd been tempted to call him a few times over the past week, but every time I dialed, I hung up again.

Because I had nothing to offer him.

And because I now understood what Seth, his husband and their children meant to Phoenix. They were his family.

I couldn't take that from him. Because even if Seth and Ronan had forgiven me, I was still a reminder of what Seth had lost, what had been taken from him. That fact didn't exactly make for comfortable family get-togethers.

And I couldn't begrudge Phoenix his family.

Another round of knocking had me getting up off the bed and grabbing my single duffle bag. It was surreal to finally be leaving the place I'd spent so many of my worst years in. I hadn't bothered telling my father I was moving out, because I didn't care what happened to him. I owed him nothing and with Dina dead and Henry gone, there was nothing tying me to this hellhole anymore. I had no clue what I was going to do, but I knew it would start at the bus station. I had a few hundred dollars in my pocket, my last paycheck from work, and I was going to use a good chunk of it to buy a ticket to anywhere but here.

I'd been tempted to move closer to Walla Walla which was where Washington State Penitentiary was, but being closer to Hank and not being able to interact with him beyond a phone and a sheet of plexiglass didn't make sense. Especially since Hank had made me promise when I'd left that place, that I'd never set foot back in it, even to visit him.

Hank had been returned to prison, but I wasn't sure if the guards would heed the warning Ronan and Phoenix's cop friend had sent their way about Gun being a threat to Hank. My hope was that Jasper was able to watch out for Hank. With T dead, I was worried Hank would become even more of a target.

I dropped my bag next to the couch and opened the door. I froze at the sight of Seth standing on the other side.

"Hi, Levi."

"Hi," I managed to get out, though even the single word seemed to be a challenge for my addled brain.

"Can I come in?"

I opened the door wider for him and then looked around the room. I needed to offer him a place to sit, but the place was a mess. Beer bottles were all over the place and our couch was so old that it was ripped and stained everywhere. Humiliation flooded through me.

"Um, do you mind sitting at the kitchen table?" I finally asked.

"Sure, sounds good."

"Do you want something to drink?" I asked, though I couldn't offer him anything besides beer and tap water. And since it was just after eleven in the morning, I doubted a beer was on the menu.

"No, thanks."

I sat down across from him and prayed the wobbly vinyl chair he was sitting in wouldn't break. "What…what are you doing here?" I asked.

"I wanted to come talk to you about something."

"Okay." I knew I probably sounded like a suspicious jerk, but he was the last person I ever expected to see again.

"Are you going somewhere?" he asked when he saw my duffle bag.

I nodded. "I'm leaving."

"Seattle?" he asked.

"Yeah. Too many memories," I murmured, then realized how insensitive I sounded. "Sorry."

He waved his hand and shook his head. "No, I hear you."

He fell silent and an ugly thought suddenly occurred to me. "Did you and your husband change your minds?" I asked. "About pressing charges?" I hated the fear that swirled in my belly at the prospect of losing the freedom I'd just found, but I wouldn't protest if he'd had a change of heart.

"What? No," Seth said quickly. "I just wanted to make sure you were okay. Phoenix told me about everything you did for Henry...I know it must have been hard to lose him like that."

I felt tears start to fall at the mention of Henry's name. I wiped at them with my sleeve. "He was innocent, you know? I just wanted him to have the best life possible."

"Better than the one you had?"

I briefly wondered exactly how much Phoenix had told him, but I realized it didn't matter, so I just nodded.

"Then why are you leaving?"

"What?" I asked as I looked up at him.

"Why don't you stay and fight for him?"

"Fight for him?" I asked. "Didn't you hear what I said? I want him to have the best life he can."

"And you don't think you can give him that?" Seth asked.

Anger went through me. I wondered if he was deliberately being cruel just to get back at me. "I never graduated high school. I'm a convicted felon. I bag groceries and stock shelves for a living and that's the best I'll ever do when it comes to a career. I'm a single, gay man with no house, no car, no money and absolutely no prospects."

"That's interesting, but you didn't actually answer my question."

I sighed in frustration. "I could have given him all the love he ever wanted, but sometimes that's not enough, you know?"

"No, I don't know," Seth returned. "After I lost my parents, I had everything you just listed. Great career, more money than I'll ever need...I would have traded every bit of it for five more minutes with my parents. Not because of how much money they had or any of that shit," he said. "Yeah, my parents were rich and successful, but that isn't what I miss every day. That isn't what made me into who I am. They loved me. Even if they'd been the poorest people on earth, they would have loved me just the same. *That's* what sticks with me. *That's* what I want to give my own children."

"Okay, yes, I thought about it for like five minutes and I thought I could give him the important stuff."

"But?"

"But I knew no one else would see it that way. They'd look at my history, my family, my future and they'd know I wasn't good enough to be his father."

"So that's all that's stopping you?" he asked.

I laughed. "Yeah, that's all," I said sarcastically.

Seth studied me for a moment and then he reached for his phone. When whoever on the other end answered, he said, "You can come on up."

I tensed as I wondered if this was all some elaborate joke to mess with me. Maybe the cops were on their way upstairs to arrest me.

As Seth got up to open the door, I forced myself to my feet. I would accept my fate, even if it was no longer the one I'd choose for myself.

But it wasn't a police officer who walked through the door.

I didn't recognize the man at all. Of course, I barely spared him a glance because my eyes were on one thing and one thing only.

The familiar red and black car seat with the scuffed handle.

The man turned the car seat to face me as he headed in my direction and my breath caught at the sight of Henry. The baby began thrashing his arms excitedly when he saw me, though he didn't let go of the stuffed caterpillar in his hand.

"Henry," I breathed as the man set the car seat on the table. I looked up at him, but couldn't find my voice to ask the question.

"Yeah, go ahead," the man said.

I quickly unbuckled Henry and lifted him up. He felt so good in my arms that I started to cry. I didn't even care that both men could see me. When I'd calmed down enough so that I could breathe normally, I looked at Seth and the other man.

"Levi, this is my friend, Zane Devereaux. He's a lawyer specializing in family law. He also acts on behalf of children in custody cases."

"Hi, Levi," Zane said as he stepped forward and shook my hand.

"Hi," I croaked. I went to the kitchen to grab a dishtowel to wipe my face because I knew I was a mess.

"Do you mind if we sit?" Zane asked as he motioned to the kitchen table. I only had the two chairs, but when I looked at Seth, he motioned me to the table and then leaned back against the arm of the couch.

"Seth was telling me about your case and I wanted to let you know what your options are. As one of Henry's only remaining living relatives, you have the right to seek custody of him."

"But…but I'm not qualified. I was in prison."

"I'll get to that in just a second," Zane said, though I had no clue what he meant. "In custody cases, the family court judge's job is to do what is best for the child. The fact that you are Henry's blood is a big benefit. But more importantly, you've been acting as Henry's father from the time he was born, both financially and emotionally. You have been the one constant in his life and the judge will take that into consideration, more so than just about anything else. You have a stable job with health insurance and you've made sure Henry's medical needs have been met…I've already confirmed that with his doctor. As for your felony conviction, there are a couple of things that have come to my attention."

Hope began to bloom in my chest the more this man spoke, but I tried to tamp it down because I wouldn't survive getting my hopes up only to have them dashed again.

"I checked out your case after Phoenix told me that the drugs were for your brother. Your court-appointed attorney pushed you towards a guilty plea when he shouldn't have. Not only was it your first offense, but they never did a drug test. Your attorney should have had a hair follicle drug test done to prove you hadn't used drugs in the previous ninety days. I've checked with the State and it turns out your lawyer is currently under investigation for a slew of infractions. That, plus the lack of a drug test, means your conviction will likely be overturned. If you're open to it, I'd like to take on your case. I'll have a colleague handle the family court case so there isn't a conflict of interest. With the new facts about your lawyer and the lack of proof that you used drugs, the prosecutor will likely knock the charge down to a misdemeanor, if he doesn't drop the case altogether. No matter which route he takes, the family court judge will likely rule in your favor once he sees the evidence."

I was completely overwhelmed by what he was telling me. "I...I can't afford to pay for a lawyer," I said as I cuddled Henry against my chest, afraid that they'd suddenly snatch him from me just because I didn't have the money all this would cost. "But I can get it...I can make payments," I added quickly.

"We'd be handling your cases pro bono," Zane said.

"What does that mean?"

"It means there's no charge."

I felt incredibly stupid because I still couldn't make sense of what he was telling me. "What, like it would be free?"

"Yes."

"But why?" I asked and then I looked at Seth. "Why would you do that for me?"

"It's not just for you, Levi," Seth said. "It's for Henry. He should be with his father."

A whole new round of tears began to fall.

"Are you okay with Zane taking on your case?" Seth asked. I was surprised to find he'd moved next to me and he was patting me on the shoulder. There was still a little bit of lingering pain from when the pipe had hit me, but I didn't care.

I nodded.

"Good," Zane said. "I've gotten the court to grant you temporary custody," he continued. "So if you're up to it, Henry will stay with you going forward."

I wanted to say yes, but reality came crashing down. I couldn't stay in this apartment a moment longer. I could maybe afford a hotel for a few days, but I'd already quit my job. My dreams were being snuffed out one by one as I considered all the obstacles in my way.

"I don't have a place to stay and I quit my job already," I whispered.

"I've spoken to Betty Carlisle and she says your job is ready and waiting if you want it back. There won't be any lapse in your employment," Zane said.

"Really?"

"And we'll help you figure out something with finding a place to stay," Seth said.

"Thank you," I managed to croak out.

"There's one more thing I want to talk to you about. Your friend Hank," Zane said.

"What about him?"

"Phoenix told us how important he is to you and what he did for you in prison. He also told us about what put him there," Seth said.

"I've contacted Hank and offered to represent him in his appeal. Like with you, I found some issues with how his plea deal was handled. I can't guarantee anything, but there's a chance we can get him a new trial. We've also managed to have Hank moved to a different prison…one in Monroe which is about thirty minutes north of the city. He'd be allowed contact visits," Zane said.

Which meant I could touch Hank. Hug him. Let him hold Henry.

"I don't know what to say," I admitted. "Thank you doesn't seem like enough."

I saw Zane glance at Seth before he returned his attention to me. "It's us who should be thanking you, Levi. And by us, I mean my entire family…Ronan and Seth's too. That little girl means the world to all of us," he said quietly and then he was standing up. He patted my shoulder and then said to Seth, "I'll wait down by the car."

As Zane left, Seth sat in the chair across from me. "I have something else I want to tell you, but I don't know if you even want to know."

"What is it?"

"Something's happened to Amani."

I stiffened and sat up, but before I could say anything, Seth continued. "Now, it's not my place to say what, but Phoenix needs you. If you still have any feelings for him-"

I didn't even let him finish before I jumped to my feet and said, "Can you give me and Henry a ride?"

I quickly tucked Henry back into the car seat and buckled him in while Seth went to grab my duffle bag. I followed him out of the apartment and down the stairs. Zane was waiting by the side of the car and opened the door for me.

The ride to the rehab center took forever, but Seth refused to tell me what had happened to Amani. He just repeated what he'd said earlier…that Phoenix needed me. Fear took hold of me as I wondered if the unthinkable had happened.

I was dimly aware of Seth following me into the building, but I didn't wait for him to keep up, though it wasn't really an issue since I was carrying Henry's car seat. I rushed to Amani's room and didn't even pause before flying through the door.

Phoenix was sitting by the little girl's bed, his back to me.

"Phoenix," I whispered.

He turned to look at me and I saw that he was crying. "No," I breathed. I put Henry's car seat down and walked right into his arms. His hug was brutally tight as he sobbed against my neck.

"It's okay," I said softly as I ran my fingers through his short hair.

"She's awake, Levi," he managed to get out.

I froze at his words. When he pulled back, he was smiling and he wiped at his tears. "She's awake," he said again and then he was tugging me towards the bed. My eyes settled on the little girl who was looking at me, but this time her eyes were actually *on* me.

"Peaches, I want you to meet someone," Phoenix said. "Again," he added with a laugh as he took my hand in his. A mix of confusion and joy went through me as understanding dawned and I jerked my gaze to where Seth was standing in the doorway. He smiled broadly at me and I finally realized I'd been had.

And I didn't care in the least. I smiled back and mouthed the words *thank you* to him. He nodded and then pointed to Henry's car seat and I nodded. I watched him take Henry out of the room, so I could put all my focus where it needed to be.

On Phoenix and his daughter.

# EPILOGUE

## PHOENIX

***T**hree months later*
"I can't do this."

"Yes, you can," I insisted as I came up behind Levi and put my arms around him. He was studying his appearance in front of the floor length mirror that was attached to the inside of the closet door. He'd dressed more formally than he needed to for family dinner, but I wasn't about to argue with him about it. He was already on edge about the night as it was.

He shook his head. "He says he's okay, but he can't be," he insisted. "Looking at me must be a constant reminder of that night."

I sighed because he and I had been having this argument for weeks. Every time Seth had reached out to invite us to family dinner, in fact. Levi had declined each time until Seth had finally showed up at our doorstep earlier in the week, Jamie and Nicole in tow, and invited himself to a playdate with Henry and Amani to force the issue with Levi.

"You're also a constant reminder that he still has his daughter because of you," I said as I turned him around to face me and loosened the top couple buttons of his button-down shirt.

"Those people will know I don't belong there," he said.

I hated that Levi's self-esteem continued to be an issue for him, but I knew it wouldn't be something he got over in a matter of days or weeks or even months. I'd finally convinced him to start seeing a therapist to discuss some of the trauma he'd faced as a child, but it was a double-edged sword because, while he was supposed to be honest with his therapist, there was one thing he could never tell her, since she'd be required to report it.

And it was the one thing that still haunted him.

The attack on Seth and his parents.

In the days after T's abduction of Henry, I'd mourned the loss of Levi. Him telling me he didn't trust me had hurt more than if he'd told me he didn't love me. The pain had been enough to have me curling in on myself. I'd managed to find enough strength to put things into motion after Seth had come to me to tell me about his plans to help Levi get custody of Henry, but three days after I'd said my goodbyes to Levi, I'd gotten the call I'd been waiting to get for more than a year.

*Amani is awake.*

Even now, the doctor's words caused my whole body to shudder in excitement. I'd forgotten everything else as I'd raced to the rehab center. When I'd run into Amani's room, she'd turned her head from where she'd been looking out the window and she'd smiled at me.

Just smiled.

Because she hadn't been able to talk then. The doctors had reassured me that she'd likely regain her speech, but that she would need time and lots of therapy. Her motor skills were compromised too. I'd held my daughter's hand as the doctors had explained it would take months, if not years, for Amani to learn to do things like talk, walk and eat again. But I hadn't cared because as I'd sat there, she'd held my hand. Not briefly as part of a reflexive movement. But really held it.

I'd been a mess for days after that.

Crying almost constantly every time Amani woke up from a nap and looked at me. I'd been terrified that she'd close her eyes and when she'd open them again, she'd be back in the vegetative state, so every time she'd looked at me and *seen* me, it had been like I was reliving that first moment all over again.

Seth, Tristan and the rest of the family had come to visit me in the days that followed, but they hadn't been who I'd needed.

That role had been reserved for one man and one man only. And he'd walked in and given me my second miracle a mere four days after I got my child back.

We hadn't talked that night about what had happened between us, but I'd known it was coming. When Tristan and Seth had come by the next day to sit with Amani so I could go home and get cleaned up, Levi had come with me. But when I'd brought it up as soon as we'd walked in the door, he'd kissed me and said that it didn't matter what had happened in the past. We were moving forward and that was it.

I'd thought for sure he'd harbor some anger towards me in the weeks that had followed, but he hadn't. When he hadn't been working, he'd been at my side with Amani.

Talking to her.

Reading to her.

Watching TV with her.

Seth had been the one to tell me that Levi had gotten Henry back, but that they'd had no place to stay, so I'd asked Levi to come stay with me, though I wasn't spending much time at the house. I'd even offered up my guest room in case Levi wasn't ready to go back to an intimate relationship, but he'd merely kissed me, told me that he loved me, and accepted my offer.

He never left.

Amani's therapy in the past few months hadn't been easy, but she'd started to regain the ability to speak. Her cognitive functions were better than her motor and physiological skills so we spent time playing games and reading books when she wasn't working with her team of therapists. A few weeks after she'd woken up, she'd gotten to go outside in a wheelchair and Levi and Henry and I had treated her to a picnic, though the food choices had been limited to the bland foods Amani was able to tolerate.

I'd finally stopped sleeping at the rehab center about a month earlier, but I still spent every day there. Levi and I hoped to go back to volunteering at the soup kitchen at some point, but between Henry and

Amani, we knew it wouldn't be as often as we would have liked. I'd donated some money to the church instead, and while I knew it helped, I still missed not being able to contribute in a more meaningful way.

Levi and Henry had settled into my home with no issue whatsoever and the one time Levi had mentioned finding his own place, I'd unashamedly begged him and his son not to move out...to stay with me and my daughter and make us a family.

He'd never brought up leaving again.

While I'd initially been worried that I'd done too much damage to our relationship to repair, Levi hadn't seen it the same way. The first full night I'd slept at home, he and I had made love. It had been just as amazing as the first time. The next night, Levi had fucked me for the first time and I'd loved every second of it. I'd never had a more passionate or giving lover than Levi, though he had a bit of dirty streak in him. After the first time he'd fucked me, we'd fallen asleep. I'd woken up to him pressed against my back, his dick notched between the globes of my ass. He'd fucked me in that exact position, but he'd told me if I didn't come, he'd reward me handsomely.

He had.

First with a toe-curling blow job.

Then again in the shower as I'd pressed him against the wall while he'd wrapped his legs around my waist.

"Daddy!"

"Yeah, Peaches, in here!" I called as I began to unbutton the cuffs of Levi's shirt and roll up his sleeves. My eyes fell on the reddened skin on his wrist. The burn was still healing all these months later, but Levi had gotten his wish. The tattoo was gone.

I pulled his wrist up to my mouth and pressed a gentle kiss against it. Levi's fingers brushed over my head and then he was pulling me to him for a kiss. The whir of Amani's electric wheelchair had me releasing him and turning to face my daughter. I smiled at the sight of Henry sitting happily on her lap.

Amani had been home for two weeks now, though I took her to rehab every day and likely would for at least a year until she fully recovered. She'd fallen completely in love with Henry and he with her. While the pair had separate rooms, they were otherwise inseparable.

"He needs changing," Amani said as she pinched her nose.

Levi chuckled and plucked Henry off her lap. Amani usually fed Henry and helped dress him, but her motor skills weren't strong enough to handle the intricacies of changing a dirty diaper.

"Daddy, can I wear this?" she asked as she looked down at her pink dress.

"It's perfect," I said. I leaned down to kiss the top of her head. "You look beautiful."

"Will the other kids like me?" she said. "Like this?" She motioned with her chin to the chair.

I bent down in front of her and said, "They're going to love you and they're going to love this," I said as I patted the chair's wheel. "Remind me to tell you about Mrs. Finney and her wheelchair on the way up there, okay? I suspect the other kids are going to want to see how fast you can get this thing to go."

"Really fast," she said with a nod.

"That's right," I said.

Levi returned with Henry. I took him and placed him back in Amani's lap. "Can you watch him while we finish getting ready?"

She nodded and carefully wrapped an arm around Henry as she maneuvered the chair around and rolled out of the room.

"I should change," Levi suddenly said and then he darted for the closet. I caught him around the waist and pulled him to me.

"No, you shouldn't."

I kissed him hard and said, "You're perfect and you belong at that family dinner because you're family. My family."

Levi sighed and wrapped his arms around my neck. "Sorry," he murmured.

"Don't be sorry," I reminded him.

He nodded against me. I knew his self-confidence was a work in progress, but he'd already grown by leaps and bounds. He'd started taking some night classes in the hopes he could eventually get his GED, though he wasn't sure what he wanted to do with his career. He was happy at the grocery store, especially since Betty had let him switch his hours to days. She'd also offered him on-the-job training so he could eventually become an assistant manager. Levi hadn't accepted yet, but more because he wasn't sure he could do it. But knowing Betty – and I did because I'd met the feisty woman several times now – she'd wear Levi down eventually.

Zane Devereaux had been a huge help in Levi's recovery as well, since he'd been working diligently to clear Levi's name. We'd learned just this morning that Levi's appeal for a new trial had been granted. Zane expected the prosecutor to drop the charges next. The talented lawyer had also continued to work on Hank's case, though it was proving to be trickier. But with Hank being in a prison where Levi could visit him often and have physical contact with him, both he and Hank had benefited just from that change. I'd met Hank on several occasions and was impressed with the man. He was still recovering from the attack three months earlier, but it hadn't changed his outlook on things. He'd cried when he'd gotten to meet and hold his namesake for the first time. The look on Levi's face as he'd watched his hero and his son meet had been priceless. When we'd left, I'd put my arms around Hank and I'd thanked him for saving Levi's life...in more ways than one. My hope was that Zane could work another miracle and Hank would get out of prison while Henry was still a child. Even if Hank eventually decided to try to reunite with his estranged wife and daughter, he'd still always be a part of our family.

"You ready to go?" I asked.

"No," he said with a laugh.

I gently lifted Levi's chin and kissed him. "I love you."

"I love you too."

I studied him for a long time, reveling in how much I really did love him. I smiled at him and said, "I'm going to do the thing."

"No," he said with a laugh. "You don't have to."

I ignored him and said, "Thanks for coming over."

His bright eyes stayed on mine as he shook his head. "God, I love you," he murmured. I lifted my thumb to stroke over his mouth.

"Thanks for coming over," I repeated. It was Levi's second favorite part of the movie he'd finally admitted to me was his favorite as a kid.

*Sixteen Candles.*

I hadn't ever seen it before, so one night I'd rented the movie and surprised him with it when he'd gotten home from class. After we'd put the kids to bed, we'd watched it and I'd finally understood his reference to me as Jake months earlier when we'd first met. As the last scene had played where the two characters finally get their shot at romance, Levi sighed over the last few lines and I'd started saying Jake's lines to him the very next day when he'd been stressed about an upcoming test.

"Thanks for coming to get me," he said.

"Make a wish, Levi."

Levi smiled briefly, but then he sobered and I saw that his answer might have been a line from a movie, but it was as real for him as it was for me.

"It already came true," he whispered.

I leaned down and kissed him. "I know, baby. For me too."

Then I took his hand in mine and led him from the room so we could go find our children and join the rest of our family for dinner.

The End

***Scroll to the next page for a Sneak Peek of Beck's story, Finding Hope***

## SNEAK PEEK

## FINDING HOPE (FINDING SERIES, BOOK 5) (M/M/M)

# PROLOGUE

## QUINN

The kid definitely didn't belong here. No question about it.

My eyes tracked his every move as he shifted past a couple of big bears who'd been loitering near the front door in hopes of snagging the freshest meat. And the kid was as close to fresh meat as you could find in a club like *The Blue Door*. Not only was there absolutely no chance he was over twenty-one, he barely looked like he was even legal. But he was trying his damnedest to play the game as he calmly made his way to the bar, ignoring the countless eyes on him.

He settled on one of the few empty barstools and pushed his shaggy brown hair out of his face as the bartender sauntered to a stop in front of him. Davey eyed the kid and I could tell he was on the same page as me when it came to the kid's age. But that didn't stop him from sliding a shot glass in front of him and filling it with what looked like the cheapest vodka Davey kept on the shelf. Only one of the barstools around the kid had been empty, but I knew it wouldn't last long. And sure enough, within a matter of seconds, a tall, scrawny looking guy with jeans that might as well have been painted on settled on the stool, only to skulk off when one of the bears from the front door ambled over and motioned to him with a jerk of his thick neck. Once the guy was gone, the bear leaned against the bar so his beefy body was practically brushing up against the kid's.

For his part, the kid seemed unconcerned as he glanced at his new neighbor just before he downed the shot. He tapped the bar and Davey was right there to refill the glass. He started putting the bottle away when the bear grabbed it and took a swig as he watched the young man swallow his second shot. I watched as the bear filled the shot glass yet again, but I didn't see if the kid drank it because I felt a hand stroking up my arm. I glanced to my right and saw a petite little blond number sizing me up. I was standing near the doorway leading to the back of the club, a clear signal of what I was looking for. I'd already been there for a few minutes and been approached by no less than three guys, but none had been my type and I'd dismissed them without a second thought. I didn't come to the city often to scratch my itch, so I was damn well going to make it worth my time and shop around for exactly what I wanted.

Like the cute little blond twink who had, by now, sidled up to me. I ignored the need to shift my gaze back to the bar to check on the kid and focused on the small hand that was sliding over my abdomen.

"Never seen you here before," the guy said, his voice a well-practiced purr.

I didn't respond because there was no point. I hadn't come here for conversation and I certainly wasn't going to entertain the guy with useless foreplay.

I was about to tell him to follow me when I felt a shiver snake down my spine. I lifted my eyes and saw the kid's gaze on me. The bear was still with him, but he seemed irritated that he hadn't managed to hold the kid's attention.

Fuck, he was gorgeous. Even from across the room, I could make out his lithe body and striking features. I couldn't see the color of his eyes, but they sat beneath full, perfectly shaped eyebrows that peeked out from the guy's hair. A slight five o'clock shadow covered a square jawline, but it was his lips that were holding my attention…and making my cock finally wake up. They were full and wide with the bottom one just a little plumper than the top.

I heard the twink next to me hum appreciatively and I had no doubt it was because he could see my cock thickening in my jeans. Too bad it had nothing to do with him and everything to do with the young man who was watching me hungrily from the bar.

Too fucking young, I reminded myself even as I fought the urge to shove the hand away that was now pressing against my crotch, grazing my hardness. I needed to just grab the little shit and take him in back and fuck him until it was his face I finally saw, not the jailbait still watching me from the bar. I saw the bear lean down to say something to him, but if the kid heard him, he didn't acknowledge it. Instead, he rose to his feet and started towards me, his gaze holding mine.

The rest of the occupants of the club disappeared as he reached me and I finally got to see that his eyes were a stunning combination of green and gold. He was shorter than me by a few inches and I knew that his age wasn't the only thing about him that didn't fit in the place. He was a city boy through and through, but not a city like Missoula. Because in Missoula, the city kids still looked like the country bumpkins they were. This kid belonged in a big place like New York with his skinny jeans, designer shirt, fancy sneakers that probably cost more than my piece of shit truck and a leather jacket that hung carelessly from his narrow shoulders.

The kid didn't speak when he reached me and I waited to see what he'd do. My twink was still feeling me up, but the kid didn't seem bothered by that fact. His eyes traveled the length of my body and I knew he liked what he saw. I suspected I fit the bill in terms of what he'd been hoping to find in an off-the-wall gay club in Montana. I hadn't bothered changing from my work clothes before heading to Missoula so I more than likely had horse shit on my boots and my hair was probably still showing the circular ring from where my cowboy hat had been pressing it down all day, despite my efforts to get rid of it by running my fingers through my dark locks. The only reason I hadn't kept the hat on was because I liked being able to see the guy I was fucking and hadn't wanted to worry about it shifting on my head and obscuring my view.

Several long moments passed before the kid reached for my

hand…the one that wasn't holding my beer. He began to pull me towards the entrance leading to the back of the club, but I tugged him to a stop, not giving too much thought to how he knew where to go for all the real action.

"How old are you?" I asked, my voice sounding heavy with lust. God, he was gorgeous. I could already feel my dick sinking into his tight heat.

No…no fucking way. I didn't fuck kids. At thirty-three, I knew better. Even knowing we were all in this shithole on a Thursday night for one reason, I still made sure there wasn't more than a ten-year age gap between me and whatever toy I chose to play with for the night. The twink, who was now hanging onto my other arm, was a safer bet.

Only problem was, I'd already forgotten what he looked like and I certainly didn't care what sounds he'd make as I fucked into him.

"You're not gonna be looking at my face when you're fucking me, so what does it matter?"

I knew he'd meant the comment as a come-on, but the way he said it wasn't quite right. I willed myself to release his hand even as the electricity fired up the limb, through my body and centered all its energy in my rock hard dick.

"Come on, cowboy," the twink murmured as his hand closed over my cock and gripped me hard. "I'll take care of you."

I ignored him as I watched the kid's reaction which was pretty easy to read.

He didn't give a shit. He was looking for a body…nothing more.

Which meant he was in exactly right place.

He sighed and dropped my hand and turned away from me and I saw the bear at the bar straighten. He was off his chair and heading towards us and my only thought was, *No fucking way*. The kid wanted to get fucked, he'd get fucked. But it wasn't going to be by that fat prick. I snagged his hand and yanked him back towards me when the bear reached us. I thrust my beer at the twink and then swung around and led my new fuck buddy through the doorway leading to the back. Now that the kid's lack of innocence had freed me, I couldn't shake my rabid lust as I searched for the perfect place to lose myself in his tight little body.

"You got a name?" I asked, though I wasn't sure why I cared. I sure as hell wasn't planning on telling him mine.

"The last guy seemed partial to 'Cockslut' but whatever makes you fuck me hardest is fine by me."

The dispassionate way he said it had me pausing, but the young man didn't seem to notice as his eyes fell on the various couples we'd passed who hadn't made it to any of the private rooms. I was ready to call the whole thing off when he tugged me to a stop. I saw his eyes skim over two big guys working a third over between them. He was being fucked from behind by one guy while a massive cock was jammed down his throat. The sight in itself was erotic enough, but the mewls of pleasure falling from the guy's mouth as he took it from both ends were enough that the few guys watching the show were going to get off without needing to take a turn. The kid's hand tightened in mine and for the first time, I saw his eyes darken with need. His excitement sent me to a whole new level and I leaned down to run my tongue along the shell of his ear before saying, "Next time...tonight you're all mine." I knew very well there wouldn't be a next time, but my words had the effect I'd intended. The kid shivered and then he was turning his attention on me. He gave me the slightest nod and then his mouth parted. I was tempted to lean down and take his mouth, but I remembered where we were and pulled him forward instead.

I'd come here to fuck, not explore. The kid could get that mushy shit from his cute little skater boyfriend or whatever guy hadn't been able to satisfy him enough to keep him from seeking the likes of me out.

I gave up on searching out one of the several curtained off areas the club had set aside for private encounters and kicked open the door to the bathroom instead. There were two stalls in the bathroom and I could see one was occupied, but the other one wasn't. My eyes lit on two guys in the corner of the bathroom near the sink. I barely noticed the guy on his knees doing the servicing because my eyes locked on the stunning blond getting his cock sucked. His gaze connected with mine before going to the young man behind me. A current of sexual awareness blanketed the air around us and I felt like I was going to come in my pants. The blond wasn't my typical type either, but I knew without a shadow of a doubt that if I'd seen him in the main area of the club, I would have likely been the man sucking him down right now... before I turned him and bent him over the sink.

It was just too fucking much. I herded the young man into the empty stall and slammed the door shut. My body shook with excitement as I finally found myself alone with my prey and I immediately turned him so he was facing the wall. As much as I wanted to enjoy playing with him, I was too lost in a haze of lust. I stripped off his jacket and dropped it on the floor and then jerked his shirt up and tucked it under his armpits, revealing the soft, pale skin of his back. I sighed as I skimmed my hands over him, reveling in the gentle slope of his back. I dropped my mouth to the back of his neck as I pressed my groin against his ass. The young man was quiet, but I could feel the tension running through his lean body.

My conscience kicked in and I forced back my need to rip the rest of his clothes off and plunge into his hot little body. "You sure you want this?" I asked softly as I gently teased his nipples.

"No," he said, and then his hands were pushing mine away. I was shocked by the turnaround, but I stepped back immediately. But instead of pulling his shirt down and turning around to leave, he worked his pants loose and pushed them down, along with his underwear. He plastered his hands against the wall and bit out, "What I want is for you to get on with it and fuck me."

God, the kid was an irritating little shit. I should just get the fuck out of there and leave him to whatever asshole came along. But one look at his tight, muscled ass and I knew I wasn't going anywhere. My mouth filled with saliva at the prospect of exploring his milky white flesh, but I doubted he was interested in anything beyond my dick shoved up his ass. I searched out my wallet for a condom and packet of lube and then jerked my pants down enough to release my dick which was slick with pre-cum.

I rolled the condom on in record time and then opened the lube. I slathered my dick with it and then stepped forward and stuck a well-lubed finger between the globes of his ass. I dropped the packet of lube to the ground and used my free hand to separate his cheeks. His pretty hole greeted me with a flutter of anticipation and I gently brushed the cool liquid over it. The guy deserved the least amount of preparation necessary, but I couldn't force myself to follow through on the silent thought.

I liked a rough fuck as much as the next guy, but I wasn't into hurting my partners.

The young man was rigid as I began toying with his hole. I heard a soft sigh escape him as I massaged him and then he stiffened and speared a sharp look over his shoulder. "Just do it already."

Whatever was left of my patience disintegrated and I pressed forward until my body was pinning his to the wall. "Be careful what you ask for, Little One," I said calmly as I nipped at his ear. I grabbed both his hands and lifted them above his head, pinning them to the wall with one hand, rendering him immobile. I pressed my other hand between the globes of his ass and pushed a finger into him. Once I was in as deep as I could go, I whispered, "You wanna top from the bottom, you're gonna have to go out there and find another cock to fill you up, 'cause it ain't gonna be mine." I pulled my finger out before shoving it back into him, causing him to groan, no doubt from a mix of pain and pleasure. I did it again as I licked a path up the side of his neck. His pulse was going crazy beneath my tongue.

"Now let's try this again," I offered huskily as I pressed a gentle kiss to his jawline. "What is it that you want?"

The young man was dragging in breath after breath, his forehead pressed hard against the wall. "I want you to fuck me…please," he whispered, his voice husky with need now instead of dispassion.

Finally…a response that worked for me.

"You want my cock inside this beautiful body of yours?" I asked as I slipped another finger into him.

"Yes…yes," he breathed as he shifted his ass back on my still fingers. I didn't move them until he was squirming against me, his ass brushing my cock. When I finally slid them out and pushed them back in, I pressed them against his prostate. He let out a startled cry and then looked over his shoulder at me, his eyes wide and unsure.

*What the hell?*

I shook my head in disbelief. Certainly someone who was as cock hungry as he was had been pleasured in this way before.

But I could tell by the way he was staring at me with a mix of confusion and need that he had no idea what had just happened.

A cold feeling went through me and I went stock still. "Is this your first time?" I asked.

He shook his head without hesitation.

"Tell me the truth!" I demanded.

"I swear it, it's not," he said quickly even as he clamped his ass down on my fingers. "Please," he begged as he tried to shift his body against mine. I knew what he wanted and gave it to him, watching him with eagle eyes as I pushed against his gland again. He closed his eyes and moaned. I watched in fascination as he pressed his mouth to his upper arm as if trying to stifle the sound.

"No," I said harshly as I released his hands long enough to force his head back. "Let them hear you," I ordered and then I nailed him again. The keening sound that fell from his lips was beautiful and my already leaking cock demanded more. I pulled my fingers free of his body and began pushing my cock into him. I made sure to slide over his prostate as I buried myself inside him and he gasped.

"Oh God!"

I was dimly aware of the silence in the bathroom and I doubted it was because all the other occupants had miraculously finished what they were doing and left. I, myself, was lost in the sound of the young man's pleasure as I bottomed out inside of him.

Never in the nearly twenty some odd years I'd been having sex had I ever been as turned on as I was in this very moment. I'd come in here to fuck this kid, but what was happening was nowhere near fucking. I had no clue how to even start attaching a label to it.

"What's your name?" I demanded as I pulled out of him and pushed back in, hitting his gland again.

A harsh sob escaped his lips as he said, "Beck."

"Beck," I repeated and then I fucked into him again, his unbearably tight ass gripping my cock like it had been made just for him. I muttered his name again and then I did what I had promised myself I'd never do in a place like this.

I kissed him.

Hard.

Deep.

Completely.

Another warning bell went off in my head when I recognized that he had no clue what to do with the tongue I'd plunged into his mouth.

Fuck, what the hell had I gotten myself into?

I kept sliding my dick in and out of him even as I gentled my invasion of his mouth and let my tongue slide over his. Several long seconds passed before he tentatively kissed me back. When his tongue finally followed mine and slipped between my lips, I let out a guttural groan and began hammering into him. When I had to come up for air, I pressed my forehead against his and I began fucking him in earnest, his sleek body meeting my every thrust. I looked down over his shoulder and saw his weeping cock standing tall from a thatch of brown hair. I was about to reach for it when I spied a couple of fingers tapping against one of several glory holes that had been punched into the wall at some point. My mind rebelled at the idea of sharing even a small part of Beck with someone else, but then I remembered his excitement at seeing the three men together in the hallway.

I let my lips slide along Beck's jaw and said, "Look down, baby."

I felt his head drop and heard him gasp when he saw the waiting fingers. "He wants to suck you," I murmured as I slowed my glides. Whereas I'd been eager to nail him and be done with it, now I was reluctant to end the encounter, despite my blinding need to come.

"Do you want that?" I asked as I kissed the corner of his mouth. He turned his head and looked at me, his eyes bright with lust and awe. And God, a look of innocence that had me wrapping my arms around him. His own hand came up to cling to my arms. "Do you want to feel it all tonight, Beck?" I asked.

Beck closed his eyes for the briefest of moments and then nodded.

Another harsh sob escaped his lips and I felt an overwhelming protective streak surge through me. How the fuck had I ever thought he knew what he was getting himself into? He was a fucking lamb among wolves.

But I knew it was far too late to stop. I wanted him too badly. And I could tell he was too far gone in his need for anything but release.

"Please," he whispered and then his eyes fell to the waiting fingers again. I maneuvered us until his dick was right next to the hole and then I carefully worked his stiff flesh through the opening. I watched a condom being rolled onto his length and felt him tense in my arms. I didn't even need to be looking down to know when his dick was sucked into a strange, hot, wet, mouth because Beck cried out in ecstasy and slammed his hips forward, hitting the wall hard. I lowered one arm to protect his lower body as he began fucking the hole and I used my other arm to brace myself against the wall. I began sliding in and out of Beck again, pushing him forward with each thrust.

"Fuck, yes! Please!" he pleaded as he began to come apart in my arms. I knew he was overwhelmed by the sensations bombarding his body and as much as I wanted to draw out the encounter, I knew he wouldn't last. I began ramming into him hard, striking his prostate on each pass and he wailed, his fingernails digging into my arm. One of his hands came up to cover mine where it was pressed against the wall and I immediately let him link our fingers. I captured his next scream of pleasure as his ass clamped down on my dick and he came. He cried out into my mouth over and over again as the orgasm tore through him with crippling force. His knees began to buckle and I had to brace his lower body with my arm to keep him upright as my own climax ripped into me.

I shouted in relief as I came deep inside of him and I couldn't stop myself from continuing to fuck into him as the orgasm crashed through me in cascading waves that seemed to go on forever. When the tension in my body finally began to relax, I slumped against Beck, pressing him against the wall. His breath came out in ragged wisps. I looked down to see the condom being pulled off his flushed dick. I saw a pair of brown work boots beneath the wall of the stall for a brief moment as the stranger on the other side climbed to his feet. I pulled Beck back enough so I could gently pull his dick back into the stall. I didn't miss the fact that there was a pool of semen on the floor beneath the wall.

I kissed the side of Beck's neck as I straightened, taking him with me. His breathing was far from normal, but he kissed me back as best he could. I carefully withdrew from him, grabbing the edge of the condom as I did and then sliding it off my sensitized flesh. I tied it off and tossed it into the garbage can next to the toilet. I pulled my own pants up before working Beck's up and then gently rolling his shirt down. I turned him around so I could button his pants because he was still too dazed to do much.

His lips were flushed and full from my kisses and his cheeks were red from the exertion of what we'd just done. His eyes were glassy as he rode what remained of the natural high. I pulled him forward and kissed him languidly and only separated when there was a knock on the stall door. Beck jumped in my hold. "Just a second," I snapped, but before I could kiss him again, there was another knock. I was about to tear into the asshole for the interruption when I glanced down and saw the same work boots standing on the other side of the door. And in my gut, I knew who it was. I didn't even consider the ramifications of what I was doing when I flicked the latch to unlock the door. It immediately swung open and, sure enough, the blond I'd noticed when we'd first come into the bathroom stood there, his own lips shiny with spit and swollen from his efforts.

The blond was a big guy. His broad chest practically filled the doorway as he stepped into the stall, as much as the small space would allow. He was wearing a pair of butter soft jeans that encased thick thighs and a narrow waist. His black T-shirt clung to a well-defined six pack and prominent pecs If my cock hadn't been completely spent, it would have been standing to attention for sure.

The man's gaze settled on me for a moment before they shifted to Beck who tensed. Embarrassment swept over his features as he realized who the guy was, but he didn't have time to dwell on it because the man dropped his head and sealed his mouth over Beck's in one swift move. Beck gasped in surprise and then began kissing him back. I should have been pissed.

I wasn't.

And I had no idea why.

They were fucking gorgeous together. The man consumed Beck's pretty mouth at first, then gentled his kiss, probably because he was realizing just like I had that Beck was new to kissing. The man's amber colored eyes skimmed over Beck as he pulled back and then shifted to me. I wasn't sure what to expect, but it certainly wasn't him pulling me forward so he could kiss me in the exact same way.

The fucker kissed like a dream. His mouth expertly took over pleasuring mine and I was leaning into the kiss, Beck pressed between us, when he slowly eased back. He nipped at my lips for a brief moment before giving me another gentle kiss and then he put a fraction of space between us. "Let's find someplace a little more private," he suggested. His eyes went back to Beck. "Just the three of us."

I'd never been in a threesome before because I'd simply never been interested. I didn't share the guys I was with, period. But it was on the tip of my tongue to agree when Beck shifted between us, his hands pushing at both of us. We immediately stepped back to give him as much space as we could.

"No!" he shouted, his voice high and uneven as his panicked eyes drifted around the stall as if seeing it for the first time. "No, it wasn't..."

Whatever pleasure Beck had gotten out of what had happened was obliterated as he went into a complete and full on panic mode. He scrambled out of the stall and his eyes darted around the bathroom, taking in the few men lingering around. I hoped like hell he didn't realize they'd probably all gotten off on the sounds of him getting off. But my hopes were dashed when color flooded his face.

"Beck," I said as I stepped out of the stall.

"No!" he yelled again, putting out his hand as if to stop me from reaching for him, which I'd actually been planning on doing. "It wasn't supposed to be like that!" he whispered in despair.

"Beck," the man beside me began, but Beck was beyond consolation.

"I have to go," he said quickly and then he was shoving past a couple of guys near the door. Shame and confusion tore through me.

He'd wanted it, damn it.

Hadn't he?

I went through everything in my head and wracked my brain for any sign I'd forced him in some way...or that I'd missed some kind of warning that he hadn't been into what had been happening between us. But there was nothing. He'd pleaded with me. *He'd* made the choice to allow the blond to help get him off. I could understand his embarrassment that others had been listening to us, but even that seemed inconsequential considering the entire situation. He'd come here to get fucked by a stranger. He'd pursued me.

"Hey," the blond said as he gave me a gentle tap. "You didn't do anything wrong."

I managed a nod. Whatever sexual energy there'd been between us was gone and even if it hadn't been, I was too blindsided to even consider acting on it. I leaned down to scoop Beck's forgotten jacket off the floor. I searched the pockets, but they were empty.

So he probably wouldn't be back for it. I could leave it with the bartender in case Beck returned on another night for it.

But I wouldn't.

Nor did I dwell on the jealously that went through me at the prospect of Beck coming back to this place in the future. Even if he did, I wouldn't know it because there was no way I could ever come back to this club. Not after what had happened in that shitty little bathroom stall.

I nodded at the gorgeous blond, but didn't speak to him as I left the bathroom. I doubted he cared because he seemed just as confused as me. And I had no doubt he'd be asking himself the same question that was now playing on a loop in my head.

*What the hell just happened?*

# ABOUT THE AUTHOR

Dear Reader,

I hope you enjoyed Phoenix and Levi's story. Be sure to check out Finding Hope next. It features Beck Barretti who you briefly met in Vengeance.

As an independent author, I am always grateful for feedback so if you have the time and desire, please leave a review, good or bad, so I can continue to find out what my readers like and don't like. You can also send me feedback via email at sloane@sloanekennedy.com

Join my Facebook Fan Group: Sloane's Secret Sinners

*Connect with me:*
www.sloanekennedy.com
sloane@sloanekennedy.com

## ALSO BY SLOANE KENNEDY

*(Note: Not all titles will be available on all retail sites)*

### The Escort Series
Gabriel's Rule (M/F)
Shane's Fall (M/F)
Logan's Need (M/M)

### Barretti Security Series
Loving Vin (M/F)
Redeeming Rafe (M/M)
Saving Ren (M/M/M)
Freeing Zane (M/M)

### Finding Series
Finding Home (M/M/M)
Finding Trust (M/M)
Finding Peace (M/M)
Finding Forgiveness (M/M)
Finding Hope (M/M/M)

### The Protectors

Absolution (M/M/M)

Salvation (M/M)

Retribution (M/M)

Forsaken (M/M)

Vengeance (M/M/M)

A Protectors Family Christmas

Atonement (M/M)

Revelation (M/M)

Redemption (M/M)

**Non-Series**

Letting Go (M/F)

Printed in Great Britain
by Amazon